A DEATH IN
THE NIGHT

D1323621

SK 2639818

A DEATH IN THE NIGHT

Book 4 in the Hampstead Murders

GUY FRASER-SAMPSON

URBANE
Publications

urbanepublications.com

First published in Great Britain in 2017 by Urbane Publications Ltd
Suite 3, Brown Europe House, 33/34 Gleaming Wood Drive, Chatham,
Kent ME5 8RZ
Copyright © Guy Fraser-Sampson, 2017

The moral right of Guy Fraser-Sampson to be identified as the author of
this work has been asserted in accordance with the Copyright, Designs and
Patents Act of 1988.

All rights reserved. No part of this publication may be reproduced,
stored in a retrieval system, or transmitted in any form or by any means,
electronic, mechanical, photocopying, recording or otherwise, without
the prior permission of both the copyright owner and the above publisher of
this book. All characters in this book are fictitious, and any resemblance to
actual persons living or dead is purely coincidental.

A CIP catalogue record for this book is available from the British Library.

ISBN 978-1-911583-46-2
MOBI 978-1-911583-48-6
EPUB 978-1-911583-47-9

Design and Typeset by Julie Martin
Cover by Author Design Studio

Printed and bound by 4edge Limited, UK

urbanepublications.com

The publisher supports the Forest Stewardship Council® (FSC®), the leading international forest-certification
organisation. This book is made from acid-free paper from an FSC®-certified provider. FSC is the only
forest-certification scheme supported by the leading environmental organisations, including Greenpeace.

A Death in the Night is the fourth volume of the Hampstead Murders. Readers are invited to sample the series in the correct order for maximum enjoyment.

PRAISE FOR THE HAMPSTEAD MURDERS SERIES

"Comfortingly old school crime fiction with a
modern twist."

Chris Brookmyre

"Mr Fraser-Sampson has presented readers with a neatly
lacquered puzzle-box filled with golden-age trickery, as
warm and timeless as crumpets and honey; a murder to curl
up by the fire with on a winter's night."

Christopher Fowler, bestselling author of the
Bryant and May mysteries

"Classy and sophisticated ... if you thought the
Golden Age of crime writing was dead, then read this."

Ruth Dugdall, CWA Debut Dagger Winner

CHAPTER 1

London, while being one of the biggest cities in the world, is really little more than a conglomeration of villages and, while passing through each, one has the opportunity to savour its particular atmosphere. The style of its architecture. Its predominant mix of shops, offices, and accommodation, and their quality of refurbishment. The ethnic mix of its residents. The standard of elegance, or otherwise, of its passing pedestrians. Such things may to many seem of little consequence, yet to anyone intent on understanding London, rather than simply experiencing it as a cardboard background to their daily activities, they are vital. For to walk just a few streets in any direction is to experience a different village altogether, with different inhabitants, different customs, and possibly even different cuisine.

Hampstead, for example, despite the influx in recent years of derivative traders and corporate financiers, preserves an atmosphere of gentle yet intellectual eccentricity, as though its solid redbrick buildings have been invaded by student squatters (though naturally from one of the better sort of universities) celebrating Rag Week. To walk into one of its pubs is to rub shoulders with writers, actors, painters, and a general melee of genteel dilettantes. Even its police station (or "nick" in Metropolitan police argot) resembles nothing so much as a line drawing from an Enid Blyton adventure story, or perhaps a Toytown cardboard model from a similar epoch.

Mayfair, by contrast, represents the very brightest, sparkliest village which London has to offer. Its designer shops rival those of Milan. Its hotels are among the most exclusive in the world, and its restaurants among the most expensive. Its passing pedestrians, male and female alike, are exquisitely dressed and shod; not that they perambulate very far or for very long, frequently alighting from or re-embarking in chauffeur driven Bentleys or Range Rovers. Mayfair, in short, does not just carry the aroma of money but fairly reeks of the stuff.

It is home to hedge funds, private equity firms, and that most discreet class of investor: the family office. Yet whereas in Zürich and Geneva the gentle murmur of money constantly increasing itself through safe and steady accumulation can distinctly be heard from behind the totemic brass name plates, it is evident to anyone with eyes to see and ears to hear that in Mayfair financial transactions are altogether more flamboyant, both in their nature, and in the manner of their execution. In any hotel lobby can be seen a variety of exotic creatures wearing handmade suits, bright waistcoats, and permanent suntans airily discussing financing deals of millions of pounds for iron ore mines deep in the jungles of various African countries. Occasionally the iron ore mine may actually exist; more infrequently still, so might the millions of pounds.

It was not ever thus. Any reader of PG Wodehouse will be aware that in former times Mayfair was where any self-respecting young gentleman went to be fitted for his suits, shirts, and shoes. It was where he played cricket with fire irons in his club. It was where he had his apartment, and where he entertained occasionally difficult aunts visiting London from their country estates. It was, in other words, a place of class, distinction, and refinement. A world of which the inestimable Jeeves would thoroughly approve, and in which he would feel totally at home. Sadly, were Jeeves to find himself in the streets of Mayfair today he would undoubtedly look around himself with dismay, as if forced to acknowledge an old friend who, since one's last encounter, has made a distinctly unsuitable marriage. For the young gentleman of Mayfair has given way to the American investor, the Russian billionaire, and the rough diamond real estate wheeler-dealer.

Yet here and there the occasional relic of former times may still be found nestling away as though hiding in the attic from storm troopers conducting a house to house search. One such is the Athena Club for female university graduates known to its members as simply "the club". Tucked into an unassuming corner position in Audley Square, its membership continues to be drawn from exactly the same sort of intelligent, well-educated woman as it was back in its earliest days when Dorothy L Sayers used to write her books in its library and take tea and anchovy toast afterwards in one of its famously comfortable armchairs.

It was one such of its members who was even now walking northwards up South Audley Street from the direction of Curzon Street, though wrestling with that most modern of accessories the mobile phone. Perhaps because of the very

A DEATH IN THE NIGHT

large number of people in the immediately surrounding area with an urgent need to book private jets to the ski slopes, she was struggling to get a satisfactory signal. She did so only when drawing near to the club, finally succeeding in making contact with her PA.

"Daphne?... Daphne? Can you hear me now? It's Liz, dear, has anyone been trying to get hold of me?"

Despite the reassuring signal bars on the phone's display, no reply was forthcoming. Instead there was first a silence and then what sounded very much like a scream. Pausing in the doorway, she took the telephone away from her ear and stared at it accusingly. Then she tried listening again, but this time there seemed to be nothing at all. Stowing the phone in her capacious handbag, she closed the door of the club behind her and approached the reception desk.

"Hello," she greeted the receptionist briskly, "can I have my key please? I'm Professor Fuller."

Though this announcement would to any bystander have seemed fairly innocuous, it was clearly less so to the woman behind the desk. She said nothing, but clasped her hands together over her nose and mouth while backing away as far as she could until she came up hard against a partition behind her. As if jolted into action by the impact, she took her hands away just long enough and far enough to emit a soft moaning noise, shaking her head and pointing at the Professor. Then, apparently completely overcome by some strong emotion, she broke away and ran into the manager's office behind and to the side of the desk.

There shortly emerged from the office a softly attractive

12

woman, currently wearing a deeply puzzled expression. On seeing Professor Fuller she stopped short and gulped hard. She opened her mouth as though to speak, but nothing came out. She gave a further gulp and tried again.

"Liz," she said at last, clutching the door frame behind her very tightly indeed, "I think you'd better come into my office."

...

On the day before this puzzling encounter took place, four people were taking afternoon tea together in Hampstead, for this was a Sunday afternoon with no work commitments to intrude upon their leisure. Currently dispensing Earl Grey tea was a woman with dark hair gathered behind her head in a way which might have looked severe had it not been at the same time so very enchanting. She was wearing a pencil skirt which, had she not been so well accustomed to wearing it and others like it, might have presented some difficulty in sitting down.

Engaged in passing plates of fruit cake and cucumber sandwiches was a man who, though older, must surely be her partner for they seemed exactly matched. He wore a Prince of Wales check suit which was the perfect counterpoint to her fitted skirt, and if one looked closely the occasional hint of a silver stud betrayed the fact that his collar was of the detachable variety.

Another man, younger, sat perched slightly on the edge of the sofa inserting a piece of cake into his mouth but watching the remaining inhabitant of the room with care and solicitude, as well he might for she had but recently been released from hospital having suffered a near-fatal head injury.

"So are you looking forward to this evening, Bob?" the older man enquired casually.

"Yes, I am as it happens," the other replied with a smile, "though I still find the idea of actually having to dance rather nerve wracking."

"Oh, Bob," the vision in the pencil skirt rebuked him. "You know very well that I've been giving you lessons. You'll be fine, don't worry about it."

"Well, I think you're being very brave," the other woman interjected with a hint of mischief. "But Karen is right you know, there really is nothing to worry about. If you get really desperate, just follow me rather than the other way round."

"Ah yes," Bob Metcalfe observed. "I'd almost managed to forget that you had your gold medal in ballroom dancing, but thank you so much for reminding me."

As the others laughed, he smiled himself. For a while recently there had been little for him to smile about, with a shattered relationship, his career in serious danger, and Lisa in serious danger of a very different kind, but in recent weeks things had resolved themselves as though by magic and the dark clouds had receded. He looked contentedly around the room. How very wonderful it felt to be among such very good friends, including Lisa who was giving every indication of becoming someone still more special. Yet niggling away at the back of his mind remained the warning the doctors had given: that Lisa would continue to require constant supervision and observation for some time yet, for the recovery process from a fractured skull was notoriously difficult to predict.

"Well, it's really good of you, Bob, to be going along with this," Lisa beamed. "Apart from anything else, it's been the most wonderful fun just shopping for an outfit. I had no idea about this whole vintage scene, how many people were involved, how many specialist shops there were, all that sort of thing."

"For me too, actually," he admitted. "When you spend all week tramping the corridors of a police station, doing something like this feels ... well, like an escape somehow."

"But that's exactly what it is, silly," Karen Willis said warmly, "It's like going to the theatre, only better. Because you're not just watching a performance, you're part of it as well."

"It's an escape all right," Peter Collins agreed, having waited politely for his turn to speak. "A chance to step outside time and space somehow and inhabit a little magic world of your own."

Lisa Atkins smiled and nodded delightedly, but the other two glanced awkwardly at each other. They were only too aware that there had been a time when Peter's little escape mechanism had turned upon him at a time of great trauma and threatened his very sanity itself. Though his recovery appeared to be complete, the memory of those awful days was all too fresh in their minds, particularly Karen's since she carried some residual burden of guilt, accusing herself of having been part of the reason for his breakdown.

"So tell me about this place we're going to," Lisa implored them, having taken more fruitcake and passed her cup to Karen for more tea. "I didn't quite understand it when Bob told me about it. Is it a ballroom or something? In a hotel perhaps?"

"No, it's a club," Willis informed her. "A women's club. The only one left, I think. It was set up for women who had been to university back in the 1920s. They've been chasing me to become a member for some time, but it doesn't really make sense for me since I live in Hampstead. It's really designed for people who live out of town so that they can have somewhere to stay when they visit."

"But while Karen was throwing one of their letters away," Collins explained, "I happened to see that they were hosting this vintage event this evening and it seemed too good an opportunity to miss. I've always wanted to see inside the club anyway since Dorothy L Sayers was such a favourite of my mother – and myself of course – and what with it being a women's club and everything this may be the only chance I get to have a look."

Again the subtlest of glances passed between Willis and Metcalfe. Collins was close to being obsessed with the character of Lord Peter Wimsey, constantly dropping into his speech and mannerisms, including referring to Willis as Harriet. Though usually harmless, and frequently entertaining, it was this alternative persona which had looked likely to overwhelm him during his illness.

"And you've been so terribly sweet, Karen, coming around with me and helping me to shop," Lisa went on. "I felt awfully guilty taking up so much of your time."

"It was nothing, truly," Willis assured her. "It was fun for me too and anyway I had nothing much to do at the nick.

That's the problem with the job; it's either feast or famine. When you're working on a case your life's not your own, but once you've finalised all the paperwork after a result there's this strange limbo period while you wait to be assigned to a new enquiry."

"When Karen says 'the job' she means the police force," Metcalfe interjected for Lisa's benefit.

"Yes, I think I'd heard that before. I can see that I'm really going to have to bone up on police slang, aren't I?"

She glanced meaningfully at Metcalfe as she spoke. Ridiculously, yet strangely enjoyably, he felt himself blush. Collins and Willis saw the glance and smiled quietly at each other. Metcalfe was still suffering from the great distress he had experienced when his relationship with Willis disintegrated under the impact of a shocking revelation, and it seemed that here might be something fine, something wonderful in this chance encounter with Lisa Atkins which could offer him the way ahead.

There was one of those companionable silences which nobody feels impelled to break. So they sat and sipped their tea and smiled contentedly at one another. Then Collins pulled an elegant half hunter from his waistcoat pocket.

"At the risk of breaking up the party," he said, "it's probably time to start thinking about getting ready."

"Surely not?" Metcalfe asked. "It's only just gone five."

"You speak for yourself, Bob Metcalfe," Lisa responded at once. "It's all right for you. All you have to do is put on a suit. I've got to wrestle with all this strange new underwear."

Startled, Metcalfe glanced at Willis, who burst out laughing.

"My fault, I'm afraid. I thought that if Lisa was going to go vintage then she might as well go the whole hog, as it were."

"Not your fault at all," she contradicted her hotly. "It was all my idea, Bob. I really want to do this properly."

"Though," she commented archly as a whirl of images flashed through his mind, "you could be a real sport and help me put it on."

Collins coughed discreetly, rose and left the room. Willis picked up the tea tray, gave Metcalfe a conspiratorial glance and followed him.

For a few moments the other two sat and looked at each other. Then Lisa stood up and brushed the hair back from her face.

"So," she said quietly but intensely. "Will you be a sport, Bob?"

There was a pleading in her glance which he wondered if he was adequate to fulfil.

"Yes," he replied with a throat which had suddenly gone dry. "Yes, of course I will."

CHAPTER 2

Within the Metropolitan police force Chief Police Officers – that is, officers of the rank of Commander or above – spend a lot of their time sitting on committees. The more senior the rank to which an officer progresses, the more committees on which they are expected to serve. Indeed, so much of the normal working week of, say, an Assistant Commissioner is taken up by such matters that they frequently find themselves regretting their advancement and wishing that they could once again be a relatively humble Chief Superintendent getting their hands dirty with operational policing.

Needless to say, the Commissioner himself sits on a number of very august bodies, including some which deal directly with national security, but others which are more administrative in nature. The membership lists of some of the latter are nonetheless impressive. The one which the Commissioner was currently addressing contained representatives of both the Home Secretary and the Mayor of London.

"Perhaps I could speak to this agenda item?" he was saying. "It's really designed to allow the committee to consider a very interesting paper which has been put forward by one of our most impressive fast track officers, Superintendent Collison."

"Isn't he the officer who's been receiving all that media

attention?" the rather severe lady from the Mayor's office asked slightly sourly.

"He's been very successful in resolving a number of complicated investigations, if that's what you mean," the Assistant Commissioner (Crime) replied calmly.

"Collison of the Yard they're calling him, aren't they?" someone else enquired, glancing askance at the Mayor's representative. "Impressive indeed, if the papers are to be believed."

"In this context his investigative skills are largely irrelevant," the Commissioner replied, "since his paper is organisational in nature. But since it relates to the organisation of our homicide investigation teams then clearly his first-hand experience makes his views very useful."

"Quite so," came a supportive murmur from the ACC.

"I've had a chance to read the paper in advance," a rather worried -looking man from the Home Office observed. "His suggestions do seem a trifle ... radical, don't you think?"

"He's suggesting some changes, certainly," the Commissioner conceded cautiously. "If they are considered radical in some circles, then so be it. But surely the question must be whether the present system is working as well as it might and, if not, whether Superintendent Collison's proposals might be of merit."

An experienced committee animal, he glanced around the table. His sense was that when it came to everyday practical matters the outsiders would always defer to the Yard, but equally some of them were known to see asking awkward questions as a validation of their presence.

"Perhaps I could ask the ACC to remind us of the present operational structure," he suggested.

"Certainly, sir. Well, as I'm sure the committee is already aware, our homicide investigations are currently organised into three major murder units: East, West and South. Each is headed by a Chief Superintendent and each comprises nine major investigation units, each headed by a Detective Chief Inspector. The Chief Superintendents report onwards up through the Yard hierarchy, but effectively to myself. However, they also have more horizontal reporting lines with the local detective and uniform branches within their areas. I'm making that sound more simple than it is, by the way, because our local operational structure is divided into separate Borough Operational Command Units, which do not always fall conveniently within the very large areas currently designated for these three units."

"All that is evident from the introduction to the paper," the Director of Human Resources pointed out.

"Quite so, Jonathan," the Commissioner said soothingly, "but as I said I thought it would be useful just to set the context very briefly."

He nodded for the ACC to continue.

"As the Superintendent points out, the present structure has a number of features which are clearly less than ideal. For example, why is there no separate unit for North London? Currently homicides as far north as Edgware might end up getting investigated by detectives from the unit for West London, which stretches as far west as Heathrow airport. You will also notice that the rank of Superintendent is entirely absent from the operational structure."

"There is a reason for that," the Director of HR cut in. "I don't think any of us were serving on it at the time, but some years ago this committee commissioned a very expensive report from some world renowned management consultants, asking their advice on organisational matters generally. One of the key recommendations they came up with was that one of the two superintendent ranks should be abolished. It so happened that homicide operations were up for consideration at the time and it was decided that this would be an excellent opportunity to start putting that advice into effect. Are you saying that their advice was incorrect?"

He gazed combatively at the ACC. The Commissioner sighed audibly. One of the many reasons why he disliked committees was the tendency of attendees jealously to guard their own turf and resist any attempt at outside review. He looked quizzically at his uniformed colleague.

"The Superintendent is saying," the ACC said carefully, "two things as I understand it, as I hope will be evident to anyone who has actually read his paper."

There was a sharp intake of breath around the table which the Commissioner affected not to notice, gazing benignly into space as he tapped his reading glasses on the table.

"First, he is saying that the original consultants' paper failed to take properly into account a number of key considerations. This was not necessarily their fault. As I understand it, and as the very full list of academic references in Collison's paper makes clear, organisational theory has moved on quite a bit over the last few years. In particular, they underestimated the problems of span of control caused by removing one rung of the hierarchy."

"Ah yes, span of control," the Commissioner said sagely. "Quite agree, quite agree."

"What exactly do you mean by that?" challenged the HR man, who was clearly not going to give up without a fight. "It's all very well to come out with these buzz phrases like 'span of control', but what do you actually mean?"

"I would have thought that someone from an HR background like you would have understood perfectly," the ACC replied, to all appearances in genuine surprise. "With a rung of the hierarchy missing, the number of individual contacts between the most senior officer and those operating below him is exponentially increased. Not only does this add dramatically to his daily workload, but it raises the very real danger of something vitally important to an enquiry yet seemingly insignificant falling through a crack because it gets lost in the noise."

"I don't think we need to get unduly hung up on that original report," the Commissioner suggested. "After all, it was only advice, and prepared by people who were not serving police officers. I suggest that we focus on the practical issues. The question is very simple: what is the best way of organising our homicide investigations?"

"As to that," the ACC went on quickly before the HR man could intervene, "Superintendent Collison's proposals are very clear. He suggests organising our activities into five areas rather than the current three: East, West, North, South, and

Central. This will have two main benefits. First, it recognises that London's demographics have changed significantly since the first report was commissioned. The population of East London, for example, has mushroomed with the building boom eastwards through Canada Water, Canary Wharf and all points onwards to Stratford – the figures are all here in an appendix."

He tapped the report with his pen.

"Second, it makes it much easier to align the interests of the BOCUs with the new, smaller designated areas of the murder investigation units. It's difficult to explain to a Superintendent in Hammersmith why he should release scarce resources for a murder investigation in Hendon Central; much easier for neighbouring boroughs like Brent and Barnet."

"It doesn't stop there though, does it?" came the dogged enquiry from the HR corner. "He's asking for a wholesale revamping of the command structure."

"Hardly wholesale, surely?" queried the Commissioner. "All he's really doing is restoring the missing level for reporting purposes, and – and I must say I tend to agree with him – recognising the real levels of operational responsibility required."

"To be clear," the ACC informed the room, "he is suggesting that each of the five regions be commanded by a Superintendent who will have responsibility for five investigation teams, each of which will be under a DCI as at present, but organised so far as possible on a local basis so that officers can work on enquiries as close as possible to where they live which, as we all know, doesn't always happen at the moment."

"But who would actually run an investigation?" queried the man from the Home Office.

"The DCI would be the SIO in day-to-day control of the enquiry," the ACC replied, "but he would report on a daily basis to the Superintendent and on an important or difficult case they would work closely on it together. To be fair, that's what tends to happen in other police forces, and it's pretty much how we used to work here in the Met as well."

"Also to be fair," the Commissioner observed, "it's what our Chief Supers – Jim Murray for example – have been trying to do but it's almost impossible with a missing command layer and having to deal with nine different SIO's. Personally, I think Collison's proposals make a lot of sense."

The other committee members stared hard, first at him and then at each other. If these ideas were to enjoy the Commissioner's personal backing then it might make sense to be seen to endorse them, at least in principle, and at least for the remainder of his term of office.

"Yes," the director of HR cut in, though noticeably less aggressively, "I was intending to raise the role of the DCS. It is unclear to me from the paper exactly what is envisaged."

"Of course we are only discussing broad principles here," the ACC said at once. "I'm sure there will be lots of practical details to work out as we begin implementation, but there will be just one DCS, who will have a day-to-day supervisory role, as well as responsibility for a pool of reserve manpower to be created by disbanding the other two existing teams. This will lessen the impact of things like sickness, holidays and maternity leave, as well as taking some of the pressure away from the BOCUs for staff secondment. So it will be the DCS who decides on the resources to be allocated to each individual enquiry, but without having to be involved on a day-to-day basis as he is at present – in theory, anyway."

"But doesn't that lessen his role?" someone asked.

"It changes it certainly," the Commissioner agreed. "It turns the role into more of an administrative position rather than a frontline investigative one, but that actually suits some officers. It means that it will be very important to choose the right person for the right position, of course, but isn't that why we have an HR department – eh, Jonathan?"

A dutiful chuckle ran round the table, prompting a thin lipped smile from the HR Director.

"Overall operational command would still devolve on the ACC," the Commissioner pointed out, "as he will of course continue to have responsibility for all operational crime matters. I'm sure we can rely on him to suggest any appropriate changes should it become apparent that we need to fine tune things as we go along. It may be, for example, that we need to insert a Commander into the structure somewhere, but I think my preference – and I would hope I speak for everyone here – would be to keep things as lean as possible."

There was an apologetic cough, presaging a fresh intervention on the HR front.

"May I remind the meeting," he said, "that the previous report was formally adopted by our predecessors on this committee, and that the phasing out of one of the Superintendent ranks remains official policy."

He gazed at the ACC with an air of sly triumph.

"Is it?" the Commissioner enquired innocently. "Then may I ask why we are still appointing both Superintendents and Chief Superintendents? Why, I remember signing some promotion papers only last week. Surely it was your office which prepared them, wasn't it?"

"It was agreed that we would continue to use the current rank structure as an interim measure, but on the clear understanding that our long-term approach would be to phase out one of the two."

"I'm really not sure about that," the Commissioner demurred. "I can assure you that's not my understanding at all. There was a report – a report about which, if I may say, a lot of us had reservations at the time – which has effectively lain on the file for a long time now. But, as Superintendent Collison's paper makes clear, it is flawed. It is based on an imperfect understanding of organisational behaviour, or at least an outdated view of it. Furthermore, the situation on the ground, particularly the very size of London itself, has changed significantly, rendering it obsolete. My strong preference would be that in future we simply ignore it."

The HR man's mouth opened and closed silently in extreme distress and indignation. One could almost sense his world falling apart around him.

"I really must protest, Commissioner…," he managed at last.

"I'm sorry," the Commissioner asked solicitously, "is your understanding not the same, Jonathan? I thought I was simply expressing the mood of the meeting."

He looked around the other attendees in turn all of whom

nodded, some dutifully but others enthusiastically. The idea of appointing professional management consultants to enquire into the internal workings of the Met had never been popular.

"Perhaps I could suggest, sir," the ACC proffered, "that if HR are not of the same mind as the operational commanders on the ground then they be given an opportunity at a future committee meeting to offer their arguments as to why the original report is still valid?"

"But on the basis that this need not delay implementation of these urgently needed reforms, naturally," the Commissioner replied with a hint of reproof.

"Naturally, sir."

The HR Director gulped, his mind flying to the pages of references and statistics nestling within what would shortly become known as the Collison Report.

"That may take some time," he said hesitantly.

"My dear chap," Commissioner replied expensively, "as long as you like. As long as you like."

CHAPTER 3

The four people who alighted from a large chauffeur driven car outside the Athena Club might just as well have been emerging from a time machine having its temporal origin in the 1950s.

Karen Willis was wearing a ball gown in midnight blue which looked as though it had been made for her. This was in fact almost true since, although she had bought it in a vintage shop, she had taken it to be altered to fit her precise measurements. The top part of the dress was heavily boned and heavily décolleté. These two features, combined with her magnificent figure, produced a result which was probably sufficiently startling to cause a traffic accident should she dawdle unduly on the pavement.

Lisa Atkins was wearing a Cinderella type dress in baby pink which set her blonde hair off to perfection. It too was quite low-cut and had Lisa, who was a very attractive woman in her own right, been standing next to anyone other than Karen Willis she would have looked quite stunning. As it was, she merely looked very wonderful.

Peter Collins, clad like Bob Metcalfe in immaculate evening dress, opened the door of the club and the two men then followed the women as they entered. They found themselves in a large entrance hall which obviously also did service as a seating area. There was quite a throng as a number of parties had arrived hot upon each other's heels, but a pleasant looking and calmly efficient woman was meeting and greeting the arrivals and passing them on out of the hall and into the body of the club as quickly as possible.

"Hello," she said with a warm smile, holding out her hand to Willis, "I'm Rowena Bradley. How very nice to see you – so wonderful that you could come. May I just see your invitation quickly, please?"

"Oh," she went on as she glanced at the four cards. "You're Karen Willis. I'd love to have a chance to speak to you later. I was very much hoping that you might consider becoming a member here."

"You're very kind," Willis replied, "but I'm not sure it makes much sense for me. I live in Hampstead, you see."

"Oh don't worry about that," Bradley said briskly. "Many of our members live in London, you know. But anyway, let's leave this until later. Who are these lovely people with you?"

Willis introduced the other three and, glancing over their shoulders, Bradley saw the door open again as another group entered the club.

"Drinks upstairs in the library," she said quickly to Willis. "Then dinner downstairs in the restaurant, with dancing in the library afterwards. Do have fun, won't you? We'll get a chance to chat over dinner – I'm on your table."

They made their way upstairs and found the library without difficulty. A waiter just inside the door offered a tray of champagne glasses. Now suitably equipped, they pressed on into the room and looked around as best they could, since it was already quite busy.

"This is amazing," Collins said in awe. "Do you realise that right here, in this very room, Dorothy L Sayers wrote some of her books? I've always wanted to see it, and now here we are."

"Yes, and it's very much her sort of place, isn't it?" Willis commented. "The club itself I mean. After all if ever there was a quintessential university woman then it must have been Dorothy L Sayers. Wasn't she one of the very first women to graduate from Oxford?"

"Yes, because at the time she was there women were not allowed to graduate."

"What you mean?" Lisa Atkins asked.

"Well, both Oxford and Cambridge were very late in deciding to grant degrees to women. It wasn't until sometime in the 1920s I believe. Until then you were allowed to take the exams but, regardless of your result, you didn't get a degree. When they changed from this ridiculous system they said that anybody who had previously passed their exams – which she did with honours – could come back and graduate. I think she was one of the first to do it."

Metcalfe sipped champagne contentedly as he looked around. While he did not share Collins's fascination, indeed almost obsession, with Dorothy L Sayers he could understand his excitement at finding himself in this holy of holies. His mind however was not wholly focused here in the room but still dwelling on the events of the previous couple of hours, which had passed off extremely enjoyably. He was still feeling the romantic afterglow of an intimacy which felt both welcome and entirely natural. He had been nervous of rushing into a new relationship so soon after the traumatic collapse of the former one, but he realised that both he and Lisa had been caught up in the onward pressure of events, and it felt good.

Lisa was even now looking around excitedly. There was something of the little girl about her, Metcalfe thought. There was a sort of teenage enthusiasm which bubbled over into her everyday conversation and right now she looked like an excited schoolgirl who had been taken to a grown-up event as a special treat. As she giggled about something with Willis he sensed something which he had not felt since he first met Willis herself; it felt like a dark, soft, comforting fuzziness deep inside, but it also felt like a deep and instinctive certainty that he was somehow in the right place with the right person.

He became aware that Willis was looking at him, and a sudden bright smile flashed between them. She knew – of course she would know – what he was feeling and she wanted him to know that she was glad.

"So we come back here for the dancing, then?" Collins asked nobody in particular, returning to the real world from thoughts of the adventures of Lord Peter Wimsey. "Yes, look, now that those people have moved I see there's a little stage at the end of the room. That must be for the band."

"How exciting!" Lisa Atkins said with a grin as she lightly grabbed hold of Metcalfe's arm. "Do you know, I haven't danced for simply ages. I'm so looking forward to it."

They circled slowly around the room in a clockwise

direction, since further people were pressing into the library behind them. As they moved towards the end of the room where the stage was they came to a halt. They looked around with that curiously detached air which people cultivate when surrounded by perfect strangers holding glasses of champagne. Willis turned to address a remark to Collins only to find that he had completely disappeared. Suddenly what had seemed like a solid set of bookshelves swung on a hinge and Collins reappeared from behind it, grinning hugely.

"A secret room, by Jove," he enthused. "I say, wouldn't this be a wonderful place to have a game of murder? It could be a locked room puzzle, with this little thing being the hiding hole for the murderer."

"A bit obvious, isn't it?" Metcalfe observed.

"Only if you know about the secret door, surely?" Collins replied a trifle huffily.

"No, I mean isn't the solution bit obvious? After all, if a murder takes place inside a locked room then surely it stands to reason that the murderer must have concealed himself in the room and then, after committing the crime, found some way of escaping from it."

"Oh no," Collins said eagerly at once, "that's not right at all, Bob. In fact, there are a number of possible solutions..."

At this point he was interrupted by the crashing of a dinner gong signalling that it was time to go downstairs. He turned from the nascent conversation with an expression of regret. For Willis and Metcalfe, however, the interruption brought a twinge of relief. For once Collins launched into any exposition based on the Golden Age of detective writing he could speak, albeit fluently and compellingly, for a considerable time.

...

Simon Collinson put down the telephone after a conversation which, while lengthy, had consisted mostly of him listening intently and occasionally saying things such as "yes, sir", "very good, sir", and "thank you, sir" at intervals.

"Bad news?" came the anxious enquiry from his wife, Caroline, who had been listening to his end of the exchange.

"No, not at all. It's very good news, actually. That was the ACC. Some committee or other has adopted my paper. The Commissioner himself was very supportive, apparently."

"Simon, that's wonderful," she exclaimed. "How clever of you."

"I don't know about that," he said, scratching his nose. "I had a sort of instinct that the powers that be might have an interest in disposing of that consultancy report, so I deliberately wrote a paper which would give them a weapon to use if that was indeed what they were looking to do. It seems I was right."

"But the way you explained it to me, you were proposing a completely new way of organising murder enquiries right across London. Isn't that right?"

"Yes, that's right. I'm surprised nobody accused me of naked self-interest, though. After all, one of the main recommendations of my paper was to reintroduce the role of the Superintendent, which of course just happens to be what I am myself."

"Well, the Commissioner must have agreed with you or he wouldn't have supported your proposals, would he?"

"I suppose not."

"Oh, Simon," she said in exasperation, "you do annoy me sometimes. Here you are having a paper accepted by the Commissioner himself and you don't even seem pleased about it. What did the ACC have to say?"

"Only that both he and the Commissioner were very happy with the paper and that the committee had agreed to implement its proposals."

"Only? What do you mean 'only'? Surely that's wonderful, isn't it?"

He laughed.

"Yes of course it is. I'm sorry, I don't know why I'm not feeling more excited than I am. It's very good news, actually. He said that they are going to give me the position in charge of North London, which is exactly what I wanted. They are even going to let me base it at Hampstead, if that's what I want."

"Hampstead? I thought Hampstead nick was due to be closed?"

"Yes, so did I," he said with a shrug, "but who knows? At the very least it sounds like it's going to get a stay of execution. Maybe they'll even change their mind completely."

"Why don't you give Bob a ring and pass on the good news?" she suggested.

"I can't," he replied. "He's off at some vintage dinner dance in Mayfair with that Lisa Atkins girl. They're going with Peter and Karen. They told me all about it."

"Yes, that's what they were doing when we first met them – do you remember? We were trying to get into a restaurant and they were on their way to a vintage dance. How nice! It would be fun if we could do something like that, wouldn't it?"

"Yes, I suppose so," he replied warily.

She picked up the book of crosswords which had fallen onto her lap when she gave up the pretence of not listening to her husband's telephone conversation. Then she put it down again as another thought occurred to her.

"Still, that's good news about the four of them going out together, isn't it? I still can't quite believe what happened. I think it's the most shocking thing I ever heard. I can't even begin to imagine what it must have been like for them suddenly to find out they were brother and sister."

"Half-brother and half-sister," he corrected her gently, "but yes, it must have been simply awful. I must say they seem to have handled it pretty well. Nobody but us knows about it, by the way, so let's make sure it stays that way."

"Of course, that goes without saying. But I am very glad that it doesn't seem to have destroyed the relationship either of them had with Peter. I have a very soft spot for him, you know."

Collison chuckled.

"I think most women do," he observed. "He really is the perfect gentleman – considerate, charming, polite and so forth – but at the same time there's something about him which seems to bring out their maternal instincts. I suppose it's the way he seems to be so completely unable to deal with life: real, everyday life that is. But you're very fond of Karen too, aren't you?"

"Yes, of course I am. She's a lovely person. I'm only sorry that she had to go through so much anguish and unhappiness wondering about what was happening to her. At least now that's over."

"Yes, Bob said that – or hinted at it, anyway. He also said that they'd all decided to treat it as a new beginning, rather than bemoaning something that had come to an end."

"Very sensible," Caroline said briskly as she picked up her crossword puzzle again.

As if on cue came the rather angry cries of a baby. They looked at each other resignedly.

"All right," Collison said wearily. "I'll go and get him."

CHAPTER 4

The restaurant of the club or, more correctly, the members' dining room, was large and well proportioned. It was looking highly elegant as each table had been covered with a crisp white tablecloth and a central floral arrangement. Yet it also had a curiously informal air, not least because the tables were all different sizes. On consulting the seating plan, the group from Hampstead discovered they had been placed on a table of six. On approaching it and sitting down, however, they saw that the remaining two chairs were as yet unoccupied.

"Rowena Bradley," Metcalfe read from the name card next to his.

"Oh, I know who that is," Willis said at once. "She's the lady who runs the club, the one who greeted us downstairs."

"She seemed very nice," Lisa commented.

"I'm sure she is. But I'm a bit nervous that she is going to give me a hard sell all evening about becoming a member."

"Well, she looked very nice to me too," Collins said distractedly as he gazed at the remaining name card. Finally he gave up and produced some reading glasses from an inside pocket. Wearing these, he found he could read the handwriting with ease.

"Dr Charlotte Tasker," he intoned. "Friend yours, Karen?"

"Friend of Rowena Bradley, more like. I'm sure I've never heard of her."

"Very nice handwriting don't you think?" Collins asked, proffering the place card. "I've often thought how jolly exciting it must be to be an expert on calligraphy. Why, you could just look at this and say straightaway that it was copperplate as taught at one of the more exclusive boarding schools for young ladies. Just think, you might even be able to identify the school in question. There are people who claim to be able to do that just from the way you speak, you know..."

He tailed off as a lady hesitantly approached the table. She looked about 40 years of age, though she could have been younger, and was wearing a rather elderly ball gown which might most kindly be described as generally unremarkable.

"Dr Charlotte Tasker, I presume?" Collins enquired, replacing her name card. "I'm Peter Collins. How do you do?"

"Oh yes, how do you do?" the doctor replied enthusiastically. "I must say I'm rather nervous at the prospect of sharing a table with five complete strangers. I don't go out very much, you see."

"But surely you know Rowena Bradley? I assumed that you were a friend of hers."

"Oh no, I've met her once or twice of course because she's always around the place – she's the manager here, you know, the real manager I mean although I'm sure she has some much grander job title – but we are not friends as such."

"Really? Well, never mind, we can all be friends together can't we? Now allow me to introduce the others."

While they were still completing this process Rowena

Bradley came bustling into the room and, standing in the middle of it, rang a small handbell which gave off a tinkling noise and quickly quelled the buzz of conversation.

"Don't worry, everyone," she called out. "I just wanted to welcome you all to the Athena Club, those of you who are not members already that is. This is a new venture for us, but when I read about these vintage events they sounded so delicious that I felt we really must have at least one in the calendar this year. Hopefully it will be such a huge success that it can become a regular feature of our events. Now please do sit down, everyone, because dinner is just about to be served. And enjoy yourselves!"

Her duty done, she turned and approached the table.

"Oh good," she said, "I see you've introduced yourself to everybody already, Charlotte. Now, perhaps Karen will do the same for me."

This done, she sat down between Metcalfe and Willis, who found herself conjecturing that this arrangement was no coincidence.

"I deliberately put myself next you when I prepared the seating plan," she said brightly, as if reading the other woman's mind. "You sound such an interesting person – aren't you some sort of famous detective? – that I'm sure you'd be a real asset to us here as a member."

"That's a very kind thought," Willis replied as waiters began serving the starter over their shoulders, "but as I said earlier, I live in town and to be honest I don't get a lot of free time so I'm really not sure that it would make sense for me."

"Well, we'll have to see if we can persuade you, won't we?"

Bradley said brightly. "And perhaps a few more people as well. It's always wonderful when we get a lot of outsiders attending an event like this. Fertile ground for recruitment, don't you think, with the club being really seen at its best?"

"I must say," Metcalfe cut in from the other side, "that I was expecting most of the people here tonight to be members."

"Oh no," Bradley explained, "we're just playing host really to one of these vintage networks who organise events at all sorts of different venues. I thought it would be fun, and I'm sure I'm going to be right. I have a feeling it's going to be a really lovely evening."

A few places away, Collins, with his customary politeness, was doing his best to put Dr Tasker at her ease.

"So are you a vintage enthusiast then, like us?" he was asking. "I don't remember seeing you at any events before."

"Oh no," she said quickly as though not wishing to be thought so frivolous as to enjoy dancing and dressing up, "it's just that I knew I was going to be staying at the club tonight anyway and since I'm on my own I thought it might be a pleasant way to pass the evening."

"And so it shall be," Collins responded warmly, "and I hope you will favour me with a dance or two."

"Oh no," she said again, sounding slightly panicked, "I don't dance."

"Ah," he said, taken aback. Becoming aware that Lisa was grinning broadly at him, he threw her an imploring glance.

"Then it's very brave of you indeed to come along," Lisa proffered by way of a rescue bid. "I do hope it won't be too boring for you. But sometimes just watching people dancing can be almost as much fun as doing it yourself."

"Oh yes," Tasker responded gratefully, "why, my mother used to say exactly the same thing. But then, I think it was because my father was never very keen on dancing himself. My mother used to say that he couldn't tell the difference between a waltz and foxtrot."

"Now that," Collins observed, nodding sagely, "might indeed be something of a drawback. The dancing equivalent of being tone deaf, as it were."

They busied themselves with their smoked salmon and then Collins tried again.

"So what brings you to London, Doctor? You live in the country, I understand?"

To his surprise, she suddenly laid down her knife and fork and burst into peals of laughter.

"Oh I'm sorry," she apologised, seeing his startled expression.

"Was it something I said?" he enquired mildly.

"Yes it was, rather," she replied, still giving little giggles to herself, "you see, you reminded me awfully of Sherlock Holmes. Didn't he say something like that the first time he met Dr Watson?"

Collins gazed at her in sudden interest and admiration.

"Yes you're quite right," he marvelled. "Doesn't he say something like 'I see you are recently returned from Afghanistan?' and then go on to explain how he knows that?"

Lisa looked on amused as the doctor nodded several times in birdlike fashion.

"Yes, quite right, quite right. It was Afghanistan, of course."

"I've always wanted to be able to say that to someone, you know," Collins mused. "A bit like 'follow that cab' to a taxi driver, but the opportunity has never arisen somehow."

By this happy accident of conversation, he seemed to have achieved his objective of relaxing the good doctor.

"I'm here to see a couple of patients," she explained. "I inherited a small private practice from my father. Oh, it's all rather rundown now. Most of the patients have died, actually. There are just one or two left, quite elderly now, and I can usually see them all – all of them who need to see me anyway – in the space of a day. So I come up to town, stay the night here at the club, make my calls during the day and then get the train back to the Cotswolds in the evening. And then that's it until the next time. Not very exciting really, is it?"

"Oh, I don't know," he said gallantly. "Why, I've always thought it must be fun to be a doctor. Diagnosing a disease from symptoms and test results must be rather like a detective trying to solve a case from the available clues, don't you think?"

She looked puzzled, gazed at his name card more closely, and then asked "but I thought you were a doctor?"

"Not a real one, no. I have a doctorate in criminal psychology, but I'm a bit of a fraud as an academic. I don't really even do any serious research now. I prefer to read and write about detective fiction."

She gazed at him with the sudden interest of one who stumbles across a kindred spirit.

"Oh, how wonderful," she breathed excitedly.

On the other side of the table, conversation was still hovering uneasily around the subject of club membership.

"Of course, it's a very different atmosphere in here usually," Bradley was explaining. "On ordinary evenings it's just members and their guests taking dinner, either at the communal club table, or individually. That's why we have different size tables, to be able to accommodate a group of just about any number."

"I suppose in the early days, when people like Dorothy L Sayers were members here, it must have seemed very natural to try to reproduce the sort of atmosphere of a senior common room," Willis suggested.

Bradley thought about this for a moment as the waiters began to clear the empty starter plates.

"Yes," she said. "I haven't really thought about it like that, but you're almost certainly right. And of a women's college, naturally. I think in the early days bringing a gentleman guest here was quite a business, even if he was your husband."

"What about if he was somebody else's husband?" Metcalfe asked mischievously.

"Oh, that was probably even more difficult," she replied with twinkling eyes. "Not so much these days, of course."

"Really?" he replied in surprise. "I would have thought that a place like this would be more..."

"Straitlaced? Not really, no. We like to think this is somewhere where our members can feel completely at home and let their hair down. Not that anything can happen here at the club anyway. Our accommodation is for ladies only, so if anybody wants to stay with their husband – or somebody else's husband for that matter – they have to go to a hotel."

"Well, I'm sure your members are all very respectable anyway," Willis said politely.

"Oh, you'd be surprised," Bradley said with a wry smile. "Why, there are two members staying with us tonight who have shared a husband for the last 20 years or so. It's pretty much public knowledge and it doesn't seem to upset anybody, least of all the three people concerned."

Willis and Metcalfe exchanged an uneasy glance.

"So tell me what other sort of events you put on," Willis enquired, consciously changing the subject.

"Oh, Karen," Bradley exclaimed in mock horror, "do you mean you haven't actually been reading all those wonderful circulars I've been sending you?"

"Some of them, certainly," she replied, colouring.

"Some of them, of course," Metcalfe came to her rescue, "otherwise how would we have known about this evening, for example?"

"Hm," Bradley observed dubiously, "perhaps I'll let you get away with that."

The three of them laughed together. I like her, Willis thought. She is one of these people who has a wonderful sense of fun bubbling away inside her.

"Well, let me see now. There are lectures, musical recitals, wine tastings, author events, private showings at art exhibitions, and even fashion shows," Bradley enumerated, counting them off on her fingers. "And should you ever want to get married, then the club makes a wonderful venue."

Again a telling glance passed between the other two: mischief on his part, but perhaps something else on hers.

"Lectures? Author events?" Willis repeated. "You know you really ought to speak to Peter Collins over there. He's a wonderful speaker. He's just written a fascinating book about poisoning in Golden Age detective fiction."

"Yes, and he's been asked to talk about it at book festivals all around the country," Metcalfe observed. "He did one recently in Hampstead."

"Hampstead? Recently? But then surely that was the crime writers' convention when that woman died, wasn't it? That really famous woman, the Queen of crime?"

"I believe it was, yes," Willis admitted reluctantly.

"But aren't you based at Hampstead?" Bradley asked excitedly. "You are, aren't you? So that must have been one of your cases then. Oh, do say it was – how absolutely thrilling!"

"I worked on it, yes, but the SIO – the Senior Investigating Officer, that is – was Superintendent Collison."

"Collison of the Yard?" Bradley squeaked, completely overcome. "You know him? Oh my God, how absolutely amazing! What's he like – to work with, I mean?"

"He's very nice and very professional. Intelligent, of course, but a lot of integrity as well."

"He must come and speak to us," Bradley said decisively. "You must come and speak to us about a career in the police as a woman. Peter must come and speak to us about how to poison our husbands and boyfriends and get away with it. It's all just too wonderful for words."

Putting down her napkin, she produced a small notebook

and gold pen from her handbag and started taking notes. Glancing down curiously, Willis noted that her handwriting was an exquisite copperplate of a kind taught at one of the more exclusive boarding schools for young ladies.

CHAPTER 5

Peter Collins glanced anxiously at his watch.

"I say," he addressed the table at large, "aren't we running rather late? Why, it's nearly half past ten already. I thought the dancing was supposed to have started by now."

"Yes, I daresay you're right," Rowena Bradley replied. "These things always overrun, don't they?"

As if they had heard his concern from afar, Collins heard the dance band strike up in the distance. He glanced enquiringly at Willis, who nodded.

"Well, if you'll excuse us …"

Collins and Willis headed for the stairs. Metcalfe and Lisa Atkins also looked at each other.

"Would you like to dance?" he asked hesitantly.

"Yes, I would, but we can wait a little bit if you like."

"They'll be round with coffee in a moment," Rowena Bradley announced. "I'm afraid I may have to slip away though, just for a few minutes."

"Are you on duty, then?" Charlotte Tasker enquired.

"Yes, I'm rather afraid I am. Our night manager has gone sick so I'm having to cover for her. I had to do it once before and it's a dreadful bore, particularly when it clashes with an event like this."

"So does that mean you're staying at the club tonight?" Metcalfe asked.

"Yes, but not in one of the bedrooms because people have to be able to reach me in an emergency, which means I have to be in the office. But there's a very comfortable armchair in there with a footrest, so I will doze my way happily through the night and then go upstairs for a shower at about 6.30. Breakfast starts at seven, so that should work out quite nicely as that's when the morning receptionist arrives. I can hand over to her and then go and have breakfast. Quite a treat actually; I usually only have tea and toast at home but here I indulge myself with bacon and eggs."

So saying she got up with an apologetic smile and left the room. Lisa Atkins flashed Metcalfe a meaningful glance which carried the clear telepathic message that they had to wait now for someone else to return to the table before they could have their dance, since otherwise they would be leaving Charlotte Tasker alone. He nodded imperceptibly and held out his cup for coffee as the waiter approached.

Rowena Bradley was away from the table for longer than they expected and they were still making increasingly laborious small talk when Willis reappeared, but on her own.

"Where's Peter?" Metcalfe asked at once.

"Oh, some other woman grabbed him for a dance," Willis replied with a laugh. "One of the perils of having a partner who's such a good dancer I suppose."

"Aren't you two dancing?" she asked as she sat down.

"We are now, yes," Lisa Atkins replied, standing up and reaching out for Metcalfe's hand.

They made their way upstairs, the music growing steadily louder as they did so.

"What sort of dance is that?" he asked nervously.

"It's a waltz, silly. It's in three, can't you hear? Come on, you can do this. You had a lesson, remember?"

Without giving him a chance to reply, she gripped him tightly and steered him into the throng of dancers.

"Don't worry," she breathed into his ear. "If you like, you can just hold me tight and move around a bit. I shan't mind at all, and nobody's watching what we're doing anyway. See?"

She squirmed against him, as if to demonstrate what she had in mind. He quickly discovered that this was in fact extremely enjoyable and did a little squirming of his own in return.

"Just one thing," she said, opening her eyes very wide. "Just in case somebody is watching, it's probably best not to hold my bottom like that."

By the time they went downstairs again, the scene around the table had changed. Rowena Bradley had returned, complete with clipboard, Charlotte Tasker still sat where she had been, but a new arrival in a short and tight black cocktail dress was sitting very close to Peter Collins, her right hand looped nonchalantly through his left arm. She was slim, dark, and attractive. She had a tightly cropped bob of black hair and piercing green eyes. She also appeared to be somewhat inebriated.

Collins was clearly uncomfortable with the situation, but unsure how to deal with it. Willis, on the other hand, looked as though she knew exactly how she would like to deal with it and was hesitating only through fear of upsetting innocent bystanders. In consequence, there was something of an atmosphere.

"This is Chloe Jennings," Collins announced rather unhappily as Metcalfe grabbed a spare chair from a nearby table and squeezed himself between Willis and Charlotte Tasker.

Jennings favoured them with a smile, but said nothing.

"We've just been dancing together," Collins continued, as if desperately trying to spark some line of conversation.

"Yes, we have," Jennings said suddenly, "and he's a wonderful dancer – so handsome too."

Moving even closer to him – so close that she seemed in danger of falling off her chair – she planted a kiss on his cheek. The pained expression which passed momentarily across his face before he politely suppressed it showed all too clearly that this was a development which he had neither expected nor encouraged.

"If only more men were like you," she said with a pout, as she shifted both shapely buttocks back onto her own chair, "but they're mostly just bastards. Total bastards."

Tasker and Bradley looked extremely uncomfortable. It was clear they were wondering who this woman was, who had invited her, and how they could get her out of the club with minimum disturbance.

"Take this bloke I'm going out with at the moment," Jennings went on, grabbing an empty glass on the table and looking around as if for something with which to fill it. "He thinks he's really something but actually he's just a complete shit."

She frowned as she realised that both the wine bottles within reach were empty.

"Why don't we go and have another dance?" she demanded of Collins, swinging around and staring hard into his face.

"I'm a little tired, actually."

"There's no need to be so polite, Peter," Willis broke in acidly. "What you really mean is that you've already promised this dance to me. Come on."

She stood up and reached out to him. As if in response, Jennings tried to grasp his left arm even more tightly, but somehow fumbled the move so that her right hand was left dangling by her side. For a moment, Metcalfe thought she might be about to fall off her chair, but she recovered herself, staring slightly wildly around the table as if wondering where she was.

As Willis and Collins left the room, Rowena Bradley came around the table and occupied the seat just vacated by Collins.

"Tell me, my dear, who are you here with? Who did you come with, I mean?"

"Oh, I'm with that lot over there," she replied, indicating a table in the corner of the room from which a lot of increasingly raucous laughter was emanating, "but they're idiots, all of them."

"But won't they be worried about where you've gone? Don't you think you should at least let them know that you're still here?"

"Oh, they'll be all right," Jennings assured her. "Anyway, I didn't like them very much. Here, what's this?"

She seized Bradley's clipboard and scrutinised it minutely, holding it closely to her face as though her eyes were having problems focusing.

"It's just a guest-list for tonight, showing who's staying at the club," Rowena said calmly, prising it free from her grasp and replacing it on the table. "Nothing to do with you. Now, if you don't want to go back and rejoin your friends, why don't you let me get you a taxi to take you home?"

"I'm not drunk, you know," Jennings said suddenly in a sharp tone of voice.

"I didn't say you were. I just thought you might like some help getting home, that's all."

"Oh leave me alone, why don't you?" Jennings exclaimed loudly as she rose to her feet and walked rather unsteadily across the room back towards her own table.

Rowena Bradley smiled sadly at the others and shook her head.

"I suppose things like this are bound to happen, but still it's rather sad isn't it? Now, why don't you young people go and do some more dancing before the band packs up?"

"Well," Metcalfe said hesitantly, "yes, we'd like that, but suppose you have to slip away again? We wouldn't want to leave Charlotte all on her own."

"Oh, surely you're not staying here just to keep me company?" Charlotte Tasker asked immediately. "Dear me, how very embarrassing. You must go upstairs and enjoy yourselves of course."

"Actually, I have a better idea," Rowena Bradley said briskly. "There are a couple of little tables upstairs beside the dancefloor and I took the liberty of putting a 'reserved' sign on one of them. So we can all go upstairs and keep each other company, even if I do get called away to go and look after any of our wretched guests."

There was a general gathering up of handbags from the female contingent and then Rowena Bradley led them upstairs, with Metcalfe bringing up the rear.

The band had just finished playing a foxtrot and Collins and Willis were heading back towards the stairs, clearly intending to return to the dinner table.

"Has she gone?" Willis demanded before anyone could say anything else.

"Yes, she has," Rowena Bradley replied with a broad smile, "and I only had to be moderately patronising to accomplish it. But there's no need to go downstairs. I was just explaining to the others. I've reserved that little table over there and we can easily fit six around it if we all squiggle up a bit."

After the requisite amount of squiggling they found that they could indeed just about fit six chairs around the table, but Metcalfe and Lisa Atkins eased the capacity problem immediately by heading back onto the dancefloor.

"Isn't it good to see Bob enjoying himself again?" Collins asked Willis.

She nodded and squeezed his arm.

"Oh, has he been through a bad time then?" Charlotte Tasker asked curiously.

"Yes, he has," Collins replied awkwardly, "but I don't

think he'd want me to talk about it. It's all rather private, I'm afraid."

"Oh, I'm sorry. I didn't mean to pry."

"Not at all. I just spoke without thinking. I'm sorry."

"Well, if his problems had anything to do with another woman, then well done him for finding Lisa," Rowena Bradley remarked. "Isn't she gorgeous? And she seems such a lovely person as well."

"Yes, she certainly is," Willis agreed. "We're all very happy for Bob – and for her too of course."

"Here, it's getting rather late," Collins said, looking at his watch once more. "It's nearly half past eleven. Isn't that when the band is supposed to stop playing?"

"Yes, it is," Bradley confirmed, "but I've asked them if they wouldn't mind doing a little overtime as it were. They said they absolutely had to stop playing at midnight, which is when we have to clear all visitors out of the club anyway, but I think you're safe until then."

"In that case," Collins said, rising and taking Willis's hand, "perhaps you'll excuse us?"

"What lovely young people," Bradley commented.

"Yes they are, aren't they? They seem to be really enjoying themselves. And all so very much in love from the look of things."

"But what about you, Charlotte?"

"Am I in love, do you mean?"

"Good gracious, no. That's really none of my business. What I meant was: have you enjoyed yourself?"

"Yes, do you know I really have. I must try to get up to the club more often. Usually I come up and down to town in a day, so I don't need anywhere to stay the night, but perhaps I should try treating myself to an evening at the theatre or something like that."

"Yes, you really should. I'm sure you deserve it. And that would give you an opportunity to meet some of the other members and get to know them. We usually have a club table in the dining room in the evening, you know. You just sit down next to someone you've never met before and introduce yourself. It's all enormous fun."

Now it was Tasker's turn to glance at her watch.

"I didn't realise how late it was until that nice Dr Collins mentioned it just now. I think it's time I turned in; I have an early start tomorrow. Rowena, would you give my apologies to the others, and say that I just slipped away as I was very tired?"

"Yes, of course I will," she replied. "I see that other people are starting to slip away anyway, so I don't think things will go on for very much longer. In fact, I think I'd better do a quick circuit just to check that everything is all right downstairs. Good night, dear."

She left the table and headed for the landing at the top of the stairs. Before she could get there, however, she felt Charlotte Tasker tapping her on the shoulder with her clipboard.

"Don't forget this, will you?"

"Oh dear, thank you so much. No, that would never do. It really is much too important."

CHAPTER 6

All in all, Rowena Bradley would later explain, it turned out to be quite the most distressing day she could remember.

It all started when the girl on the reception desk reported that though Mrs Fuller had requested an alarm call at seven thirty she was failing to answer the telephone in her room. A maid, or room assistant as they were supposed to be called these days, was promptly dispatched to knock on the door but similarly received no reply. She went downstairs and reported this to Rowena Bradley, who was still awaiting the arrival of the day manager. Distracted by a lady member who was anxious to check out but had a query about her bill, one with which the receptionist was unable to deal, she grabbed the duplicate key for room 16 from the board in her office and pressed it into the hands of the maid, knowing she could trust her to be both polite and discreet, for she had worked at the club for many years.

Once upstairs again, the maid knocked once more on the door, very firmly this time, and on once more failing to elicit any response she unlocked the door and opened it slightly, calling through the crack to enquire whether she might enter the room. The room was dark and silent, so she opened the door about halfway and felt along the wall for the light switch.

A few seconds later she ran quickly from the room, clutching her hands in front of her and saying "Dios mio" repeatedly.

As she reappeared on the ground floor, still in great distress, everybody stopped what they were doing and stared at her.

"What on earth is the matter, Maria?" Rowena Bradley asked her, already instinctively fearing the worst.

"The lady in room 16," Maria responded breathlessly. "She dead, I think."

At this she was seized by the shoulders and ushered quickly into her office by Rowena Bradley, who lowered her into a chair and, turning to the goggling receptionist who had come unbidden to the doorway to gaze at this harbinger of fate, told her to call Dr Tasker in her room and be quick about it.

Thus it was that Dr Tasker, who was just leaving her room to head downstairs for breakfast, was interrupted and redirected as a matter of urgency to see Rowena Bradley instead.

"Charlotte, dear, I am so sorry to trouble you but it seems that something unpleasant may have happened to one of our guests. I know I should probably phone somebody, but would you mind taking a look at her for me?"

She prised the room key from the grip of the maid, who was now in the full flood of tearful hysterics, and handed it to the doctor.

"I'll join you as soon as I can," she promised, "but first I need to find somebody who can look after Maria. Do you want me to phone for an ambulance?"

"Better let me take a look at her first, I think."

With that, Charlotte Tasker headed resolutely upstairs. Pausing only to collect her bag from her own room, she made her way to room 16. In fact the key was unnecessary as Maria had clearly left in such a hurry that not only had she neglected to lock the door behind her, it was even slightly ajar. The light was now on and as she opened the door she saw at once the form of a middle-aged woman sprawled on the floor beside the bed, mostly obscured from the waist upwards by bedclothes.

As she placed her doctor's bag on the bed she heard Rowena say "oh good God" from the doorway behind her. Turning, she saw her glance briefly at the body on the floor and then go and stand in the corridor, looking dazed.

"Don't worry, I can take care of this, Rowena," the doctor called to her from inside the room. "I'm pretty sure she's dead, but I just need to make sure. It will only take a moment."

Kneeling beside the woman, she felt for a pulse but there was none. She uncovered the woman's face, which was unmarked and bore a peaceful expression. Then she shook her head briefly and allowed the bedclothes to fall back into place.

Rejoining Rowena Bradley in the corridor, she said calmly "she's dead all right, I'm afraid."

The other stared at her in horror.

"My God, this is awful," she replied. "I've read so much about this happening in other places but I never thought we would have to deal with it here. What do we do?"

"It all depends on whether she has seen her doctor within

the last few days. Do you happen to know if she was being treated for anything?"

"No I don't, but I could ask her husband I suppose. Oh God, poor Andrew. I suppose I'll have to call him and break the news."

"If she hasn't seen her doctor recently, that complicates matters. When one of my patients dies I can just certify the cause of death myself, but this is different. I think the easiest thing would be for me to notify the local coroner. It's almost certain that she had a heart attack during the night and fell out of bed – perhaps trying to reach for the telephone – dragging the bedclothes on top of her, but it may be that he will want a post-mortem carried out just to be sure."

The other stared at her once more, shaking her head helplessly.

"You're in shock," the doctor said firmly. "Why don't you go back downstairs and leave things to me? There are one or two things I need to do before I can contact the coroner, but I'll lock the door behind me when I've finished."

Rowena Bradley nodded silently and headed back to her office. Maria had apparently been escorted elsewhere, for the room was empty. She closed the door behind her and, with a trembling hand, found the number she was looking for and dialled it. Andrew Fuller answered almost immediately.

"Andrew, dear, it's me – Rowena. Look I've got some awfully frightful news for you. I'm afraid it's Liz."

"Liz? What is it? She hasn't found out has she?"

"No, nothing like that. Oh Andrew, she's dead, my darling. I've just seen her lying on the floor of her room. Fortunately we have a doctor staying with us and she took a look at her for me, but there was nothing she could do."

There was a long silence. She found herself starting to sob.

"I'm really not sure what to say," he said at length. "I'm completely stunned. I suppose I should come round straight-away, but I'm in court at 10 o'clock. I'll ask for an adjournment and see if I can come then."

"Yes," she gulped. "Oh Andrew, I'm so sorry..."

At the other end of the line there was only silence, and then a click as he hung up.

After she had sat staring into space for some five minutes or so there was a little knock at the door and it opened to admit Charlotte Tasker.

"I've done everything I can," she announced. "I managed to lift her onto the bed, by the way, and I opened the window; it was quite warm in there and I didn't want her to – well, deteriorate."

The other woman nodded, though secretly aghast.

"Now we need to find the phone number of the coroner's office and give them a ring. I don't know if they'll be in this early, but we can try."

The phone call produced nothing but a recorded message inviting callers to try again after 10 am.

"But what can we do?" Rowena asked in despair as she glanced at her watch. "That's over an hour and a half away and even then it will presumably take them some time to ... to come and fetch her. We can't have her lying around up there all that time. Apart from anything else, we're fully booked tonight and I need to get the room cleaned. Oh dear, doesn't that sound dreadful? She was a friend, after all. Yes, a friend..."

She started sobbing quietly again.

"Not to worry," the doctor said comfortingly. "I can get the body removed to a hospital mortuary. That way it will be available to the coroner if they decide to ask for a post-mortem. I'm sorry, I wish I could issue a death certificate, but I can't. Other than the fact that it's natural causes I have no idea how she died, nor do I have any idea of her medical history."

"But it will be dreadful having to bring her body out through the club," Rowena replied tearfully. "Why, there'll be all sorts of people about."

The doctor thought for a moment.

"Don't you have a backdoor? A service entrance or something like that?"

"Yes we do."

"Well there you are then. Don't worry, these people are very used to being discreet. They can put her in a bag and bring her quickly down in the lift – standing up, as it were – and out through the back entrance before anybody knows what's happening."

"Well, we don't really have a choice do we?" Rowena said resignedly. "We can't leave her up there."

It turned out pretty much as Dr Tasker had foretold. The two men were indeed professional, discreet and efficient. In only about 10 minutes from start to finish, they had gone up in the lift, come down again with an accompanying package, and left the building through the rear entrance.

The doctor sat down and wrote a brief report for the coroner of what she had seen and done, copying out Elizabeth Fuller's name and address from the club records and explaining that she was not the deceased's GP but was simply staying at the club and had been asked to check that life was extinct, which she had done at 7.51. Remembering her pathology lectures, she had taken a reading with the rectal thermometer which she carried in her bag, which she recorded as having been 24°C, still comfortably above the ambient temperature of the room. From this she advanced the suggestion that death had probably occurred some nine hours previously, which would be consistent with the advanced state of rigor mortis she had observed in the body.

She recorded that in her brief examination she had not noticed any obvious marks on the body, and that the position of the body and the bedclothes might be indicative of the deceased having suffered a sudden heart attack during the night and fallen out of bed while reaching for the telephone in a strange and darkened room. She had conducted a quick search of the bathroom and the deceased's handbag but have not found any evidence of her being on any medication. At the foot of the report she jotted down her professional details and then left, somewhat delayed, to make her intended house calls upon her own patients.

Andrew Fuller QC, having obtained a brief adjourn-ment of his fraud trial at Southwark Crown Court, arrived as promised around eleven o'clock and spent some time alone with Rowena Bradley sitting sombrely over a pot of tea before departing again about an hour later to restart the wheels of justice.

It was about half an hour later that the lady pushed through the doors struggling with her mobile phone.

"Hello," she greeted the receptionist briskly, "can I have my key please? I'm Professor Fuller."

Though this announcement would to any bystander have seemed fairly innocuous, it was clearly less so to the woman behind the desk. She said nothing, but clasped her hands together over her nose and mouth while backing away as far as she could until she came up hard against a partition behind her. As if jolted into action by the impact, she took her hands away just long enough and far enough to emit a soft moaning noise, shaking her head and pointing at the Professor. Then, apparently completely overcome by some strong emotion, she broke away and ran into the manager's office behind and to the side of the desk.

There shortly emerged from the office the softly attractive form of Rowena Bradley, wearing a deeply puzzled expression. On seeing Professor Fuller she stopped short and gulped hard. She opened her mouth as though to speak, but nothing came out. She gave a further gulp and tried again.

"Liz," she said at last, clutching the door frame behind her very tightly indeed, "I think you'd better come into my office."

CHAPTER 7

"So let me get this right," Professor Fuller asked in a tone of disbelief. "I'm dead, am I?"

"Well someone died during the night," Rowena Bradley replied, desperately trying to keep a grip on reality, "and we thought it was you because she was in your room, you see."

"But why did you think she was me just because she was in my room? And anyway, it can't have been my room, can it? I was asleep all night and I think I would have woken up and said something if a dead woman was carried in and dumped beside me."

"Yes, yes, I know," Bradley concurred, fidgeting nervously with a pen on her desk. "It's all quite bewildering, isn't it? I don't know what to think anymore."

"Well, what did she look like? Did she look like me? Is that how the confusion arose?"

"I don't know," came the embarrassed response. "I didn't look, well not properly anyway. I just saw the body of a woman lying on the floor – not even her face – and I'm afraid that like everyone else I just assumed it was you because we had you registered in room 16."

"I was in room 24," Fuller informed her crisply. "That's not even on the same floor is it?"

"No, it isn't, but Liz, how on earth could this have happened?"

She pulled the daily list of guests across the desk towards her, and inspected it.

"I don't understand any of this. Look, according to this room 24 was occupied by Angela."

"Angela Bowen?"

"Yes, of course. Didn't you know she was staying?"

"Yes, of course I did. As a matter of fact we ended up checking in together as we both happened to pitch up at the club at the same time."

They both stared at each other, realisation starting to dawn.

"But then...?" Bradley began, but tailed off.

"I'm just trying to remember what happened. We were chatting, I expect – yes, we must have been – and I suppose that each of us must have picked up the wrong key by mistake. I just looked at the number on mine and headed for 24. Angela must have done the same and assumed that she was checked into 16."

They stared at each other again.

"So that means it must be Angela who died, surely?" Bradley said at length.

"That would seem a reasonable supposition," the Professor said dryly, "but since the club seems to have killed somebody off by mistake once already today, perhaps it might be a good idea to make sure?"

"But how can we do that? They've taken the body away.

It's not here anymore. Oh, how I wish Charlotte hadn't had to go out. She would know what to do."

"Charlotte? Who's she?"

"Oh, Charlotte Tasker. You don't know her, of course. She was at the vintage dinner dance last night. She's a doctor, you see, so when poor Maria came running downstairs saying someone was dead I thought it would be easier to ask her to take a look than wait for anybody to come from outside. After she finished examining the body she filled in a report for the coroner's office and naturally she just copied down your details from the reception desk. You were registered in room 16, so it was your name that went in her report."

"I see," Fuller said heavily. "Just as a matter of interest, can I ask how many other people believe me to be dead? Has the news spread? Shall I be reading my obituary in the afternoon editions, anything like that?"

"Well," Bradley said hesitantly and then looked at her in sudden horror. "Oh, Liz – Andrew..."

The Professor nodded in resignation.

"Of course, of course. Naturally the first thing you did was to phone my husband and pass him the sad news."

"Yes, of course I did. He was just here. He had to get an adjournment of his case. Oh Liz, I'm so sorry, he thinks you're dead."

"Well, we'd better find a way to disabuse him as quickly as possible, hadn't we?"

She looked at her watch.

"Did he say what court he was in?"

Bradley thought hard for a moment.

"I think he said Southwark Crown Court."

"Yes, I know it. Well, I'd better get over there so that I can wait outside the courtroom for them to finish. You never know, I might be able to get a note sent into him. I can hardly just walk in bold as brass and sit down, can I? He'd probably have a heart attack on the spot."

"Oh Liz," Bradley said miserably. "This is all my fault. If only I hadn't been such a silly coward about looking at the body I would have known straightaway that it was Angela, not you."

Fuller shrugged.

"Always assuming that it was Angela Bowen of course. How did she die anyway?"

"We don't know. Charlotte said it was natural causes but she couldn't make a guess at what exactly because she didn't know anything about her medical history. Was she on any medication, do you know?"

"I haven't the foggiest idea. Andrew would know, presumably. I'll try to remember to ask him when I see him – provided he doesn't drop dead himself when he sees me."

Now it was Bradley's turn to look at her watch.

"But the court won't finish, or rise or whatever it is they do, for ages will it? Why don't you stay and have a cup of tea before you go? After all, we need to decide what we're going to do about poor Angela."

"I'll take a cup of tea with pleasure, or even perhaps a glass of something stronger. After all, it's not every day that one dies. As for Angela, I'm not sure why you're saying 'we'. There's nothing I can do, is there? If this Tasker woman has reported me dead to the coroner's office then I assume that someone needs to get onto them and tell them there's been a mistake. It should be quite an interesting conversation, don't you think?"

"Yes, I imagine it will be," Bradley said helplessly. "It's not going to be an easy thing to explain, is it?"

"Now don't upset yourself," Fuller said more kindly. "Why don't we both have a glass of something to steady our nerves? Then we can do whatever has to be done."

Rowena Bradley rose rather unsteadily, removed a bottle of sherry from the cupboard, and poured them both a generous measure. The bottle rattled nervously against the glasses as she did so.

"I suppose," the Professor observed after her first mouthful, "that you will have to go through this whole wretched business all over again: informing the next-of-kin, I mean."

"Yes, I suppose so. Who was her next-of-kin, do you know?"

Fuller laughed briefly and took another sip of sherry.

"I would imagine that the only person in the world who would have any real interest in the matter would be my husband, wouldn't you? But, come to think of it, I think she did mention a cousin, or aunt, or something. In the Cotswolds perhaps? Andrew will know, I expect."

"Oh God, this is all such a mess," the other moaned. "I honestly still can't quite believe all this is really happening. It feels so much like a bad dream. I can't tell you what a turn it gave me to see you standing there."

"Reports of my death have been greatly exaggerated," the

Professor quoted sardonically. "Yes indeed, it must have been quite a shock for you. At least it explains the reaction of the receptionist. For a moment I thought I must have grown two heads or something."

The conversation having reached a natural pause, they occupied themselves with finishing their sherry in a companionable silence. Bradley offered the bottle with an enquiring expression. Fuller thought briefly but, though clearly tempted, shook her head.

"Better not. You'd better not either. Still a lot to do this afternoon."

Bradley replaced the bottle in the cupboard and then sat down again and started scrabbling through the papers on her desk.

"Charlotte made a note of the telephone number here somewhere, I'm sure."

"The coroner's office, you mean?"

"Yes – ah, here it is I think."

She dialled the number and it was only as there was an answer at the other end that she realised she really had not thought of how to phrase what it was she had to say.

"Oh, good afternoon," she began uncertainly. "This is Rowena Bradley from the Athena Club. I'd like to talk to somebody about a death which occurred here during the night."

There was a pause while she was transferred, after which she had to repeat this opening gambit.

"Has the death been reported to us by the deceased's GP?"

the official enquired. "Normally they just issue a death certificate and deal directly with the hospital mortuary."

"No, there was a doctor staying with us at the club and she certified the death, but she prepared a report to your office because she wasn't the lady's GP and she couldn't form any conclusion about how she died."

"Where is the body now?"

"It was taken away earlier to the mortuary."

"Has anybody identified it, do you know?"

"Well, yes and no," Bradley said awkwardly. "You see, I'm afraid there's a bit of a problem there."

"A problem?"

"Yes, you see – oh, this is very awkward – well, it turns out the lady wasn't who we thought she was."

There was a silence of the other end of the line. Feeling that further explanation was clearly called for, she went on, feeling increasingly foolish.

"You see there was a mix-up with the room numbers. The body was discovered in room 16 and that was registered to a Professor Elizabeth Fuller, so naturally that's who we thought it was."

"And it wasn't?"

"No, in fact Professor Fuller is here with me right now. What we think happened was that she accidentally changed room keys with another guest, a Professor Angela Bowen. That's who we now think the body must have been."

"I see," the disembodied voice said uncertainly. "Would you mind waiting a moment please while I have a chat with a colleague?"

After a lengthy pause the voice spoke again.

"We'll have to look at the doctor's report, of course, but it sounds as though there will need to be both a formal identification and a post-mortem. We'll ask the hospital mortuary to make the necessary arrangements. Now, is there anybody there with you who could formally identify the deceased? Anyone who knew her well?"

"Well, there's Professor Fuller – they were colleagues for a while, you see – but I don't think it would be very convenient for her just at the moment. You see, she has to go and tell her husband that she's still alive."

There was another silence and then the voice commented, "yes, I see", sounding even more dubious than before.

"Apart from her, there's only me. I've known both Liz and Angela for years. I suppose I could get away a little later. Oh dear... yes, I suppose it will have to be me then. Where should I go?"

"Give us half an hour or so to make the necessary arrangements and I will call you back. What is your number?"

She gave it and rang off.

"Oh Liz," she said gazing at her mournfully with her hand still on the telephone. "How wretched. I've got to go and identify the body."

"I'm sure it won't be too bad," the other said sympathetically. "I expect it's just a question of looking at her face quickly and confirming that it's her."

"But suppose it's not?" she asked, sounding suddenly panicked. "Suppose it's somebody else entirely? A total stranger?"

"Don't be silly, Rowena," Fuller admonished her. "Of course it must be Angela. Who else could it be? She surely wouldn't allow a complete stranger to use a bedroom which she had booked for herself. Well, yes, I know that actually I had booked it myself, but you know what I mean."

"Yes, I suppose you're right. You must be."

Fuller gazed at her steadily for a while as if appraising her emotional state.

"Have you ever seen a dead person?" she enquired.

"No, never. That's why I didn't take a good look this morning, you see. I was too scared. Stupid of me, I know. Why, if only I'd done what I should have done, none of this mess would have happened. Why, have you?"

"Yes, when my mother died. My father was away from home at the time so I had to deal with things until he got back."

She considered the situation for a moment.

"There is another way of doing this," she proffered, "but it's only a suggestion, mind."

"What is it?"

"Well, I was just thinking that we could always swap. I could go to the mortuary and identify Angela, while you go down to court and break the happy news to Andrew."

"Why yes, Liz, that's brilliant. Actually, it's so much better isn't it? You see I could go and sit in court without causing any upset at all and I might even be able to pass him a note."

"You might at that," she nodded in agreement. "All right then, that's settled. I'll take the phone call when it comes and go and take a look at Angela. You get down to Southwark Crown Court and speak to Andrew."

So it was that a little later Andrew Fuller QC's Junior felt someone tugging on the fabric at the back of his gown. Turning, he was handed a note by one of the instructing solicitors, who indicated a rather agitated looking lady sitting in the public gallery. He in turn tugged at the back of Andrew Fuller's splendid silk gown and, when the great man turned from observing a cross examination which was in his opinion being very poorly handled by the other side, passed him the note.

In the course of a glittering legal career many surprises had been sprung upon this particular Silk. Witnesses had retracted statements previously given, opponents had produced damning evidence the existence of which had never previously been suspected, and on one memorable occasion a suspect had collapsed in the box with a heart attack just as Fuller was saying "and I put it to you..." at the dramatic climax of a long string of accusations. Yet nothing in that prior career had prepared him for what he read when he opened the neatly folded piece of paper.

Liz is alive. Yes really, I just had tea with her,
it was all a ghastly mistake.
Angela is dead, we think. Liz has gone to look at her to
make sure. Make sure that she is Angela, I mean, not make
sure that she is dead.
Oh Andrew, isn't it all too terrible?
Rowena

CHAPTER 8

The Westminster public mortuary sits on Horseferry Road, at number 65 to be exact, almost precisely in the middle of a triangle whose apex is Victoria station and whose other two corners are bounded by Vauxhall Bridge and Westminster Bridge respectively.

The morning after Andrew Fuller had been passed a note further up the Thames at Southwark, Sandeep Patel, one of the duty pathologists, was reading the newspaper in an empty room; empty that is apart from two currently unoccupied post-mortem tables and a variety of surgical equipment. He looked up as his colleague Sandra opened the door and looked in.

"We've got one for you," she announced. "Just been identified, and the coroner's office want a PM."

"Is it a suspicious death? If it is then you know it should go next door, not here."

The "next door" to which he was referring was the U.K.'s first purpose-built forensic facility for cases where someone was suspected of having died as a result of criminal activity. It was named after Iain West, who was the closest thing to a film star that the forensic profession had yet produced.

"No, it's natural causes according to the GP who attended. It's just a matter of finding out what."

She gazed around the room suspiciously.

"I thought this room was supposed to be unoccupied? What's that in the fridge?"

"Actually, it's my dinner," he admitted defensively. "I didn't think it would do any harm. After all, the room wasn't being used, as you say."

"You know it's against the regulations," she said tartly. "I've told you about this before. There's a risk of contaminating any specimens – you should know that. Anyway, it's unhygienic isn't it? I hope you're not planning on inviting anyone to have dinner with you. I can't imagine anyone would want to eat something that's been lying around in a pathology lab."

He gulped. He had been hesitating for six months now and he felt that if he was ever to get a chance to ask her out then surely this was it.

"Actually," he began.

As if already aware of what it was he was about to say she stared at him in sudden disdain.

"In your dreams, mate," she commented briefly.

It was his first experience of female intuition. As she turned on her heel and stalked out of the room she nearly ran into the mortuary trolley which was being wheeled down the corridor outside. While Dr Patel was regathering what was left of his male self-respect, the attendants deftly slipped the body onto one of the tables and then went on their way with the empty trolley.

He slipped a rectal thermometer into position and then picked up the folder which had come with the body and read Charlotte Tasker's report. Also contained was an identification report. He spotted at once that the former was in the name of Elizabeth Fuller while the latter referred to an Angela Bowen. Puzzled, he glanced from one to the other and then he spotted a supplemental note explaining that initially the deceased had been wrongly identified. He shook his head in surprise, and then read the doctor's note carefully twice before turning to the cadaver.

"You should be done now," he said lightly to the thermometer as he removed it.

It read 4°C which was, he knew, the temperature of the refrigerated unit in which the body had been stored overnight. He shrugged but entered the result into the relevant box of the PM form anyway.

That done, he went over the body minutely looking for marks much more intently and expertly than Dr Tasker had done, but with the same negative result. Again, he noted this on the form. The next stage of the process was to examine the eyes, which he did. At this point he stopped and thought for a few moments and then picked up the phone, after checking which extension to dial.

"Sandra?" he said when she answered. "I'm not happy about this one. I think she should go next door, just in case."

So it was that the next stage in the deceased's journey was by a connecting passageway to the Iain West Forensic Suite next door where a few hours later she was examined by a very august pathologist indeed, so august that not only was he a Professor of Pathology at Guy's Hospital but he also rated an assistant, with whom he was even now discussing the case.

"So Dr Patel thought there might be something for us to take a look at, did he?"

"Yes, he thought the eyes were unusually bloodshot. I've taken a quick look myself and I tend to agree with him."

"Do you? Well, I'm sure you're right but let me just take a look for myself."

He bent over the body, gazing into each eye in turn with the aid of a powerful torch and saying "hm" at intervals.

"You're quite right, both of you," he said as he stood up. "They are much more bloodshot than I would expect. Let's see what we can find in her nose, shall we?"

His assistant produced some swabs and painstakingly wiped around both nostrils, inside and out. She carefully placed each in a separate sterile container and labelled them neatly.

"Right," her colleague said heartily as she finished her task, "let's open her up, shall we?"

…

Detective Chief Superintendent Jim Murray looked tired as he gazed across his desk at Simon Collison.

"Great paper, Simon. I think your proposals make a lot of sense."

"Thank you. I do believe it will make for much greater efficiency to have the teams split into five like this – and to restore the missing layer of management of course."

"Of course, of course."

He squinted at Collison and gave a quick bark of a laugh.

"You being the missing layer of management, naturally?

All you've done is to restore the rank of Superintendent to its proper function."

"I'm aware that some may regard my conclusions as self-serving," Collison said stiffly.

"No need to be defensive with me, Simon. They're sound proposals and I'm entirely in agreement with them. The fact that they may advantage you personally is just a happy coincidence as far as I am concerned."

"Thank you, guv. That's good to know."

"And do call me Jim when we're alone. God knows, Tom Allen does and he's only a DCI."

"Tom Allen is a law unto himself. But I will, and thank you."

"Now, Simon, since all this was your idea I need to ask your advice."

"Go ahead."

"Well, I have a slightly tricky situation to deal with. The transition is still taking place and I don't even have all five Superintendents in place yet. In particular, I don't have anyone covering the new Central division and I have what could be a very difficult case to allocate. Under your guidelines, as I understand them, the sort of case that would be headed by a superintendent as SIO."

"Or perhaps by a very experienced DCI. Tom Allen, perhaps?"

"Perhaps, yes. But this is a suspicious death in a rather special location and I have the feeling that it's going to need very careful handling. Tom is a fine police officer, as we both know, but I have a hunch this may require someone with a little more, how shall I say ..."

"Finesse?"

"Yes, exactly, finesse. In short, Simon, I'd like to allocate this case to you even though it technically falls outside your district. I say "technically" because there is actually a Hampstead connection. Although the death took place in Mayfair the woman whom the deceased was originally believed to be actually lives in Hampstead – for part of the time, anyway."

"Was originally believed to be? I don't understand."

Murray sighed.

"I'm not ruddy surprised. To tell the truth, there's a lot not to understand about this situation. That's another reason why I want someone like you to handle it. The facts briefly are that a woman died during the night at a club in Audley Square: the Athena Club to be precise. A GP who was staying at the club certified death by natural causes and authorised the removal of the body. Since then two problems have arisen. First, it seems the deceased wasn't who they thought she was. Second, we're not so sure about the "natural causes" any more. Of course because nobody had any suspicions the room was cleaned and reoccupied, which means that the crime scene – if that's what it was – was completely compromised and is of no real use to us at all."

"Wow, what a mess," Collison exclaimed.

"Mess is the right word all right. To be honest, I'm worried this may be a bit of a hospital pass I'm giving you. If I was in your place I'm not sure I'd know where to start. I've arranged to have the inquest adjourned, by the way, so that's one thing you won't have to bother with at least."

"Do I assume that because the death was believed to be from natural causes no statements have been taken from anybody who was at the scene?"

"Correct, and to complicate matters still further I guess that a lot of people who were there that night will have moved on and could be anywhere in the world by now. Some members use it as somewhere to spend the night before going to the airport. That's what the woman who runs the place says, anyway."

"So you have spoken to her, at least?"

Murray shook his head.

"Not really. Just a quick chat to get some background."

He consulted his pad.

"Rowena Bradley, she's called. You'll see that I made a note of our conversation for the file. By the way, she happened to notice that one of your mob was there at a function the night before: that Willis female."

"Oh yes, of course. They told me they were going. It was some vintage thing, I believe. A dinner dance or something like that."

"They, did you say?"

"Yes. She and her partner, Peter Collins. He's helped us in the past, remember? And Bob Metcalfe went as well. I think he was squiring that poor girl who got hit on the head."

"How is Bob? He went through a difficult time of it with that business. Didn't they start a disciplinary process?"

"Yes, but then abandoned it, and rightly so in my view.

What he did was an error of judgement at worst, and no valid complaint was ever made by anyone who was involved. He was suspended for a bit while things were getting sorted out, and I think that was tough for him. He had some personal stuff going on as well which I'd rather not talk about if that's okay with you."

Murray gave him a hard stare but then nodded.

"If you think it's nothing I need to know about then I trust your judgement, Simon."

"It's something personal which was told to me in confidence and in my honest opinion it has nothing to do with the Met at all."

"Then, like I say, I trust your judgement. What about Willis? She's very much on the fast track as far as the ACC is concerned, you know. Like you, of course."

"She's first rate. She's got a fine mind and she's very professional."

"Not just a fine mind," Murray observed with a grin. "I think she's probably the most attractive woman I've ever seen. Not that we're supposed to notice these things anymore."

"I don't think anyone expects us not to notice, Jim. We're just supposed not to comment on it."

"Political correctness gone mad," the other growled. "It's a different police force to the one I joined, Simon."

"There have been a lot of changes, certainly," Collison said cautiously, "even in the time I've been in the job, which isn't as long as you of course. But most of the changes have been for the better, I think. Look at Karen, for example. It's not so long ago that she wouldn't have been allowed to play any serious role in an investigation at all. Even now there are people in the force who don't take women officers seriously."

"I won't disagree with you, Simon. Looking back on it, the sort of racism and sexism around the nick back then was appalling, particularly in CID. I'm not condoning it for a moment, it was wrong, but it was just part of the spirit of the job, the place and the time ... there's some fancy name for that, isn't there?"

"Zeitgeist, perhaps?"

"That's it. There you are you see: the benefits of public school and University. No wonder you're marked out for great things, Simon, when you can pluck words like zeitgeist out of the air."

They both laughed.

"But seriously, Simon, when I see the way things are going I begin to feel a bit like a stranger in my own home. I'm not at all sure that I'm cut out for this anymore. It used to be about catching villains and banging them up. Now it all seems to be about reports, and committees, and targets, and guidelines ..."

"Isn't that just the flipside of promotion, though? The more senior you become, the more removed you are from actual policing on the front line and the more your responsibilities become supervisory, managerial."

"Yes of course, but I think there's more to it than that. Nearly 30 years I've been in the job now, and the force has changed almost beyond recognition. It's almost as though it's become two forces which get shoved together and somehow have to coexist. There are the bright young things like you and Willis who can make Superintendent in 10 years or so, and the hardened old coppers who probably get stuck at DS and must know in their heart of hearts that they're not ever going any further. Sometimes I feel that I'm really one of that second bunch who's just somehow accidentally got squeezed up to DCS."

"That you've risen beyond your station, you mean? Do you really believe that? Surely not. I know the ACC thinks very highly of you, for a start."

Murray shrugged.

"Oh, I don't know. Maybe I'm just feeling a bit down in the dumps. Is there some smart German word for that as well?"

Collison reflected for a moment.

"Not really," he observed. "I'm no expert, Jim, my degree was in law not psychology, but I don't think it has anything to do with your career in the police force. It sounds to me like pretty typical middle age angst."

CHAPTER 9

On the way back to Hampstead, Collison called Metcalfe on his mobile.

"Bob? Simon Collison. We've just been handed a case by Jim Murray. Something over at the Athena Club by the way. Isn't that where you lot were the other night?"

"Yes, it is. What's happened?"

"Suspicious death apparently. It may even have happened while you were dancing the night away downstairs. See who you can grab will you? I'm just on the way back to the nick now. We definitely need Karen on this, particularly as she was there the other night and I think she knows the lady who runs the place. See if you can get Evans and Desai as well, will you? The DCS is sending the file round by courier. Can you tell the desk Sergeant to intercept it when it comes in and give it to you? Let's get together, please, as soon as I'm there."

As soon as he arrived, Collison put his head around the door of Metcalfe's room.

"Let's get together in my office, shall we? Bring Karen if you can."

Willis had obviously been expecting the summons for she joined them only a minute or two later. She was wearing a bright purple blouse which in the bright morning sunlight coming through the window seemed to fill the room with a rich, imperial iridescence.

"Right," Collison said as he opened up the folder. "Let's see what we've got here. First, a note from a Dr Charlotte Tasker identifying our victim as Elizabeth Fuller and concluding that she died of natural causes. It now seems that both statements were incorrect. Who is this woman, do we know?"

"If you mean the doctor then yes, guv," Metcalfe confirmed. "As a matter of fact she was on our table at dinner and made a bit of a nuisance of herself. We couldn't get rid of her all evening. It was almost as though she was afraid to be on her own. She even went to the loo with Karen."

"Oh Bob," Willis chided him gently. "Don't be unkind. I think the poor woman was just very lonely, as well as a bit frightened at not knowing anybody else there."

"Is there anything we need to look at there – with the doctor I mean? After all, it does seem a bit strange that she made not one but two inaccurate statements about something so important as a sudden death."

"No, I don't think so, guv," Metcalfe replied, looking questioningly at Willis who nodded in agreement.

"Okay, well clearly we need to explore how she came to get both things wrong, but let's leave that for the moment. Second we have a record of formal identification of the body later the same day as an Angela Bowen. By some strange coincidence the identification seems to have been given by none other than Elizabeth Fuller. Oh it seems they are both professors by the way. Perhaps they were colleagues? Plainly we need to find out everything we can about both of them."

He picked up the next piece of paper.

"This is a note by the pathologist who first examined the body, referring it for detailed post-mortem as he was uncomfortable with a verdict of death by natural causes. He refers to excessively bloodshot eyes."

They exchanged glances. They all knew that this could be a symptom of smothering. Collison took up the next document.

"And here is that post-mortem report. It agrees with the first view and says death could be consistent with smothering. Nasal swabs have been taken and will be analysed. Other than that, there is nothing to suggest any particular cause of death. Heart, major blood vessels and other organs all appear normal taking into account the age of the victim."

"Finally we have a quick note by the DCS of his initial conversation with Rowena Bradley – I think that's the lady you met the other night, isn't it? She explains that both Elizabeth Fuller and Angela Bowen were staying at the club that night and that somehow their rooms got switched around, thus leading to the false identification. She asked Dr Tasker to investigate since she was staying on the premises too. Once the doctor had certified death she, Bradley that is, asked her to arrange for the removal of the body as discreetly as possible. This was apparently done shortly afterwards, with the body being taken to the local mortuary: Westminster in this case."

"Does she say why it was Elizabeth Fuller who went to identify the deceased?" Willis asked curiously. "I would have thought it would have been more appropriate for Rowena Bradley to do it herself."

"No she doesn't. Clearly there's a lot we don't know that we need to know."

"How do you want to proceed, guv?" Metcalfe asked.

Collison thought for a moment.

"Have you managed to grab any other bods yet?"

"I've put in a request to find out where Desai and Evans are, and have them transferred to this team. But, other than that, no."

"Okay then, you stay here and start the incident room. Pull the best team together that you can. Let me know if you have any problems and need me to tell an SIO to release someone to you. Karen, why don't you go and do a preliminary interview with Rowena Bradley?"

"Of course, guv. Anything in particular?"

"Just everything, Karen. Everything you can think of."

Willis headed off on the underground to Green Park. Hyde Park Corner might have been slightly closer, she reflected as she struggled through the crowds of tourists heading to and from Buckingham Palace, but once away from the hustle and bustle of Piccadilly this was a nice walk, along Curzon Street and skirting the hidden jewel of walkways and pavement restaurants that was Shepherd Market on one side, and the machine-gun guarded Saudi Embassy on the other.

Rowena Bradley was hovering nervously in the hallway of the club. She was not actually wringing her hands, but everything about her mien suggested that she might just as well have been.

"Oh God, isn't this all just too dreadful?" she said as soon as Karen made her appearance.

"Yes, it must have been terrible," Willis replied sympathetically, "but there's a huge amount we need to know, Rowena, so please let's sit down and make a start?"

"Yes of course, let's go to my office. I'll order some tea."

Once in the office Willis settled a notebook on her crossed legs and thought about where to begin.

"For a start, why don't you explain the mix-up with the rooms? It's very unusual, you know, for a body to be wrongly identified in a case like this."

"Oh gosh, I know, I'm so sorry. It's all my fault really. I should have taken a proper look at her as she lay there on the floor, but I couldn't bring myself to. I funked it, I'm afraid."

"But if you didn't look at her, how do you know she was lying on the floor? Who told you?"

"Oh I saw her all right, but the top half was all covered in bedclothes so I couldn't see the face. To tell the truth, I just ran straight out of the room. I couldn't bear to see any more."

"I see. Well, let's come back to that – the discovery of the body – shall we? Let's stay focused on what happened with the room numbers."

"Well, I discussed it with Liz immediately after she made her dramatic entrance; it was all rather frightening, you see, what with us all believing her dead and everything. She remembered that she and Angela checked in together at the same time and she thinks that what must have happened is that one or the other of them picked up the wrong key by accident, with the other person then naturally assuming that the key that was left was theirs."

"So Elizabeth Fuller never actually occupied room 16, even for a bit?"

"It seems not, no. She went straight to room 24. When Charlotte – that's Dr Tasker – made her report for the coroner's office she simply looked at my daily guest list, saw Liz's name against room 16, and proceeded accordingly. I think she asked the receptionist for her address. It wasn't until Liz walked into the club about midday alive and kicking that anybody realised the mistake."

"Okay, let's come back to that in a minute. Can we fill in some of the background first? What can you tell me about Elizabeth Fuller, for example?"

"Oh, I've known her for simply ages. We were at university together, in fact, although we didn't know each other very well then as we were studying different subjects. But we had friends in common, so we definitely knew each other a bit; we went to the same parties and that sort of thing."

"Is she married? Children?"

"Yes. She's married to a rather wonderful man called Andrew. You may have come across him, or at least have heard of him. He's a brilliant lawyer, you know."

"I've heard the name, certainly. What sort of man is he?"

Bradley looked slightly nonplussed.

"What sort of man? I'm not sure what you mean. If you mean 'what sort of person' I would say that he's highly intelligent but not the warmest person in the world, not someone to take fools gladly if you know what I mean."

"How long have they been married?"

"Oh, quite a long time now. About 20 years, I think."

"Any children?"

"No, none. I think they are both quite wedded to their careers. In a way they are both quite selfish characters. No, that sounds wrong. Not selfish, but self-reliant perhaps. They both had what they wanted and felt children would get in the way, would be a distraction. That's what Liz told me anyway."

"And what sort of marriage has it been, do you think?"

Bradley considered the question.

"Not a very conventional one perhaps, by some people's standards. But then, they've never set much store by other people's standards, either of them. They're both very bright and very good at what they do and that's really all that matters to them. It wasn't the most passionate of marriages, certainly."

She fell silent and looked at Willis who gazed back at her silently until she felt compelled to go on.

"Oh dear, this is all very difficult. They are both friends of mine you know. Well, I don't think the physical side of things has ever been very important to Liz. She did mention to me once that she didn't find any real pleasure in it. So I think from a very early stage there's been a sort of agreement between them that the marriage will be a largely social one – after all, they both really enjoy each other's company – but that so far as ... well, other things were concerned then Andrew would be free to pursue his interests discreetly elsewhere."

"And has he?"

"Oh yes, very successfully I think. He's a very handsome man you know and there's something about him – a charisma or whatever you want to call it – that indefinable something which some men have. It's charm and self-confidence and lots of other things as well. Do you know what I mean?"

"Yes, I think so. Though personally I tend not to find that sort of man attractive. I like a certain degree of vulnerability. Above all, I like someone who's kind and that sort of man rarely is, is he? Not really, I mean. They may well feign sympathy or interest to get what they want, but once they've had it then you find out pretty soon that they were just putting it on for effect."

"Oh dear, do you think so? Well, maybe you're right, I wouldn't know."

"So Andrew Fuller made a habit of pursuing other women, and you think that his wife knows about this and is happy about it?"

"Oh no. No to both, I think. I don't think he pursues women, rather the other way round. I've often noticed that when a woman meets him for the first time she lights up a little – I'm sure you know what I mean. Her eyes sparkle and she makes a point of laughing at whatever he says. They set out their stall, shall we say, and who's to blame him if he takes advantage of the opportunity? He's a man after all, and we all know what men need; they can't help it."

"Hm," Willis said noncommittally. "But you said the second bit was false as well. What did you mean by that?"

"Oh, I think you asked if Liz was happy about the situation. Actually, I think in the broad sense of the word she was, but I would prefer to say content, or comfortable, or relaxed. You see, she has very strong feelings for Andrew herself so I'm sure she must experience the occasional pang of jealousy when she sees him with other women."

"And yet she doesn't want to do anything about it – to compete as it were?"

"No, as I said, I think that side of things simply doesn't interest her. Oh, I think she went through the motions right enough in the early days, but I think it became obvious to both of them that that's all it was – going through the motions – and sooner or later they came to this sort of tacit understanding."

"I see."

Willis was about to add something, but the phrase 'let he who is without sin cast the first stone' came to mind and she strangled the intended comment with a sardonic smile.

"Just by way of background, partly because I'm curious and partly because I think it will help me understand the situation better, has there ever been a period when Andrew Fuller has been, well ... having an affair with a woman who happened also to be a friend of his wife? And if so, did Elizabeth Fuller ever find out about it?"

"Oh yes, rather. In fact, that's what makes this whole situation so wretched. You see, Angela Bowen was Andrew Fuller's mistress, and had been for some time."

Willis gazed at her in astonishment, her pen paused in midsentence.

"And Elizabeth Fuller knew about this?"

"Oh yes, absolutely."

"I see," Willis said automatically as she regained her

composure and her pen continued on its course. "Hang on a minute, just let me get all this down, will you?"

"Now then," she continued, "let's try to pin down exactly what we know about what happened that night; the night of the vintage party, that is. The doctor seems pretty sure that death occurred sometime between 10 PM and midnight. As I remember it, you were with us part of that time. Weren't you actually on duty, though?"

"Yes, as I explained at the time, the regular night manager had gone sick and so I was deputising. That's why I was flitting in and out all the time. I wanted to be sure that everything was all right, although of course everyone knew where they could reach me if I was needed."

"We left just before midnight, I think. Can you tell me any more about your whereabouts, either before or after that?"

"Gosh, let me think. I suppose I really should have expected you to be asking these sorts of questions. I should have jotted down some notes or something to try to help me remember."

"It's just routine, really," Willis assured her. "Please tell me everything you can remember, no matter how trivial it may seem. Start about 10 o'clock and go on from there."

"Well I think at 10 o'clock we were still having dinner, weren't we? And I know I didn't leave until after that so I must have been with you all in the dining room until about half past. That's when I started moving around, though I kept coming back to the dancing because it was such fun. I came here to my office a few times just to check that nobody was asking for me, and about 11 o'clock I went and checked that the back door was secure."

"And was it?"

"Oh yes, although you can open it from the inside of course."

"I'll take a look at that later if I may. Now, I wonder if it might be possible to track the movements of any other people: Angela Bowen and Elizabeth Fuller for example? Is there CCTV in the bedroom corridors?"

"Yes there is, but I'm afraid it won't be much use to you. You see, we dim the lights from 10 o'clock onwards because people have complained about them shining under the doors and keeping them awake. When the nightlights are on, you can't see anything on the CCTV. Oh, you might see the occasional shape but nothing you could make out distinctly."

"I see," Willis said again. "Well that's disappointing, naturally. Did either of the ladies happen to mention to you whether they had any plans to go out that evening, or to see anybody here for that matter?"

"No I don't think so. I spoke to both of them briefly early on in the evening, before the event started. Angela said she had a bit of a headache – I offered her some pills but she said she had some of her own – and that she was planning to spend a quiet evening in her room. Actually, I have a feeling that was something of a cover story, for I saw her having a drink in the bar with Andrew just before people started arriving. I suspect they went up to her room afterwards. Not strictly against the rules to entertain a gentleman guest, although they are supposed to be out of your room before 10."

Again Willis's pen halted involuntarily.

"Do you mean that Andrew Fuller visited his mistress here at the club that evening even though his wife was staying here separately at the same time?"

"Oh dear, yes, it does sound rather racy when you put it like that doesn't it? But you have to remember that things were all very civilised between the three of them. He might even have told Liz in advance that he was planning to see Angela that night. I don't know – you'd have to ask him yourself."

"And was that the only time you saw him that evening?"

"Yes, I think it was. I didn't see either him or poor Angela again."

"And what about Elizabeth Fuller?"

"She said she was going out to dinner – she would normally have eaten here of course but the restaurant was being used for the event – dinner with a friend, I believe, though she didn't say who."

"Did you see her at all during the evening – say after the event started?"

"No, I didn't. So I don't know what time she got back. It must have been before midnight though, because we lock the door then and anybody coming back after that time has to ring the night bell to be let in."

"Doesn't that inconvenience people?"

"No, not really. Our members are not the sort of people who stay out late at night clubs or anything like that, and anyway everyone knows that this is a club not a hotel. It's not a problem, by the way. Remember there is a night manager so it's only a question of them crossing the lobby to open the door."

"But it must have been open later than midnight that night because people presumably took time to drift away from the event, didn't they?"

"Yes, you're right of course. I think I remember the last people leaving at about half past midnight and I locked the door then. So Liz must have been back by then, at least, because nobody rang the bell that night. I was very grateful for it because I was asleep in the office. I kicked my shoes off and made up a sort of bed for myself in the easy chair."

"And nothing occurred during the night to disturb you?"

"No, nothing at all. In fact I can remember feeling surprised that I slept so well given the rather cramped circumstances. I got up about 6.30 and went to have a shower in one of the bedrooms that we keep for staff – it's a rather cramped one on the top floor which is really too small to offer to a guest. I was down again in time for the start of breakfast at 7 o'clock. But no, I can't remember anything happening during the night, certainly not anything which made enough noise to disturb me anyway."

"And what was your first indication that something was wrong?"

"Well, Liz – or rather Angela but of course we thought it was Liz at the time – had booked an alarm call for 7.30 but the girl at the desk couldn't get her to answer. I was busy with something out in the lobby so I gave the duplicate key to Maria, who was just passing through the hall, and asked her to go in very discreetly just to check that everything was all right. She came running downstairs a couple of minutes later looking completely distraught and saying that she thought Liz – or rather Angela – was dead."

"What happened then?"

"Well at once I remembered that Charlotte was staying with us. You remember Charlotte from the party of course? As it happens she was just leaving her room to come down to breakfast and I took the key from Maria, gave it to her, and asked her to go and see what was happening. I thought it would take me a few minutes to finish up what I was doing with the guest I was talking to, but as it happened she pretty soon realised something was seriously wrong and insisted that I should follow Charlotte upstairs myself."

"So Doctor Tasker went into room 16. Could you see her at that stage?"

"No, she was just out of view. But she couldn't have been in the room more than a few seconds before I arrived because she'd only just had time to put her bag down on the bed."

"And when you went into the room, what did you see?"

"Oh, it was awful. Liz – or rather Angela – was lying beside the bed on her side but with the whole upper part of her body tangled up in bedclothes so it was impossible to see her face. Of course I realise now that what I should have done was to ask Charlotte to uncover the face so that I could see for certain who it was, but I was just expecting it to be Liz you see, so naturally I just assumed that's who it was."

She paused and gazed at Willis uncertainly.

"To tell you the truth, I panicked and ran out of the room. Charlotte came out a few seconds later and said that she was dead all right but that she needed to examine the body. I came back downstairs and waited for her. I was in a sort of daze and I can remember Maria being rather hysterical and having to be looked after. Charlotte came down a little later and said there was no obvious cause of death and that she would write a report for the coroner's office."

"Okay, let's think about how anybody might have had access to room 16. How many master keys are there, for example?"

"Oh my dear, we don't have anything as modern as master keys. There is a key – a real key I mean, not one of these plastic things – for each room which is given to the guest and which they are supposed to leave with the desk if they go out. Then there is a duplicate key for each room which is kept here in my office. They're not used very much. We have quite an old-fashioned system in the morning whereby as each guest checks out their key is given to one of the chambermaids who in turn returns it to the desk once the room is made up. So when we needed to get into room 16 I gave Maria my key, the duplicate key."

"And you say that you slept pretty much all night in your office, so it wouldn't have been possible for anybody to slip in and remove the key without your knowledge?"

"Well, I suppose that technically it might have been possible if they were very, very quiet, but I'm a pretty light sleeper so I think I would have woken up."

"And when you went into room 16, do you remember seeing the guest's key anywhere? Beside the bed for example, or in the lock?"

"I think it was lying on the floor, but I can't be sure. Like I said, I panicked and ran out of the room almost immediately. Silly of me I know."

"All right, I'll make a note that we need to ask both Maria and Dr Tasker about that."

Rowena Bradley gazed hesitantly at Willis as if there was something which she very much wanted to ask but wasn't quite sure if she should.

"Charlotte said death was by natural causes ..."

"Yes, she did, didn't she?"

"But this interest which the police are taking in the matter ..."

"Yes?"

"Well, does this mean that her death was ... well, something else?"

"To be honest, we don't know for certain at the moment and I couldn't tell you even if we did. I can tell you that we are treating her death as suspicious."

Bradley stared at her in horror.

"But that's dreadful! Who would want to harm Angela?"

"That's very much what we would like to find out," Willis replied evenly. "At the moment everything seems very confused which is why we need to know as much as possible about what went on."

"Do you suspect Andrew? You don't, surely?"

"We don't suspect anybody at the moment. We're only just beginning our investigations. By the way, you mentioned to DCS Murray that you told Andrew Fuller some time that morning that his wife had died. How did he take it?"

"He was very upset, naturally. Oh, he didn't subside into floods of tears or anything like that. He's not that sort of man. He's always very in control of himself. In fact, to people who don't know him really well he can come across as being a bit cold. He's not, not really, but it can seem that way."

"And it seemed that way to you that morning?" Willis asked.

"No, because I know him. I've known him and Liz for years. So I could see that he was very upset, poor man. He and Liz are very close, despite the way in which they've chosen to run their marriage."

"And how did you manage to get a message to him later, when you found out I mean? He was in court, wasn't he?"

"Yes, that's right. He managed to get an adjournment for the morning but then went back for the afternoon session. Liz and I discussed it and decided that I should go and see him while she went to identify poor Angela."

"Yes, we wondered about that, why did you choose to do things that way round? Wouldn't it have been more natural for Professor Fuller to go and see her husband while you went to the mortuary?"

"Yes, I suppose it would, but you see Liz knew she couldn't just walk into the courtroom, not with Andrew believing her to be dead, whereas I could. She would have had to wait outside until the case attended for the day and even then it would have been a terrible shock for him when he saw her. So we agreed that I would go into court and try to pass a note, which I did."

"Ah, that explains that, then."

"There's something else as well actually," Bradley confided awkwardly. "Liz knew that I was terrified of having to look at a dead body. She done it before and I think she volunteered to go as much for the sake of my feelings as for Andrew's. As it was, she must have got finished pretty quickly because she was waiting outside court at about 5 o'clock when I came out. I left her and went home so that she and Andrew could be together."

"All right," Willis commented, noticing that she had already filled several pages of a notebook. "We will be needing to speak you again of course, and I'd also like you to sign a formal version of what I've just been jotting down once I've prepared it, but I think that's everything for now. I'd like to see room 16, please, and I'd better take a look at that backdoor as well."

CHAPTER 10

Collison decided to hold an initial team meeting later that afternoon after Willis had returned to the nick. Priya Desai and Timothy Evans had both by now arrived, released from other duties, and so at least they were now a 'team' in more than name only.

"Priya, Timothy, very good to see you both again. We've been asked by DCS Murray to form a special team to investigate a case which falls outside our official area, with myself as SIO. The facts of the case briefly are that two nights ago a lady guest at the Athena Club in Audley Square died during the night. A doctor who was a fellow guest certified death by natural causes as a result of which the body was removed in the ordinary course of events to Westminster public morgue and the room cleaned and reoccupied, thus rendering it effectively useless as a crime scene. By the way, it seems that both DI Metcalfe and DS Willis were attending a function at the club that evening – perhaps even when the murder took place."

"Murder, guv?" Desai queried. "I thought you just mentioned natural causes."

"Yes I did," Collison replied grimly. "It appears that the good doctor got that wrong. It so happens that she also wrongly identified the corpse."

Evans whistled with melodramatic amazement.

"To be fair to the doctor, whom we actually met that evening by the way, the post-mortem report does say that there were no obvious signs of foul play," Willis interjected.

"But what about the dodgy ID, Sarge?" Evans asked. "How on earth did she come to get that wrong?"

"Again, it really wasn't her fault. What seems to have happened is that two women booked into the club at the same time. There was a mix-up; each picked up the wrong key and went to occupy the room that had actually been allocated to the other. So when the doctor asked for the details of the lady in room 16 the receptionist quite innocently gave her the name and address of the wrong woman."

"Talking of the post-mortem," Metcalfe said, holding up a slim folder, "we now have the final report. I'll circulate it of course but to summarise the important points: the deceased's eyes were unduly bloodshot suggestive of death by smothering, and microscopic fragments of cotton material such as is commonly used in bedding including pillow covers were found in the woman's nostrils. The killer point though – no pun intended – is the high level of carbon dioxide in the blood. In the light of all these indicators the pathologist is prepared to state that in his opinion death was indeed caused by smothering."

"Could it be accidental?" Desai asked. "Is that possible?"

"The pathologist says not," Metcalfe replied. "Apparently accidental smothering is virtually unknown outside cases involving very young children who either get caught up in their bedclothes or fall down the side of the mattress. No, it looks like murder all right."

"There's one other thing which may be significant," observed Collison, who had also had an opportunity for a quick glance at the report before Willis's return. "The deceased was about three months pregnant."

"Pregnant?" Willis queried in amazement. "I understood from Rowena Bradley that Angela Bowen was quite elderly."

"Not really: she was 43. Unusually old to be pregnant, certainly, but not exactly rare these days given modern medical techniques."

"I see. It will be interesting to find out just who knew about that. It could have a bearing on what Rowena Bradley told me about the deceased's relationship with Andrew Fuller."

"Hang on, hang on," Collison said quickly. "What are you talking about?"

"I'm sorry, guv, I haven't had a chance to tell you of course but it seems that Angela Bowen was Andrew Fuller's mistress, and had been for some time."

"Why don't you brief us verbally on what you found out, Karen?" Metcalfe suggested. "I know you haven't had a chance to write it up yet but at least it would give us something to think about overnight."

"Okay, well the deceased had been Andrew Fuller's mistress for some time, according to Rowena. The wife – Elizabeth Fuller that is – apparently knew all about it and was quite comfortable with the arrangement. I was told that the physical side of the marriage never really worked out but that they enjoy each other's company as friends and saw no reason to get divorced. The wife and the mistress were apparently friends and former colleagues and so it was a very cosy arrangement for all concerned. Elizabeth Fuller and Angela Bowen actually checked into the club together that afternoon, as I mentioned, and that's how the false identification arose. Rowena Bradley accepts that she should have looked at the body herself, but couldn't bring herself to do it."

"You mean she never actually saw the body?" Collison asked.

"She did see the body, guv, but not the face. The death was apparently discovered by one of the chambermaids – we've yet to interview her – and then Dr Tasker went upstairs to inspect the body for herself. Rowena Bradley followed her into the room almost immediately and saw the body sprawled by the side of the bed but with everything from the chest upwards swathed in bedclothes, so she never saw the face. We are assuming that's the way the maid found things a few minutes earlier, but obviously we need to check that."

"What do we know about Dr Tasker?" Desai asked. "Is there any way she could be involved somehow?"

"No, she just happened to be staying at the club, that's all. In fact DI Metcalfe and I met her the previous evening at a dinner dance. She was on our table. She seemed very nice. A perfectly respectable GP with a private practice which she inherited from her father. She was in London to see some patients the following day. But by all means run her through the computer and see if you can find anything. We obviously need to interview her too."

"Go on, Karen," Collison urged. "What else do we know?"

"The doctor was of the view, having taken the body's temperature, that death occurred sometime around 11 PM the previous evening: say, between 10 and midnight. At that time the dinner dance was still in full swing, though neither Angela Bowen nor Elizabeth Fuller attended it. Elizabeth Fuller told Rowena Bradley that she was going out to dinner with a friend, but we don't know if she actually did, or at what time she returned to the club. Angela Bowen said she had a headache and was going to have a quiet night in but Rowena Bradley saw her having a drink in the bar with Andrew Fuller, and believes they may have gone up to her room together afterwards. She believes that his wife knew he was going to be there that evening with the deceased, although she can't be sure about that."

"We obviously need to find out where both the Fullers were around the time of death," Collison observed. "I've already asked DI Metcalfe to arrange for both of them to be interviewed tomorrow. What else, Karen?"

"I was obviously concerned about possible access to room 16," she went on. "If Andrew Fuller was there at some time, I think we can safely assume that he was let into the room by Angela Bowen using her key. However, for anyone else there would be two ways of getting in: either she would let them into the room herself – which I'm guessing would presuppose it was someone she knew, or at least expected to see there – or they would have needed to let themselves in using the duplicate key."

"You mean using a master key, such as a chambermaid would have?" Metcalfe asked.

"No, they don't have master keys. There is the room key itself, which is given to the guest and left behind when they go out of the club, which allows it to be given to a chambermaid to clean the room. There is also a duplicate of each which is kept on a keyboard in the manager's office. Access to this would be fairly simple as the office itself is not kept locked. However, on the night in question Rowena Bradley was covering for the usual night manager, who was sick, and she spent most of the night asleep in that room, probably from about half past midnight to about 6:30 AM. She says that she is a light sleeper and finds it difficult to believe that anybody could have crept into the room without disturbing her. So that seems to confirm – assuming a duplicate key was used, that is – that the murder must have occurred sometime before half past midnight, which would be consistent with Dr Tasker's view based on body temperature."

"What about access to the building itself?" Desai asked.

"Yes, good point, Priya, I asked about that too. Normally the front door is locked at midnight and anybody coming back after that time has to ring the night bell and wait to be let in. There is a service door – which also operates as a staff entrance – at the rear of the building which gives into a little mews, which can always be opened from inside but is usually kept secured except when deliveries are taking place. I looked at it myself. It's a simple Yale lock and Rowena told me that she checked it was closed before she bedded down for the night."

"Okay, very good," Collison said. "Now, I know we still

only have a very sketchy outline of the facts, but what are our initial thoughts?"

"The change of rooms could be significant," Willis said at once. "Was the killer intending to murder Angela Bowen, or were they expecting to find Elizabeth Fuller? And, once they realised their mistake, why go through with it? Why not just make some excuse and go away?"

"Perhaps they were already too far committed," Desai suggested. "After all, you can't really start smothering someone with a pillow and then suddenly say 'whoops, sorry, wrong person' now can you?"

"And if that's true, then is Elizabeth Fuller still in danger I wonder?" Collison asked thoughtfully.

"Andrew Fuller seems to be pretty much in the frame, doesn't he?" Metcalfe said. "It looks like we can place him in the room itself and if the deceased had suddenly sprung the pregnancy thing on him then that would give him motive."

"Agreed," Collison responded. "Hopefully a lot of these things will start to become clearer when we have a chance to interview the Fullers tomorrow. But what about more practical matters? What else do we need to do?"

"We obviously need to trace as many people as possible who were staying at the club that night," Willis proffered. "I have the list and ordinarily it wouldn't be difficult as they are all club members and we have their contact details, but Rowena thinks that some of them may have been going abroad the next day in which case God knows where they are or how long they will be away."

"Nonetheless, we clearly need to do it," Collison agreed.

"Priya and Timothy, you make a start on that tomorrow. Hopefully we'll soon have some other bodies to assist you."

"I suppose we also need to contact everyone who was at that event," Metcalfe said. "After all, there would be nothing to stop them going upstairs to where the bedrooms are, and the estimated time of death puts it right in the middle of the period just around when we were finishing dinner and starting to go upstairs to dance. We need to find out if anyone saw anything, and exactly which parts of the club they visited. I've got three or four new bods due to join us tomorrow morning, guv. With your permission, I'll put them onto that. I'm sure we can get a list from the organisers."

"Yes, do," Collison nodded. "The other thing we obviously need to do pretty quickly is to get a full picture of the background of Angela Bowen. Assuming this wasn't a case of mistaken identity then somebody somewhere had a motive for killing her. We need to know what it was. Karen, why don't you get onto that in the morning after you've written up your report?"

"Right you are, sir. It may be quite a task actually. Rowena Bradley said she had few friends and no close family, though she did mention a relative in the Cotswolds and I'm trying to trace her. I got the impression that both she and Liz Fuller were very much wrapped up in their work."

"Angela Bowen seems to have indulged in outside activities as well," Collison observed with a smile. "I'm going to be very interested to see what Andrew Fuller has to say about that. Did he know that she was pregnant? And, if so, what was she proposing they should do about it?"

"Speaking of Andrew Fuller, guv," Metcalfe said, "I've been talking to his chambers but it seems he's in court on a fraud case, which is likely to run a few weeks."

"Tell his clerk we can meet with him at his convenience after the court rises tomorrow evening," Collison replied briskly. "Lean on him if you have to. Say that you're sure Mr Fuller would want to give the police every assistance, that sort of thing."

"Will do, guv. It seems Mrs Fuller is around in London at the moment so I've got her booked to come in at 10 o'clock. Would you like to sit in? It would be helpful actually, since we're still a bit shorthanded as yet."

"Yes, let's you and I do both interviews, Bob. By the way, everyone, let's not just naturally assume that the key to this lies in Angela Bowen's relationship with Andrew Fuller, and indeed with his wife. Let's keep an open mind. I know how easy it is to get drawn up a blind alley just because it seems like the obvious solution."

He looked around at the others who did their best to nod sagely. Then he glanced at his watch.

"Okay, let's call it a day. I've got a feeling that we're all going to be working some long hours over the next few days, so let's go home and get some rest."

CHAPTER 11

"Now then, Professor Fuller," Collison explained, after Metcalfe had turned on the tape recorder and made the customary announcements. "I'd just like to make clear to you what's happening. We are making enquiries into the death of Angela Bowen, and this is a formal interview which will be tape-recorded, but we have asked you to come here as a witness, not a suspect. Should that situation change at any time then we have an obligation to tell you so at once, caution you, and advise you of your right to legal representation. However, as I say, that is not the case at present. Do you understand?"

"Yes, quite clearly, thank you."

"Good, then we can start. When did you first learn of the death of Professor Bowen?"

"Shortly after lunchtime. I went back to the club and asked for my key and the receptionist reacted as if she'd seen a ghost, which I suppose she thought she had. Then Rowena came out of her office – Rowena Bradley that is – and she looked pretty shocked as well. She took me into her office and told me they thought I had died during the night. It wasn't me of course, but that's what the doctor had put on the forms."

"Yes, we would like to dig into that a little more deeply if we may. Do you have any idea how the mix-up happened?"

"Yes, I've been thinking about it more and more since I found out what happened, and I'm pretty sure I can explain it. You see Angela and I just happened to arrive at the club more or less at the same time and so we checked in together. That is to say, I checked in first and then she did, but I stayed there chatting to her while the girl did everything she had to on the computer, and I left my key lying on the desk. I think what happened was that she put Angela's key on the desk as well, next to mine. Whoever picked up their key first – and I think it was me – must have just picked up the wrong one. I looked at the number on mine as I walked away from the desk and I presume she did the same; they're on different floors you see. I took the lift as I needed to go up to the second floor, but she didn't come with me so I assume she must have taken the stairs to the first floor."

"What time was this?" Metcalfe asked.

"It must have been sometime around 5 o'clock."

"And did you stay in your room after checking in?" Collison enquired. "And, if so, for how long?"

"I did some work for about an hour and then I felt like a break so I went downstairs and had a cup of tea in the hall."

"So that must have been about 6 o'clock?"

"Yes, but I don't remember exactly. After all, it didn't seem important at the time."

"Did anybody see you? Did you talk to anybody?"

"Yes. Rowena was passing through and she sat and had a little chat with me, for about ten minutes or so. We're old friends you see. We were at university together."

"Can you remember what you talked about?" Collison asked.

"Oh just idle chitchat I think. She asked me what my plans were for the evening and I explained that I was meeting a friend for dinner. She asked me if I knew Angela was staying at the club and I explained that I did because by chance we had checked in together."

"Could I ask who you were planning to meet, and when and where?"

"Another old university friend actually. A lady called Deirdre Thompson. She lives in South Kensington and we met at a restaurant in Shepherd's Market. It's the little Italian one just on the left hand side as you go through the alleyway. I'm afraid I can't remember its name. We met at 7:30 and I returned to the club about 9:15."

"I appreciate this must seem a frightful imposition," Collison said apologetically, "but I'm afraid we will have to ask you for Mrs Thompson's name and contact details. We need to build a picture of where everybody was absolutely for certain, you see."

"Yes, I do see. I'll happily give you what you need."

"Thank you. That's very kind of you. Now, you say you returned to the club about 9:15. What did you do then?"

"I watched television for a while, but not very seriously. There wasn't much on. Then I read a book for a while and then quite soon – about 10:30 I think – I went to bed."

"And just to be quite clear, Professor, did you leave your room at any time thereafter?"

"The next morning yes, quite early. I had a meeting out of

London and I wanted to get an early train. So I was gone by 7 o'clock."

"Would anyone have seen you? Did you have breakfast, for instance?" Collison asked.

"No. Breakfast doesn't start until seven, and when I left there was nobody on the desk. I just left my key and went out into the street."

"And just for the record, between going to your room at about 9:15 the previous night and leaving the club just before 7 o'clock that morning, you didn't leave your room at any time?"

"No. I went to sleep almost immediately when I went to bed and I set my alarm clock for 6:15, which is when I woke up."

"All right, thank you. Now I apologise for having to ask you about some very personal matters, but what can you tell us about the relationship between Angela Bowen and your husband?"

"I suppose you might describe her as his mistress, although that makes it all sound much more wicked than it really was. I'm sure you must been told about this already: by Rowena, presumably."

"Nonetheless, we need to hear it from you please," Collison pressed her gently. "For example, how long has the relationship been going on? As far as you know, that is."

"Oh, there was never any great secret about it, Superintendent. Andrew and I have been married for about 15 years. Almost at once it became apparent that … well, let's just say it became apparent that we were never going to be very much good at the physical side of things – my fault entirely, not his – and I knew that Angela had always found Andrew very attractive. Why not, after all? He's a very handsome man. So it was actually my suggestion that, since we were all friends already, Andrew and I might enjoy the companionship we had together, and that he might find whatever else he was looking for with her."

"And they both agreed to go along with that?"

"Yes, at once. Oh, it was a little awkward at first, but we soon got used to it. As I said, Angela had always fancied Andrew, and she didn't have anyone else in her life, so the arrangement suited her very well. As for Andrew, to be honest it probably wouldn't have mattered whether it was Angela or anybody else. I'm very much in love with my husband, but I know him for what he is. He's a pretty typical man. He needs constant sex, and he doesn't much mind where he finds it."

Collison and Metcalfe gazed at her silently. She returned their glance and laughed softly.

"I'm sorry, am I offending any male sensibilities? In any event, perhaps I should soften that a little. You see, Andrew has always been surrounded by doting women. Both his mother and his older sister believed he was the most wonderful creature that ever walked the earth, and nothing that he wanted was ever too much trouble for them. I'm afraid he came to expect that of other people as well. So it's not just that he needs physical attention, and believes that he has the right to it wherever he finds it. I think it's also that he craves affection, recognition, whatever you want to call it.

He's the grown-up equivalent of a very pretty but very spoiled little boy."

"Do you happen to know," Collison asked cautiously, "if your husband was at the club that night?"

"I didn't see him there, if that's what you mean. But when Angela and I were discussing our plans for the evening – when the keys got swapped – she did mention that she was going to see him for a drink. She didn't say what other plans they may have had the evening, and I didn't ask."

"Just so we can properly understand the nature of the relationship," Collison persisted, "was there ever a time when your husband raised the possibility of leaving you to go and live with Angela Bowen?"

"Good gracious no. Andrew just wanted sex, not commitment. His relationship with Angela suited him fine just the way it was. It left the way clear for him to see other women as well. Oh yes, I've always known about that, though I've never asked for any details."

"Did he ever talk about seeing other women as well as Angela Bowen?"

"No, he didn't have to. I know what sort of person he is. As long as a woman is tolerably attractive he would be quite incapable of saying 'no' if she offered herself. As I said, I think it gives him a sort of ... validation, I suppose. He has a very powerful ego – I suppose that's what makes him such a successful barrister – but it needs feeding, and I think female adulation does that for him."

"Well, thank you for being so honest with us, Professor. There are just a couple more questions which I need to ask."

"Go ahead."

"Can you think of any reason why anyone would want to kill Angela Bowen?"

She shook her head decisively.

"No, none whatsoever. Believe me, I've been thinking about this very deeply and I have absolutely no idea why anyone would have wanted to kill poor Angela. I don't think she had an enemy in the world."

Metcalfe looked enquiringly at Collison, who nodded.

"Did you know that she was pregnant?" Metcalfe asked bluntly.

She stared at him in amazement, and then looked from him to Collison and back again.

"Pregnant?" she echoed. "Surely not? There must be some mistake."

"No mistake," Metcalfe assured her. "It showed up during the post-mortem."

"No, I had no idea." The Professor said vehemently. "How far pregnant? I mean, would she have known about it?"

"About three months," Collison replied. "So yes, I think she must have done. Are you quite sure she never said anything to you about it?"

"Yes, I'm absolutely certain."

"What about your husband? Do you think he might have known?"

"How would I know? You'll have to ask him yourself. Certainly he never mentioned anything to me. I think I would have remembered, you know."

"Very well, now I'd like to touch on a rather delicate matter."

"Even more delicate?" she asked sardonically.

"Well," Collison said with an awkward shrug, "delicate in a rather different way perhaps. You see we have a legal duty to warn somebody if we think they may be in danger. To be honest, I'm not sure whether that duty really applies in this situation or not, but I feel there is something I should raise with you."

"Yes?"

"Well, bearing in mind that you and Angela Bowen had switched rooms without anybody knowing about it, it does occur to us that whoever killed her might in fact have been intending to kill you."

"My God! What a dreadful thought."

She stopped and glanced abstractedly around the room. Then something clearly occurred to her.

"But that's absurd surely? They might have gone into the wrong room intending to kill me, but once they discovered that they'd got it wrong why wouldn't they just slip away again?"

"Who knows? Perhaps Angela Bowen had already got a good look at them and worked out what they were intending to do. In that case they may have had to go through with it just to cover their tracks. After all, how would you explain being in somebody else's bedroom in the middle of the night?"

"I suppose so," she said dubiously.

"So perhaps I could ask the same question again," Collison

went on. "Are you aware of any reason why somebody might want to kill you?"

She stared at him aghast.

"No I am most certainly not," she said emphatically.

"Please stop and think," Collison urged her. "This really could be frightfully important. As I say, we need to form an assessment of whether you may be in danger or not."

"I see," she murmured uncertainly.

She clasped her hands together and gazed resolutely at the table top for a few moments.

"No," she said finally. "I honestly can't think of any reason why anyone would wish me harm. Oh, a few students disappointed in their grades perhaps, but that's hardly a matter for murder is it?"

"It wasn't when I was at university, no," Collison concurred with a smile. "Very well then, Professor, I don't see that there's any reason why we should form a view that you are in danger, not at the moment anyway. But if anything does occur to you subsequently that may be of even the faintest relevance then I do urge you to get in touch with us straightaway and pass it on. As you've just heard, you may have a direct personal interest in doing so."

She nodded.

"I'm sorry," he said, "but for the tape could you please just say that you understand what I have just told you?"

"I understand," she replied firmly, looking at the tape recorder.

CHAPTER 12

Collison and Metcalfe went that evening to the chambers of Andrew Fuller. As they walked through the narrow streets of the Temple, they were reminded of a previous occasion when they had attended a 'con' with Adrian Partington on the very first investigation they had worked on together.

Though they were punctual, they were kept waiting.

"Sorry gents," one of the clerks told them, "Mr Fuller is back from court, but we're trying to find a room for you."

Collison knew of the occasionally chaotic hot desking that went on in barristers' chambers. Unless counsel were very senior they rated only the use of a desk in a communal office. But, Collison wondered, surely an eminent QC like Andrew Fuller would have his own room?

"Superintendent Collison?" came the sudden enquiry as Fuller himself came into the waiting room from the corridor. "I'm so sorry to keep you waiting. My office is being painted, believe it or not. But don't worry, I've managed to kick someone out of the conference room."

"Pleased to meet you, Mr Fuller. I know you by reputation of course. May I introduce Detective Inspector Metcalfe?"

As they made their way to the meeting room the narrowness of the corridor made further conversation impractical so it was only as they were taking their seats that Collison was able to deal with the formalities of their visit.

"It's very good of you to see us like this," he said. "Normally, if we were having this interview at the police station that is, we would be able to use a tape recorder. But as it is DI Metcalfe will take notes and once he has typed them up he will send a copy to you for your inspection. If you see anything there that you don't remember having said, or which appears to you to be a mistake, then please let us know as soon as you can."

"I understand," Fuller said with a nod. "Now how can I help you?"

"As you know we are making enquiries into the death of Angela Bowen. Early indications were that she had died of natural causes but I have to tell you that we now have a post-mortem report which strongly suggests that she was murdered."

"Good God! How?"

"I'm afraid we can't make that information public. But suffice it to say that the pathologist is very confident in his diagnosis. Now, could we make a start by asking you when you last saw the deceased?"

"Yes, I saw her at the club that night. The night she died."

"So I understand," Collison replied evenly. "May I ask exactly whereabouts in the club you were, and between what times?"

"I arrived about six, I think. I went straight from court. The judge rose just after five but I had to hang around for a while and speak to my instructing solicitors. So, yes, six would be about right."

"And did you go up to Angela Bowen's room?"

"Not at first, no. I called her on my mobile as I arrived and we met in the bar for a drink. Then we went out to dinner."

"May I ask where you went?"

"We went to Scott's, just round the corner in Mount Street. I rang ahead on my way to the club and booked a table for 7 o'clock. They know me there. I eat there quite a lot when I'm in town."

"And do you have any idea what time you left, and what time you arrived back at the club?"

"Not exactly. Someone at the restaurant may be able to remember. I would say it was probably sometime before nine and that we got back to the club at around 9 o'clock."

"And is that when you went up to her room?"

"Yes it is."

"It would be helpful for us," Collison said carefully "to know the exact nature of your relationship with the deceased."

Fuller smiled nervously.

"She was my mistress, if people still use that rather melodramatic term. It was well known, I think. We've been seeing each other for a good 10 years or so. My wife knew all about it, and was comfortable with the situation. It was her suggestion originally, in fact."

"And I understand that she and your wife were friends – even before you started seeing each other, I mean?"

"Yes they were. I don't mean to say anything disloyal about my wife, but she has certain ... sexual difficulties. I'd rather not go into details; it's a private matter between the two of us. I believe it may derive partly from something which happened to her when she was young but, as I say, it's personal."

"And you say that it was her suggestion that you and Angela Bowen should embark upon this relationship?"

"Yes. I'm a normal man with all the urges of a normal man. Liz knew that I could never be content with a purely platonic relationship, no matter how convivial we found each other's company, so she came up with this as a pragmatic solution."

"And you say it was well known?"

"Well, we didn't advertise the fact," Fuller said dryly, "but I suspect most people had heard something about it. Like I said, it's been a long time now."

"Okay, thank you for being so honest with us about that. Now, let's pick up the narrative shall we? You went to her room at about 9 o'clock. At what time did you leave?"

"It was about 11. A bit naughty, I know, because I don't think 'gentlemen visitors' are supposed to be in the rooms after 10 o'clock, but I sneaked down to the basement and let myself out through the service door. There's a mews at the back which leads down to Farm Street, and I managed to pick up a taxi around there to take me home."

"To your London home in Hampstead, would that be?"

"Yes I'm normally there during the week, unless it's the long vac and I'm not in court."

"Nobody actually saw you leave the club?"

"No. At the time I thought I was being rather clever but with hindsight of course I wish I had brazened it out by going through the main door. Come to think of it, I probably could have done with no problem because I think there was some sort of event going on. There was music coming from somewhere – dance music, I think."

"There was indeed, Mr Fuller. In fact DI Metcalfe here was tripping the light fantastic at that very event. But be that as it may. I suppose we may be able to trace the taxi driver. Was it an ordinary black cab? And did you pay by cash or card?"

"Yes, a London cabbie, and I paid by cash. I always do in a taxi. I can't be bothered to start fiddling around with the card machine."

"And, forgive me but I must ask this, when you left was Angela Bowen alive and well?"

"Yes, she had just had a shower – we both had, actually – and she was ready for bed. So far as I could tell there was absolutely nothing wrong with her."

"We haven't been able to make contact with her own GP yet. Do you happen to know whether she had any medical problems, or whether she was on any medication?"

"Nothing that I knew about, no."

"Forgive me, but I must ask this question too: can you think of anybody who might have wished to murder Angela Bowen?"

"No, absolutely not. In fact, I don't think she knew that many people. She was a bit of a loner."

Collison pretended to pause for Metcalfe to catch up, but in reality he was considering the situation. He knew that he had two surprise shots in his locker and it was important to use them for maximum effect. Perhaps now was the time.

"So do I understand you to say," he asked, conscious that he was starting to sound like a barrister himself, "that this relationship with Angela Bowen was essentially symbiotic – that you each got out of it what you needed?"

"Yes, I suppose you could describe it like that."

"And yet we have evidence," Collison went on, gazing directly at him, "that on occasion you saw other women as well."

Fuller started and then shifted uneasily. A hit, Collison thought with satisfaction.

"Well," Fuller began. Then he paused and looked pointedly at Metcalfe's notebook.

"Does this really have to be on the record?" he asked.

"Yes I'm afraid it does," Collison replied formally. "I would remind you that this is a murder enquiry. You are entirely free to refuse to answer the question, of course."

"No, I'm happy to cooperate," Fuller said at once.

"Very well. Then I'm assuming from your reaction that what we have been told is correct …?"

"Well, you know how it is," Fuller answered breezily.

"No, Mr Fuller, I don't know how it is. Tell me."

"Well, as I said, it's been a long time. 10 years at least. That's a long time to be faithful to any woman, regardless of whether she is your wife or your mistress. There are times when you fancy a change, something different. And if it comes along, then why not?"

"And did Angela Bowen know about these 'something different' occasions?"

"No, of course not. At least, I don't think so. If she did, she never said anything."

"You see, Mr Fuller, as I'm sure should be obvious to you

as an experienced barrister, one of the things we need to try to establish is whether you yourself might have had any cause to wish harm to the deceased."

Fuller gasped. He seemed genuinely taken aback.

"Well ... yes ... I mean I realise of course that you have to do that, but why on earth would I possibly want to murder Angela? The relationship suited me perfectly. Angela, God rest her soul, was a lovely lady. Oh, she wasn't obviously beautiful or anything like that, but she was always very eager to please if you know what I mean. The last thing I would ever have wanted to do was to bring it to an end.".

"But what if she had found out about one or more of your other women? Would she really just have taken that in her stride, or might she have got upset? Might she not have taken the view that here she was giving you everything you wanted, and that it was a pretty poor show for you to go and seek little extras elsewhere?"

"Like I said," Fuller said shortly, "she didn't know. Leastways, if she did then she never said anything to me about it."

"Very well," Collison acknowledged. "So are you saying that during that last meeting, which lasted for about five hours on the evening in question, there were no cross words between you? No argument, no heated discussion, nothing like that?"

"No. Actually, Angela and I never had arguments. It was one of the great attractions of the relationship. In all those years I can't remember even one example of us falling out over anything."

Collison paused once more.

"Did you know that Angela Bowen was pregnant?"

The question, though quietly asked, seemed to explode inside the room with the force of a hand grenade. Fuller, who had reddened a little during the previous exchange, suddenly paled and opened his eyes wide.

"Dear God, no," he gasped. "Surely you're joking. It's impossible."

"Why impossible?"

"Because Angela couldn't have children. That's what she told me, anyway. That's why we never used any contraception. Not so far as I was aware, anyway. I suppose she could have been on the pill without telling me ... but no, that's ridiculous, why would she?"

"I'm trying really hard, Mr Fuller, but I find it very difficult to understand why a woman who is in a long-term relationship to which, you say, she believes the father of her child to be entirely faithful, should not want to break the news to him that she is going to have a baby."

Fuller stared at him speechlessly.

"You see one of the things we do during an investigation is to form a hypothesis. We keep testing it until we find something which proves it false, and then we start all over again with a different one. And it might be rather tempting in this case to start with a hypothesis that Angela Bowen did indeed tell you that evening that she was going to have a baby, and that you were the father, and ask you what you intended to do about it."

"I just told you, she never said a word about it."

"But suppose she did, Mr Fuller? Suppose she wanted you to leave your wife and marry her in order to give her child – your child – respectability and a stable family environment? You might not have liked that idea very much. Meeting someone for sex once or twice a week is one thing. Caring for a child full time is quite another. Milk, sick, noise, inconvenience ... and certainly very little sex. Not what you were looking for at all, eh?"

"But it didn't happen like that. What you told me just now came as a complete shock. I didn't know, you have to believe me."

Fuller stared hard at Collison as he said this. The tension in the room was palpable now. Overall, Collison was satisfied with the effect his two surprise gambits had achieved. At the same time, however, he felt a sense of frustration. That had he had just one more lever the door might have come crashing open. As it was, he had shot his bolt for the moment. It was time to consolidate the position and take time to consider what should happen next. He clasped his hands in front of him and returned Fuller's gaze.

"As you know very well, Mr Fuller, we are under a duty to inform those we interview whether we are doing so viewing them as a suspect or as a witness. At the moment, we are treating you as a witness, and a very important one given that you seem to have been the last person we know of to have seen the deceased alive. That is why this interview has not been conducted under caution, as you must be aware."

Fuller nodded, but uncertainly as if he knew there was more to come.

"In the light of what you have told us today my colleagues and I will be considering over the next day or so whether we need to change that stance. If we do, then we will invite you to come to the police station and be interviewed again under caution. In that case, you will of course be entitled to have a legal representative present should you wish. I know that you understand these matters, but I would like to ask you formally to confirm that for the record."

"Very well. Yes, of course I understand," Fuller replied tetchily. "I'm a QC for God's sake."

"Thank you very much, Mr Fuller," Collison said smoothly. "In that case I don't think we need to detain you any longer."

CHAPTER 13

"So are we saying that the husband's favourite, sir?" Evans asked the next morning as Metcalfe finished reading his notes of the previous evening's interview.

"He seems our best suspect so far, yes," Collison replied. "It's difficult to get past the fact that he was the last person to see her alive. He says he left her room at 11 o'clock and we think that's bang in the middle of the period when she must have been killed. By the way, while I think of it, we need to make absolutely sure of the time of death. Priya, could you please speak to the pathologist this morning and double-check what he thinks on that?"

"We don't even know for sure that he left at 11, guv," Metcalfe pointed out. "We've only got his word for it."

"Yes, and doesn't it seem a bit strange that he didn't go out through the front door?" Willis observed. "I went down to the Ladies shortly after 11 and there were a lot of people milling around. So it's not as though he would necessarily have been noticed leaving the club. Or rather, nobody would have thought twice about it. They would just have assumed that he'd been at the event. Okay, he wasn't wearing evening dress, but he was presumably wearing a suit if he'd come from court ..."

"All we can do is try to trace the taxi driver," Collison

replied. "Timothy, can you get onto that please? We looking for someone who picked up in Farm Street around 11 o'clock and dropped his fair off in Hampstead."

"Right you are, guv," Evans said, making a note.

"I have a feeling that a key factor here is going to be Angela Bowen's pregnancy," Collison commented. "Did she tell Andrew Fuller or not? If she did, then that might have changed everything. He'd been having a cosy little relationship with her for the last ten years or more with never a threat of commitment. If he were suddenly confronted by a woman telling him that she was about to have his baby and demanding that he leave his wife to help her bring it up, that would be a very different kettle of fish, wouldn't it?"

"But he claims that she didn't tell him," Metcalfe reminded him.

"I know that's what he said, and on the surface he seemed quite convincing. But don't forget that he's a very experienced criminal court lawyer. A lot of his job is acting, and particularly seeming upset at the drop of a hat. On balance, I'm not sure that he convinced me. What about you?"

"I'd probably go the other way," Metcalfe admitted, "but I must confess I hadn't considered what you just said. Maybe he was play-acting for us after all. I don't know."

"You raise an important point though, Timothy," Collison said. "We clearly need to come to a formal decision about whether we are going to re-interview Andrew Fuller under caution as a suspect. Right now I'm inclining to 'yes', but my instinct is to defer that decision as long as we can. Thoughts, anyone?"

"I'd suggest completing the interview process first, sir," Willis ventured. "There's the doctor and the maid for a start. I've got the maid lined up for this morning and I also have a call out to the doctor."

"I'd agree with that, guv," Metcalfe said quietly. "Also, we kill two birds with one stone. We get a more complete picture of events and we can also use the ongoing process as an excuse not to come to a decision yet on whether to treat Andrew Fuller as a suspect."

"Yes, okay, that all sounds sensible," Collison replied. "Now, what do we think about Elizabeth Fuller?"

"She too was on the premises when the murder took place," Desai observed. "But she doesn't have any obvious motive, does she? Angela Bowen was her friend and it was she who suggested the arrangement in the first place. It seems as if it had run to everyone's satisfaction for a long time, so what incentive would she have suddenly to upset things now?"

"Well now, Priya, I've been thinking about that too. What if Angela Bowen told her that she was pregnant? They were friends after all. So I do have this alternative hypothesis that she may have told Elizabeth Fuller she was going to have a baby, and asked her how she thought Andrew would take the news."

"Wow, yes," Willis exclaimed. "Suppose she was suddenly panic stricken that Bowen was going to demand that Fuller divorce his wife to marry her? It seems clear that she has always been very much in love with her husband and that the only reason she suggested this three-way relationship was to keep him for herself, as a companion at least. If she was suddenly threatened with the possibility of losing him, who knows what she might have done? She might have listened out for him to leave the building and then gone downstairs and knocked on her door."

"She might indeed," Collison agreed. "That's something else that gives me pause for thought, you know. If we have another viable suspect then can we really treat the husband as one?"

"The problem is, of course," Metcalfe said thoughtfully, "that in order to decide between these two possibilities we need to know what the deceased said to whom, and there's no way of finding out from her, is there? So it looks like we're stuck with what the suspects themselves are telling us."

"So that's the first two possibilities as I see things," Collison went on, "but in my view there is a third, and it raises a very serious concern."

"You mean did someone murder Angela Bowen thinking that she was actually Elizabeth Fuller?" Willis asked.

"Yes, that's exactly what I mean. They might actually have killed her by mistake – in which case they must have been someone who had never seen either woman before – or they might have already put themselves in such a compromising situation by the time they realised their mistake that they felt they had no option but to carry on and finish the job. In either case, it raises the possibility that Elizabeth Fuller may currently be in danger. After all, the case has been reported in the papers this morning so they will presumably already have discovered that they got the wrong woman."

"If it was someone who really did believe until this

morning that they had killed Elizabeth Fuller, then as you say it must have been someone who was a complete stranger to both of them," Willis reasoned, "but why would a complete stranger have a motive for murder?"

"Yes, that's been troubling me too," Collison said. "I rather think that if we go down this avenue we have to choose my second conjecture, namely that they did realise their mistake but that for whatever reason it was too late to pull out. Either way, the question we need to address is who would want to kill Elizabeth Fuller, and why."

"We did ask that, guv, and she said she had no idea," Metcalfe interjected.

"Agreed, and I tend to believe her, but suppose it's some unbalanced individual who has taken undue offence over some seemingly trivial occurrence? Or some woman who's become obsessed with Andrew Fuller? Or even – it seems bizarre but we have to consider the possibility – some psychopathic serial killer who roams hotel corridors gaining entrance to people's rooms and smothering them?"

"We can deal with that last point easily enough," Metcalfe commented. "We'll run a computer search for similar offences. I must say, it seems very unlikely given the level of security in hotels nowadays."

"I agree, and I'm sure we would have heard about it anyway, but let's run the check anyway so that we can tick that particular box."

"Excuse me, guv," Desai said suddenly, "but suppose there was such a nutter at work, and suppose that the killings were diagnosed as natural causes – as this one was initially – then presumably nothing would show up on the computer, would it?"

"Damn, I wish I hadn't mentioned it now," Collison said with a smile. "All right, Bob, let's widen the search to include unexplained deaths by natural causes; in the last two years, say."

"Other points to report, guv," Metcalfe said, looking at his notes. "We're trying to trace everybody else who stayed the night on that floor. It looks like at least two of them were heading off abroad the next morning, but I'm confident we'll get to them all sooner or later. I'm also getting the guest list of the dinner dance from the event organiser. You never know, if this was planned in advance then somebody may have used the event as a way of gaining access to the premises."

"Yes, I hadn't thought of that. It would be helpful to know how far in advance Angela Bowen booked a room. Could you deal with that please, Karen?"

Collison consulted his own notes.

"I've been thinking about the keys," he commented. "Unless our murderer was relying on Angela Bowen to let them into her room – and it seems hard to believe that she would have invited a complete stranger in at gone 11 o'clock – then somebody must have got hold of the duplicate key to room 16. It seems that may not have been too difficult if Rowena Bradley was flitting around. She may even have gone into her office at some stage and not even noticed that the key was missing from the board. After all, why should she? Was there any CCTV in the hall outside her office, Karen?"

"There is one CCTV camera only, and it's not a very satisfactory set-up," she reported. "It only has a partial view of the hall – at the foot of the stairs to be exact – and is one of the old sort of cameras that takes a still photograph every two minutes or so. I'm having the film checked for the period between 10 o'clock and midnight, but I'm not holding out any great hope of coming up with anything."

"That's unfortunate, to put it mildly," Collison observed. "If we can't place somebody removing the key from Bradley's office then we're thrown back on Mr and Mrs Fuller, our two existing suspects. Andrew Fuller admits that he was in the room anyway, while Angela Bowen would presumably have opened the door to Elizabeth Fuller without question. She might have said that she wanted to borrow some face cleanser, or something like that."

"I still can't quite believe that we were there at the time, actually on the premises," Willis said. "While we were enjoying ourselves dancing, somebody was killing Angela Bowen in her room. If only we could remember something that might give us a lead, but my mind's a complete blank."

"Nonetheless, I think you and Bob should make formal statements setting out whatever you can remember. Lisa Atkins and Peter as well."

"Of course, guv, I was going to suggest that myself. I'll try to remember if there were any specific times that Rowena left the room, because that might give us more of a handle on when someone could have removed the key from her office. It could be difficult though, because I wasn't wearing a watch and I don't remember there being a clock upstairs in the library. In fact it was only when I asked Peter to tell me the time that I realised how late it was."

"I'll do the same," Metcalfe said. "I was wearing a watch, but I don't remember looking at it very often. And time did seem to pass very quickly, didn't it? Apart from when I was lumbered with that wretched doctor woman, that is."

"Yes, and the fact that she may have a better grasp of the timeline is the reason why I'm looking forward to taking her statement," Willis remarked. "After all, she was with us all the time, wasn't she? And I don't remember her dancing much, either. Peter asked her a couple of times, of course ..."

She broke off and looked accusingly at Metcalfe.

"I asked her once," he said defensively. "After all, I was talking to Lisa and anyway Peter's a much better dancer than I am."

"Hm, that's as may be but the fact remains that she's probably more likely to remember specific times then we are. I do remember looking over at the table a few times while I was dancing with Peter and she seemed to be deep in conversation with Rowena each time."

"Okay, then the order of business for today seems to be to interview the doctor and the maid, find Andrew Fuller's cabbie, chase the CCTV footage, run a PNC check on deaths in hotel rooms, and track down fellow residents from the night of the murder," Collison said, jotting the items down for himself as he did so. "Bob, I'll leave it to you to assign individual responsibilities. Let me know during the day if anything turns up, will you? I have to go and brief DCS Murray."

CHAPTER 14

"Dr Tasker," Willis began formally for the benefit of the tape recorder, "thank you very much for agreeing to travel into London and be interviewed. I just want you to understand that you are not being treated as a suspect and therefore this interview will not be under caution. We are however very keen to ask you certain questions since you are obviously a key witness to what happened. Do you understand what I have just said?"

"Yes, I do."

Willis gestured to Evans.

"Also present is DC Evans," he piped up.

"Okay, let's begin," Willis said briskly. "Now first of all, can you tell us how it was that you came to examine Angela Bowen?"

"Yes. I was about to go down for breakfast when the phone rang in my room and it was the girl on the desk with a message from Rowena Bradley. She was in a bit of a state. Apparently one of the guests had been reported dead by one of the chambermaids and Rowena wanted me to go and take a look."

"What time was that – do you remember?"

"Well, my alarm went at seven and I got straight up and

went in the shower. I was just finishing getting dressed so I would guess that it was sometime around 7:30."

"And you went downstairs straightaway?"

"More or less straightaway. Within a few minutes, certainly."

"What happened then?"

"Rowena gave me the key to the room – room 16 it was – and asked me to go and see how things were. I realised at once that the maid was hysterical and needed someone to look after her, so I suggested that Rowena stayed where she was while I went on my own. In the event though she must've found somebody to pass the maid off to pretty quickly because she ended up fairly close behind me. I only just had time to get my bag from my room and then get to room 16 before she was there too."

"Can you remember whether the door was open or shut? And locked or unlocked?"

"It was open. Presumably the maid had left in such a hurry that she hadn't thought to close it. I pushed it fully open and went in. I saw at once the body of a woman – I say 'body' I suppose because with the benefit of hindsight I now know she was already dead – lying beside the bed, almost as though she had fallen out of it. Most of the upper part of the body, including the head, was wrapped in bedclothes. I wondered if she had experienced some sort of cardiac event and had got tangled in the bedclothes as she fell out of bed."

"Okay, it's probably better if you just tell us what you did rather than what you thought. Can you tell us precisely what happened next?"

"Yes I heard Rowena come into the room behind me and say 'oh my God' or something like that. She seemed very shocked so I told her she could wait outside while I made my examination. She nodded and went out. I knelt down beside the body and felt for a pulse, but there wasn't one. Her arm as I felt it was noticeably cold, much colder than it should have been had she been alive. Once I was sure she was dead, I went out into the corridor where Rowena was waiting and broke the news to her."

"Can you remember what she said?"

"Not exactly, no. I do remember that she thought almost immediately about the husband. At that time, of course, it was assumed that the dead woman was Professor Fuller. I'm very sorry about that by the way, but it really wasn't my fault."

"Don't worry, we'll come to that in due course, but for the moment just carry on telling us what you can remember."

"Well, I explained that there were a few things I had to do in order to be able to prepare a note for the coroner, so I went back into the room while Rowena went downstairs. I took a rectal thermometer from my bag – my father taught me always to carry one, he was very old-fashioned about such things – and inserted it. While I was waiting for that, I examined the body fairly closely, particularly the head and face, but I couldn't find any marks to indicate a blow, or anything like that. In fact there was nothing I could see to indicate anything other than death by natural causes."

"Were her eyes open or shut?" Willis asked curiously.

"They were open."

"And you didn't think that their being bloodshot was suspicious in any way?"

"To be honest, no I didn't. I've never worked as a police surgeon, or a pathologist, or anything like that. Like I said, it just looked like natural causes, which is what I said in my note."

"Okay. Then what happened?"

"Once the time was up for the thermometer I took it out and made a note of the temperature, which was 24°C. That was pretty much all I could do, but before I left the room. I turned off the central heating and opened the window because it was quite warm in there and I wanted to preserve the body as well as possible as I knew there may well have to be a post-mortem."

"You've told us that Rowena Bradley gave you a key to the room," Willis said, consulting her notes. "Presumably that would have been her duplicate key that is normally kept in her office?"

"It was a duplicate key, yes, because the original was in the room. I don't know where she normally keeps it, but if you say it was her office then so be it."

"Ah, that's interesting. So you saw the guest key? Where was it? On the bedside table?"

"No, actually it was on the floor about halfway between the bed and the door. I thought that was a bit strange at the time. I wondered if she had been scrabbling around in the dark and had knocked it off the bedside table in the process."

"Did you move it at all?"

"Yes, I'm afraid I did. I picked it up and put it on the

bedside table. I'm so sorry. You see, at the time I had no idea it might be a crime scene. If I had, of course I would have been much more careful not to disturb anything."

"That's okay," Willis said sympathetically, "nobody is blaming you for anything that happened. Now tell us how the body came to be misidentified, will you?"

"Well, it really was the most ridiculous thing. You see the only person who had seen her face was me and of course I didn't know her from Adam, so I asked the receptionist for the name and address of the lady in room 16 and copied them down into my note. So far as Rowena and the receptionist knew, the woman in room 16 was Elizabeth Fuller. I understand the mistake wasn't discovered until later in the day."

"Yes, that's right. By the way, what inference did you draw from the temperature of the body – as to the time of death, I mean?"

"Oh, that's quite simple," the doctor replied. "It's something everyone learns at medical school. You start with the normal body temperature of 37.5°C and then deduct 1.5°C for every hour that passes until you get to the actual recorded temperature. In this case there was a difference of 13.5°C, which meant that death had occurred approximately nine hours earlier. Counting back from just before 8 AM that would give a time probably between 10:30 and 11:30 the previous night."

"Yes, we wanted to ask you about that. Of course around the time of death we were together weren't we? We were dancing, or at least I was for most of the time. In fact, because

I was dancing so much and I wasn't wearing a watch I really don't have a very good recollection of exactly what happened when. Can you help at all?"

"Well, of course I'll try but I'm really not sure that I can remember anything in particular that might be of interest. I remember that we all went upstairs together from where we were sitting for dinner. That must have been about half past ten, wasn't it? I remember somebody grumbling about it being later than advertised which would leave less time for dancing."

"Yes, that's pretty much how I remember it too. But what about after that? Can you remember anything that happened upstairs? Can you remember anybody leaving the room and coming back, for instance?"

"I think Rowena did a few times, didn't she? She was on duty of course. I didn't leave the room myself except once, to go to the loo. And I think either you or the other girl came with me, didn't you? I remember both going downstairs and upstairs again with somebody else. Surely that was you, wasn't it?"

"Again yes, my recollection is the same. I'm really not sure what I'm looking for here. After all, the bedroom was in a different part of the club and there is no direct access to it from the library. You'd have to go downstairs to the hall and then back up the other staircase. Ah well, it was worth a try I suppose."

"How dreadful," Dr Tasker murmured, "to think that we were dancing and enjoying ourselves just a short distance away from where someone may have been murdered."

"No 'may' about it, I'm afraid," Willis responded briskly.

"The post-mortem report is pretty definite about the cause of death."

"Which was smothering, presumably? If you're talking about the eyes being bloodshot, that is?"

"I'm afraid I can't discuss the detail of the report," Willis said firmly. "This is a murder enquiry, you know."

"I'm sorry, I didn't mean to pry. I was just putting two and two together."

"That's all right. Now, can you tell us where you went when you left the club?"

"Yes, I went to make house calls on two patients, one who lives in Marylebone and one in Holland Park. To be honest, I don't have that many patients left. It's a practice which I inherited from my father. Not many people want an old-fashioned private physician any more, and those who do are dying off. I've lost two or three in the last few months actually."

"So most of your patients are elderly then?" Willis asked.

"All of them really," Tasker said with a laugh. "You might say that my practice is in terminal decline. I've only got about a dozen patients left, so it's very difficult to make things pay."

"Doesn't that worry you?" Evans cut in curiously.

"No, not really," she said, looking at him. "You see, my father left me a very large house which I really don't need, so I'm planning to sell it, buy a little place at the seaside somewhere, and put the rest away as a sort of pension pot. I've had a few small bequests from patients over the years as well. It used to be customary in private practice, and I'm glad to say that my father's patients take great pains to keep the tradition alive."

"How often you come into London?" Willis enquired.

"Only as often as I need to see my patients really. Oh, and I did a little bit of consultancy work for a court case a little while ago. In fact, I met Andrew Fuller – that's the husband, isn't it? – really, what a coincidence!"

"Hang on," Evans said, "are you saying that you knew Elizabeth Fuller's husband?"

"Yes, but it was only when I read about him being a famous barrister that I made the connection. But anyway, I don't really know him. I just met him a few times, that's all. I had been examining someone who was injured in an accident and was trying to claim damages from the person responsible. I had to go and see Andrew Fuller in Chambers a couple of times to advise him on the other side's medical evidence."

"When was this?" Willis asked.

"Oh about six months ago, I think. I could easily check the dates in my diary if it's important."

"But, just be clear, you never met Elizabeth Fuller?"

"Oh no, never. It was just a couple of professional meetings, that's all, I didn't know him socially, as it were."

"Right," Willis said, thinking quickly. "Yes, I think it would be helpful to have those dates please. Just for the sake of completeness you understand?"

"Yes of course, no problem at all. I will check my diary when I get home and give you a ring if I may."

"Thank you very much, that would be great. Perhaps we could also have the names and addresses of those two patients you saw that day as well? Again, we do need to check on every detail I'm afraid."

"You won't go worrying them, will you? They're both quite frail you see."

"We will have to contact them, yes, just to corroborate your statement, but I promise we'll be very gentle and discreet."

"Very well," Dr Tasker said resignedly, "but please do your very best, won't you? There's one of them in particular that I'm very worried about."

"I promise we will," Willis assured her. "Now, we're going to type up everything you told us into a formal witness statement and when it's ready we'll need you to go through it very carefully and then sign it once you're happy with it, but since you live out of London we can do that by post or email if you like."

"Yes of course, I'm very happy to do anything I can to help. I can't help thinking that some of this is my fault somehow."

"Interview terminated," Willis announced, looking at the clock, "at 1646."

CHAPTER 15

By the time of the regular meeting the next morning some further new members of the team had arrived, bringing the total number up to around a dozen. The new arrivals listened nervously as Collison asked Metcalfe "okay, Bob, what news?"

"Most importantly, guv, we've interviewed both the doctor and the chambermaid. You may have had a chance to see the transcripts which went on the system yesterday evening."

"I haven't, I'm afraid. I was with DCS Murray until quite late. Why don't you give me the gist?"

Metcalfe nodded to Willis.

"We didn't get much at all from the maid," she reported. "We understand that she was pretty hysterical at the time. All she can confirm was that the door was locked and that when she unlocked it and went in she saw the deceased sprawled beside the bed. Her description, such as it was, corroborates exactly what the doctor said. The bedclothes were wrapped around the upper part of the body. She only stayed in the room a second or two and then she turned and ran out, neglecting to close the door behind her. I got in touch with her again following our interview with the doctor and, after a bit of prompting, she also remembered seeing the guest key lying on the floor about halfway between the bed and the door."

"Okay, not very helpful then," Collison commented. "Now, what about the doctor?"

"Not a lot that we didn't know already, I'm afraid. She was called in her room at about 7:30, told what had happened, and asked if she would come down to get the duplicate key and take a look in room 16 with Rowena Bradley. When she went down she saw at once that the maid was hysterical and needed someone to look after her. So she offered to go up to the room by herself."

"Did she go straight there, do we know?" Collison queried.

"She says she went back to her room first to collect her bag. In the couple of minutes or so that it took to do that Rowena Bradley must've found somebody to hand the maid off to, because the two of them arrived at room 16 almost together, with Tasker just ahead. That all gels with what Bradley told us, by the way."

"Okay, go on."

"She checked that the deceased was indeed dead and then went to report this to Bradley, who had run out of the room in some distress and was waiting in the corridor. She says Bradley thought at once of the husband. Tasker explained that there were a few checks she needed to make before she could complete her report, and suggested that Bradley went back downstairs to get on with things. Tasker went back into the room, and the rest was pretty much as she laid out in her note for the coroner."

"What did she say about the time of death?" Collison

asked. "We really do need to be as precise as possible about that."

"Her calculation would suggest sometime around 11 PM, guv. I spoke with the pathologist afterwards and he agreed her conclusion. I pressed him and eventually he conceded that provided the room had been kept at a reasonably stable temperature then she was probably accurate within half an hour or so each way."

"So between 22:30 and 23:30 then?"

"That's what it looks like, yes."

"Okay. Thank you, Karen. What else do we have, Bob?"

"First item, guv: Evans has traced the cabbie. He confirms that he picked up a fare who matched Fuller's description in Farm Street at about 23:05. He can be pretty exact about the time because he was listening to a phone-in on Radio London and they'd just had the break for the news. He took him to Church Row where he was paid in cash, just as Fuller said. I've checked and Fuller does indeed own a house there."

"Okay, good. What else?"

"Second: we've examined the CCTV film from the camera in the hallway. As expected, it's pretty useless. There are a couple of shots of Rowena Bradley heading towards and away from her office at 22:46 and 22:58 respectively but that doesn't tell us anything new as we already know that she was popping in and out for the couple of hours or so after we left the restaurant at 22:30. The CCTV camera in the corridor where room 16 is situated is useless too. As Bradley told us, the lights are dimmed almost to nothing and after that it's too dark for the camera to pick up any proper image."

"I hope there is some good news somewhere," Collison observed grimly.

"Yes and no, guv," Metcalfe replied apologetically. "The good news is that we've managed to get a full attendance list from the organisers of the dinner dance. They've been very helpful, in fact. We also have from the club a list of all the members who stayed the night. The bad news is that there are about 120 names on the first list and over 30 on the second. Even with the new bods who've joined us we just don't have the resources to tackle anything like that. We'd need a major incident room and a team of two or three times the size."

He broke off and, in the ensuing silence, gazed sadly at Collison. The latter was suddenly struck by an idea.

"Hey, I've just remembered something," he said thoughtfully. "You know I've just been preparing a paper for the Met, and that I had somebody from Cass Business School helping me? Well this chap, John Watt is his name, was telling me that one of his colleagues there has produced some very sophisticated statistical software which is intended for use in the digital marketing space. It's apparently able to handle large amounts of data and identify what might at first appear to be completely random connections. The idea is that if you can identify something which your potential customers have in common, even if it's nothing to do with the product or service itself, you can use that as a sort of backdoor to gain access to them, often much more cheaply than through conventional advertising."

He gazed around the room and was met mostly either

by blank stares or people looking very hard at their notes. Obviously he wasn't explaining this very well.

"Well, it's probably not that important for our purposes that we should understand exactly how it works," he said quickly, "although of course we do have something similar already which sits within the Met's own system. The problem is that all it has to go on are our own records, and as we all know they have their limitations. First, if someone has never been involved in an investigation before then they won't be on the system. Second, it all depends how that information has been categorised and entered. Remember the Yorkshire Ripper case? When he was first stopped by the police, years earlier, and was found to be carrying a hammer it was assumed that he was going out housebreaking, so it was classified as burglary equipment. So even though there was only a card index system back in those days, no match for a hammer was found."

"So how does this work exactly then, guv?" Desai enquired.

"Well, I remember John saying that it needed to be hooked up to as many information sources as possible. Apparently that's very expensive for anybody other than a very large business. Even the business school has not been able to test it properly because of restrictions which apply to their licence agreements. Their databases are intended for student or research use only, whereas this software has been developed for commercial application. I remember thinking at the time that this wouldn't be a problem for us. After all, we already have access to just about every information source in the country. Assuming our IT chaps can hook it up then this might be a brilliant opportunity to try it out."

"Sounds promising," Metcalfe agreed cautiously. "How do you want to proceed, guv?"

Collison thought for a moment.

"I'll give John a ring just to check whether they would be happy to play ball. I can't imagine that they wouldn't be. After all, think what a wonderful sales pitch it would be for them to be able to say that it had been used by the police in a murder investigation. Assuming they're okay at that end, I'll go through the ACC to get at our IT people. They're likely to deal with it much more urgently if it comes straight from the top. Put that down as an action point for me please, Bob."

"Very well, sir. In that case how do you want to handle these lists in the meantime?"

"I do think that we need to find every guest who slept at the club that night, and take a statement from them. I appreciate that one or two of them may have gone abroad, but it should still be possible to contact them and arrange for them to come in once they're back in the UK."

"Right you are, guv. That's what we've already started doing actually. I have the first few lined up for tomorrow morning."

Collison stood up and went to stand beside the whiteboard, which he perused thoughtfully.

"So where are we?" he asked, as if thinking aloud. Then, picking up a marker pen he started to jot some items down.

"First, we can be confident that we have a pretty precise time of death. We seem to be looking at a window of about 30 minutes either side of 23:00. That places Andrew Fuller right in the frame, of course."

"Second, that takes us to known suspects. It looks like we are limited to two, both of whom had opportunity. Andrew Fuller admits to having been at the murder scene for at least a large part of our time of death window. His wife, Elizabeth, was staying in the club at the same time and it would have been perfectly possible for her to listen out for her husband to leave and then go to room 16 herself. Since Angela Bowen would have been well acquainted with the sound of her voice she would presumably have opened the door without question when Elizabeth Fuller called out to her."

He hefted the marker pen in his hand and scratched his nose ruminatively.

"Third, and what I really don't like about this situation, are the number of things that we don't know but really need to. Did Angela Bowen tell one or both of the Fullers that she was pregnant? If so, when? If so, what was she proposing? It seems to me that we can't begin to construct a motive for either of our suspects without cracking this somehow. But how? The only person who could tell us for sure is Angela Bowen, and she's dead. Any thoughts anyone?"

Perhaps unsurprisingly, there were none. He turned back to the board and began speaking again.

"Speaking of opportunity, did somebody gain access to Rowena Bradley's office and remove the duplicate key to room 16? After all, if the murderer was somebody other than one of the Fullers then it would have been difficult to gain access to the room without it. But what can we do about this? It seems the CCTV camera is useless. We can't even be precise about the timing, can we? It could have been lifted at any time."

"Hey, now there's a thought," Willis exclaimed spontaneously. "It's true that Rowena was moving around after dinner, and going in and out of her office in an unpredictable manner, but until 22:30 she was sitting down in the restaurant having dinner with us. Anybody who knew that might have been able to slip into her office quite easily when the receptionist wasn't looking – perhaps busy with a phone call or having slipped away for moment to go to the loo."

"Yep," Collison agreed laconically. "That's about the size of it."

"So what you're saying, sir," Desai piped up, "is that just about anybody could have taken the key?"

"Yes. They'd have needed quite a bit of luck of course, not to get spotted going into the office when they took it or coming out again when they put it back, but yes."

"A lot of luck surely, sir?" Evans conjectured. "I think there was a receptionist on the desk until 11, wasn't there? So to get away with it twice, as you say, would be pretty improbable, wouldn't it?"

"Unless both visits to the room occurred after 23:00?" Metcalfe suggested.

"But after 23:00 Rowena Bradley was wandering about, sir," Evans persisted. "So they would still have needed to get lucky twice, wouldn't they?"

"There's a lot in what you say, Timothy," Collison conceded. "Whichever way you look at it, getting the key and then putting it back again would have been a hugely risky enterprise. And if this was premeditated, rather than done on the spur of the moment, then it's difficult to imagine somebody actually planning to do this. Oh dear, is this all a huge red herring I wonder? Is the key really important after all?"

"It's only important," Willis said slowly, as though trying to work things out for herself, "if our perp is somebody other than one of our two suspects. We've already agreed that either of them could have gained access to room 16 without it. But for anybody else it would be vital, wouldn't it? Without it, they'd have to try to bluff their way into somebody's room in the middle of the night, which would hardly be easy."

"We asked the receptionist if she had seen anybody go in or out of Rowena Bradley's office after the function began," Desai reminded them, having checked her notes. "She said she hadn't seen anyone, other than Bradley herself."

Suddenly Collison was struck by another thought and could not resist a smile.

"Remember the case of the invisible man," he said softly with a meaningful glance at Willis. "I'm sure Peter Collins would remind us of it if he were here."

"Oh yes!" she said at once.

Some of the team shifted uneasily in their seats. The newcomers had heard of Collison's approach to running an investigation, but were not sure what was expected of them by way of response. As if sensing their unease, Collison grinned and explained.

"The case of the invisible man is one of GK Chesterton's

Father Brown stories. Somebody was murdered in a house which was being kept under guard against exactly such an eventuality. After the murder was discovered the guards swore blind that they hadn't seen anybody go near the house. What Father Brown was able to establish was that they had not taken any notice of what they had expected to see. The murderer had dressed as a postman, and the watchers had thought nothing of it when they saw him approach the door. Bob, let's find out if there was a cleaner operating at that time, shall we? Or perhaps a waiter with coffee on a tray, or anything like that. Anybody who might have looked as though they had a legitimate reason to be there."

"Right you are, guv," Metcalfe acknowledged.

CHAPTER 16

The ACC listened intently while Collison outlined his idea, nodding from time to time.

"Sounds good," he commented, "but why has nobody done anything like this before I wonder?"

"I understand this is a completely new sort of software," Collison replied. "It's all to do with something called big data, which makes use of the fact that there is more information about everybody available today than ever before."

"Yes, that's the one aspect of this which troubles me a little," the senior man observed. "What about privacy, data protection, all that sort of thing? The Commissioner is very sensitive to any suggestion that we are compromising individual freedom, you know. We have enough allegations about a police state already."

"Yes, I asked about that. Insofar as you are looking to make use of data which has been compiled as a result of people's online transactions, or browsing habits, I think there could be a real concern. But we're not. All we are looking to do is to tap into official databases which are largely or entirely a matter of public record anyway: Companies House, the Land Registry, that sort of thing."

"But don't we have access to those already?"

"Yes we do, sir, and that's why I don't think there should

be any real issue here. All we are doing is hooking them up to a sort of search engine which can interrogate them for random matches when applied to a large body of data, such as the guest lists we're talking about here."

"Very well then, Simon. Just give my office anything you need signed and we'll do the necessary."

"Thank you, sir, I'll do that straightaway."

"How are you getting on by the way?" the ACC asked suddenly. "I'm sure I don't need to tell you how sensitive this case may be, what with a senior QC involved and everything. I happen to know from a chum at the Home Office that Fuller is being considered for appointment to the High Court bench. That's for your ears only, by the way. I'm not supposed to know anything about it."

"Understood, sir. It's a tricky one actually. Right now we only have two suspects: Fuller and his wife. Fuller was actually in the woman's room around the time of death, while his wife was staying elsewhere at the club and could easily have gained access to the room herself. There really are no other obvious candidates, not so far anyway."

The ACC grunted unhappily.

"Well, just do the best you can, Simon. Have you interviewed Fuller under caution yet?"

"No, we haven't, but I'm strongly considering doing it sometime soon."

The ACC grunted even more unhappily.

"Let me know before you do, will you? Not that I'm trying to clip your wings in any way you understand, I just need to be kept informed, that's all."

"I do understand, sir, and of course I will."

"Was there anything else?"

"Yes, as a matter of fact there was. While I'm here I wonder if I could ask your advice about Peter Collins?"

"What about him?"

"Well, I'd very much like to involve him in the investigation. You know how helpful he's been in the past. But I'm very conscious that he's not a member of the team and therefore technically I'm not allowed to discuss the case with him. There is also the matter of him being a witness ..."

"He's not a witness to anything material, is he? And anyway that didn't stop him getting involved last time. I think you need to use your own judgement on that. Just remember that if events take an unexpected turn and it looks like he may be a material witness after all then you may have put yourself in a rather difficult position."

"I appreciate that," Collison said quietly.

"As for the rest of it, he is still an approved police psychological adviser, isn't he? I remember authorising him some time ago when you used him to give you that profile. If he's still on the list then you can make whatever use of him you like, subject to you and Jim being happy to sign off on the budget of course."

"Thank you, sir. I was hoping that's what you would say. And I'm sure he'd be happy to give his services free of charge as before, so budgetary sign off is not an issue."

"Well there you are then. As I say, I think it's a matter entirely for your own judgement. Do keep Jim Murray informed though, won't you? Between you and me I think he's feeling a little awkward in his new position. Still trying to work out exactly what it is he's supposed to be doing. Frankly, I sympathise. Before all that nonsense with the management consultants, homicide teams used to report directly to me, or if you go back far enough to the Commander (Crime). Jim's role now seems to be entirely admin and personnel. Privately, I think he's hating it."

"I think you're right," Collison agreed unhappily, "and I'm very sorry about it. When I drew up the proposed new structure I never really stopped and thought about how it might affect the DCS personally. Now I'm feeling rather guilty about it."

The ACC shrugged.

"Nothing to feel guilty about, certainly. We all get further and further away from front-line policing each time we get promoted. I think your scheme makes a lot of sense."

"I'm glad you think that, sir. But ..."

He paused and looked at the other man uncertainly.

"Go on."

"Oh dear, I just realised that this is going to sound awfully like me trying to teach you how to do your job, sir, and it really isn't intended like that at all ..."

"Go on," the other said again.

"Well, it does seem to me that the new structure needs a different sort of officer as DCS. Not a good, traditional copper like Jim but someone who is more happy with an administrative sort of role."

"That had already made itself apparent to me," the ACC observed with a smile, "and naturally I'd like to try to do something about it. But it's not always easy juggling the pieces around when you're dealing with senior officers and all sorts of pending promotions and retirements."

"Are there lots of those around at the moment?" Collison asked, wondering why the ACC was telling him this.

"No more than usual," he replied vaguely.

Collison called Collins on his mobile as he walked away from Scotland Yard towards Westminster tube station.

"Peter, how are you? Listen, I'd very much like to get you involved in this case and I have clearance from the ACC to reactivate you as a police adviser, if you'd be willing."

"My dear old Parker bird, that would be spiffin'," came the response, which would have taken aback anyone who was not used to Collins dipping in and out of his Lord Peter Wimsey persona.

"Great, when can we get together?"

"I'm free now if you'd like to come round. Or I could meet you somewhere?"

"No that's fine, I'll come to you. It will take me about half an hour, I expect. I can get the tube from Westminster and change onto the Northern Line."

So it was that a little later the two men sat together in the living room of the house in Frognal.

"It's a little before teatime, I know," Collins said, "but I've made Earl Grey and anchovy toast. I trust that's acceptable?"

"Very acceptable indeed," Collison concurred.

He waited while Collins poured the tea.

"How much do you know about the case already?" he asked.

"Hm," Collins replied thoughtfully. "Isn't that a rather dangerous question? After all, surely Bob and Karen aren't supposed to be discussing it with me at all are they?"

"Good point, Peter," Collison acknowledged. "That was silly of me. Sorry."

"Why don't you just assume that I know nothing other than what I said in my statement, and bring me up-to-date?"

"Great, yes, let's do that," Collison agreed and launched into a concise summary.

Collins munched daintily yet thoughtfully on his anchovy toast as Collison drew to a close.

"So you have two clear suspects," he mused, "either of whom may have committed the crime. Have you considered, I wonder, the possibility that they may have murdered the deceased together?"

"No, we haven't but we should," Collison replied, chastened. "For some reason we hadn't thought of that."

"It just seems to me that if we are going to consider the possibility that Bowen may have told either or both of the Fullers about her pregnancy, then they may have had a chance to discuss it together and come to the conclusion that drastic action was necessary. Perhaps Fuller, as an experienced criminal lawyer, might have remembered how difficult smothering can be to detect ... but let's not get ahead of ourselves. More tea?"

"All good ideas, Peter. And yes please."

"There's something else I think you need to consider," Collins advised as he carefully poured tea.

"You mean I've missed something?" Collison enquired mischievously.

"Perish the thought, old man. But yes, perhaps."

He sat back and raised his cup to his lips. Then, finding that the tea was still slightly too hot to drink, he set it down again.

"Have you considered how either or both of the Fullers might have gained access to room 16?"

"Yes, of course. We know that Fuller was already in the room as – a guest, shall we say – of Angela Bowen. We also know, or at least presume, that Bowen would have opened the door to the wife since they were old friends."

"Very good," Collins nodded, "but have you also considered how they may have come to leave the room?"

He suddenly darted a very significant look indeed at the occupant of the sofa opposite. The latter stared back at him blankly.

"Well," he began hesitantly, "if you mean how were they able to leave the room without being observed, it was a fairly quiet time of the evening and the corridor lights were dimmed."

"No, I don't mean that at all," Collins replied rather dreamily. "I mean how were they able to leave the room and lock the door behind them, given that the room key was found on the floor inside the room."

"My God," Collison gasped. "Of course – "

"I am assuming of course," Collins remarked sardonically, "that Angela Bowen, having been but recently bumped off, was unable to walk across the room, lock the door from the inside after her visitor had departed, and carelessly drop the key on the floor on her way back to bed. Ergo if she did not lock the door, who did?"

"And whoever did, must have done so from the outside," Collison chipped in.

"You see the point exactly."

"But this changes everything," Collison said excitedly. "We've been assuming that either of the Fullers – or both, as you say – could have committed the crime without needing access to the duplicate key in Rowena Bradley's office. But that's not right, is it? They would have needed it just as much as anybody else would have done."

"Correct."

"Which means that access to the office both before and after the time of death remains the key issue."

"No pun intended, I assume. But yes, again, correct, so far as I can see anyway."

Collins took a thoughtful sip of Earl Grey.

"Of course there is someone who could have gained access to the key without arousing any suspicion whatsoever."

"Really? Whom do you have in mind?"

"Rowena Bradley herself, naturally. We already know that she was slipping in and out of her office from about 22:30 onwards. She could have taken the key at any time and returned it later. Perhaps she was looking out for Fuller to slip away through the back door. Perhaps she knew that he was in the habit of doing so when he visited Bowen at the club ... but again, let's not get ahead of ourselves."

"But Peter," Collison exclaimed, staring at him, "there's

no suggestion – is there? – that Bradley had any motive for killing Bowen."

"Nor is there, old Parker bird, but don't you think it might be worth doin' a spot of sleuthin' just to make sure? After all, if the key represents opportunity then right now she looks like the only person who could have had guaranteed access to the room."

He gazed mildly at Collison as he finished his tea.

"Anything else?" Collison asked almost facetiously.

Collins appeared to take the query seriously. He stapled his fingers and stared hard at the wall.

"Yes, I rather think there is," he said slowly. "You see if either or both of the Fullers had a motive, and Bradley had opportunity, then what's to stop Bradley having done it jointly with either of the Fullers, or come to that with both? Yes, Charles, what's to stop the whole bally lot of them having done her in together?"

CHAPTER 17

"Well, folks," a somewhat chastened Collison said the next morning, "it looks like we've overlooked something rather fundamental."

The team gazed at him uncertainly and then at each other.

"I went to see Peter Collins yesterday, having got permission from the ACC to use him as an adviser on the case. For those of you who haven't met Dr Collins, he's an academic psychologist whom we've used before as a profiler. I was wondering if he might have any insight into the motives of any possible suspects and obviously in order to do that I had to share with him all the facts as we know them so far. As it happens, he wasn't able to help me on the question of motive but he did point out something which should have occurred to us earlier."

Metcalfe and Willis, who had already discussed the matter with Collins overnight and had already had time to come to terms with what they had missed, still looked uncomfortable nonetheless.

"We've been focusing on how the killer gained access to room 16," Collison continued, "but what we failed to realise was that the killer would not have been able to lock the door behind them when they left without having the duplicate key in their possession. If you remember the maid's evidence, the door was locked when she knocked on it and she needed the key to open it. But we know both from her and from the doctor that the guest's room key was lying on the floor, about halfway between the bed and the door. So once again we are back to the issue of someone having to obtain the duplicate from Rowena Bradley's office, and then return it later."

"But we said yesterday that for somebody to do that – once, let alone twice – would be hugely risky," ventured Evans, looking confused.

"So we did," Collison said helplessly, "and so it would. Any thoughts anyone?"

"I'm cheating because obviously I've had a chance to talk to Peter about it," Willis piped up. "For those of you who don't know, by the way, Peter Collins is my partner. Having clarified the importance of the duplicate key, he also made the suggestion that we might want to consider Rowena Bradley as a possible person of interest."

"Rowena Bradley?" echoed Desai. "But why? What possible motive could she have had? I thought she and Bowen were friends?"

"You're right of course," Willis replied, "there's no motive at all so far as we know. But we haven't really looked, have we? We haven't been thinking of her as a possible suspect. All Peter is pointing out is that she is the one person who could have had access to the key at any time. After all, it's kept in her office."

"Peter also makes the point," Metcalfe said, "that she could have been an accomplice to the actual murderer, whether that was the husband or the wife."

"Or indeed both together," Collison concluded. "Something else we haven't considered, incidentally. Personally I agree with Peter. I think we need to get Rowena Bradley in for a formal interview. We need to find out everything we can about her relationship with the deceased and with our two suspects. There really is no getting away from this wretched key, and she seems like the only person who could have got hold of it without running the risk of being caught in the act."

"I'll organise that, guv," Metcalfe promised, jotting down a note. "Now, shall we review where we are generally?"

"By all means, Bob," Collison agreed. "I'll go first shall I? We have approval from the ACC to use the business school software and all the relevant documentation is being processed today. With a bit of luck we should be able to arrange for someone from the Business School to come in tomorrow to load it on our system and show us how to use it. I'm hoping, by the way, that it really will turn out to be as simple as I'm making it sound, but we should be prepared for some delay and a few teething problems. I understand from the IT people that getting it to interact with many different information sources at the same time could be problematic, to say the least."

"Thank you, guv," Metcalfe said. "I'll take responsibility for our end of that myself. Now, other news. We've started working our way through the list of other guests who were staying at the club that night. In particular, we've taken full statements from most of the people who were on the same floor as our victim. None of them remember hearing anything unusual, although all of them say that there were occasional footsteps in the corridor up until about midnight, though only one or two of them were precise about that so it's not really conclusive."

"What about other sudden deaths in hotel rooms?" Collison asked.

"Nothing really, guv. Oh, there are deaths right enough, but nothing that looks out of the ordinary and no more than you would expect. Again, not conclusive I'm afraid, but there's nothing to indicate that we have some serial killer on our hands with a grudge against people who spend the night in hotel rooms."

"I didn't really expect there would be," Collison observed mildly. "How about the list of people attending the vintage event?"

"It's a long list," Metcalfe commented sourly. "Over a hundred names. I was going to suggest running it through the software program as a first step. If we really want to go through it person by person then we're going to have to request a lot of extra bodies."

He looked questioningly at Collison, who shrugged.

"If that's what it takes then that's what we'll do. But I agree: let's try the software first."

"That's all I have at the moment," Metcalfe said, looking up from his notes.

"OK, I'll leave you to press on with the interviews then, Bob. But could I have a word with you and Karen in my office when you have a moment?"

"I'm thinking of trying something a little unorthodox," he

said when they reconvened upstairs, "but I don't think there's any need for the whole team to know about it. I want to tell you two, however, and I'd be interested in your thoughts."

"Okay, guv," Metcalfe acknowledged.

Collison leaned back reflectively in his chair and put his hands behind his head.

"I can't help feeling that we really don't know enough about the Fullers and their rather unconventional living arrangements. Oh, I'm sorry, no personal slight intended to either of you."

"None taken," Willis said quickly with a glance at Metcalfe, "and for what it's worth I agree. Given that they are our prime suspects at the moment then it's likely that whatever the motivation for the killing might have been, it was something to do with the relationship between the three of them."

"What do you have in mind, guv?" Metcalfe enquired.

"I've been thinking about Adrian Partington," Collison said slowly, "and wondering if he might be prepared to have a full and frank discussion about one of his colleagues at the bar, strictly off the record."

Metcalfe nodded. Partington had been at university with Collison, had been part of the legal team on his first case as Superintendent, and had recently acted for Metcalfe personally on a potential disciplinary enquiry.

"It sounds like a good idea. After all, what have we got to lose?"

"Good, I'm glad you agree. I'm going to try to see him later today. He's not in court; I checked with his clerk."

So it was that Collison and Partington sat together

that afternoon over the combination of Assam tea and rich fruitcake for which the Chambers were justly famous.

"The whole bar's talking about it of course," Partington said as he brushed half an almond from his waistcoat. "I mean, it's not every day that a prominent QC finds himself a suspect for the murder of his mistress, now is it?"

"What are they saying?" Collison asked.

Partington gave a quick chuckle.

"In public everyone is being terribly supportive. Rallying round a highly reputable member of the senior bar. All a dreadful misunderstanding. Sure it will be cleared up very soon, all that sort of thing."

"And in private?"

"In private they're not so sure. It's pretty unthinkable that a QC would stoop to murder, but then stranger things have happened. And he's not exactly a conventional character, is he?"

"I suppose not, although of course I don't really know him. How would you describe him?"

"As a lawyer, he's pretty damn good. As an advocate, especially in front of the jury, he's brilliant. I've certainly heard nothing like him, and I've been led by just about every decent silk in London."

"And as a man? A human being?"

"Ah, that's where things get a bit difficult. The phrase 'larger than life' could have been invented for him. He seems to spend a lot of his time in restaurants, nightclubs, and casinos. And where women are concerned ..."

Partington fell silent and chuckled again.

"Well?"

"He can't keep his trousers up," Partington said bluntly. "Everyone at the bar knows that. All the instructing solicitors too. It's as if he wants to bed every half decent–looking woman he meets."

"And does he?"

"As I understand it, yes," Partington said simply. "One chap I know thinks he does it almost like collecting postage stamps or something. Each woman is another one to stick in the album."

"That sounds rather extreme," Collison protested.

Partington shrugged.

"Perhaps. I'm not suggesting any impropriety of course. The women concerned seem to love it as far as one can make out. There's definitely something about him that women find very attractive."

"What sort of women are we talking about?"

"This is starting to sound like the catalogue aria from 'Don Giovanni', don't you think? All sorts I think. He's been pretty active with the female bar, for a start. They say he chooses his pupils personally, and they're always female and usually very attractive. There's quite a high rate of churn as well. You know, they get handed off to another barrister halfway through. You can draw your own conclusions."

"Hm. Age?"

"Again, not much of a pattern. As I say, he has quite a reputation with young women lawyers, but if the rumour mill's to be believed then he's apparently had the middle-aged wives of a lot of his colleagues as well. It's really quite extraordinary that the tabloids have never run a big story on him."

"Is he discreet?"

"Oh yes, he's not one to brag and he seems to have been pretty lucky in choosing women who aren't the kind to kiss and tell. But inevitably word gets out."

"Do you know anything about his marriage?"

"Oh, everyone knows about that. They have some sort of ménage à trois. He has a long-term mistress who is also a good friend of the wife. It's all supposed to be a big secret, but it's pretty much public knowledge."

"Yes, so I understand," Collison said thoughtfully. "I wonder how much either of the two women know about his extracurricular activities?"

"You never know," Partington said with a smile. "Women are strange around him. I remember one case where one of the instructing solicitors – a good-looking woman, by the way – was gazing at him all gooey eyed right the way through the trial. I'm sure he must have had her sooner or later, but it didn't look as though she would have needed much persuasion."

"What makes him tick, do you think? Is it just a never ending quest for sexual conquest, or is it something else? What about his career for example?"

"He does seem to be the sexual equivalent on alcoholic, whatever that might be. A nymphomaniac perhaps – or does that apply only to women? Anyway, whatever you call it he seems to suffer from it. So far as his career is concerned he's right at the top of it, and he knows it. He has huge amounts of self-confidence, but whether that's drawn from his success or vice versa I couldn't say."

"Is he capable of murder do you think?" Collison asked bluntly.

"Oh, Simon, what a question. If I were put on the spot I would say that he seems a thoroughly decent and even gentle man. But what is it that makes anyone capable of killing anyway? And whatever it is surely it's within all of us, isn't it? I think we could all envision situations in which we would kill: to protect our family from attack, for example."

"Yes, I suppose so. But to kill a helpless, unsuspecting person in cold blood – that's different isn't it? Particularly if it's someone you love, or are supposed to love. Usually when a partner murder happens it's a frenzied attack born of some sudden huge anger, but this isn't like that. This seems all rather cold and premeditated, even if the decision to kill had only been taken very recently, as it might have been."

"But surely," Partington replied, casting a covetous glance at the last remaining piece of fruit cake, "that's all in a day's work for Collison of the Yard isn't it?"

CHAPTER 18

"Now then, Miss Bradley", Metcalfe began. "Oh, I'm sorry, is Miss Bradley correct?"

"Yes, quite correct. It's my maiden name. I went back to it after I got divorced about 10 years ago."

"Thank you, that's fine. Now my colleague, DC Desai, and I would like to ask you a few more questions based on the statement you gave DS Willis, which I have here."

"Well I'm eager to help of course," Rowena Bradley said with a tense smile, "but I think I told Karen everything I know."

"I'm sure that's right," Metcalfe replied soothingly, "but in a case like this it often helps to go over things more than once. Also, rather than what actually happened on the night in question we'd like to focus a little more this time on your relationship with the Fullers. It would be really helpful if you could tell us everything you know about them."

"But I think I've already done that, haven't I? But by all means ask me whatever you like and I'll do my best to answer."

"To start with, I wonder if we could dig a little more deeply into the origin of the ménage à trois which they had with the deceased. When exactly did it begin?"

"Almost as soon as they were married, I think. For some reason Liz just found the whole physical side of things a bit of a nightmare. She told me it was all a bit of a disaster – in fact I think those were her exact words – but of course I never asked for any details."

"And these sexual difficulties, did they suddenly spring up out of nowhere once they got married or was it something that had always been a problem?"

"I really haven't the slightest idea," Bradley said looking shocked. "You'd have to ask Liz about that. I do know that she was always a bit old-fashioned about sex. We'd known each other some time and I'd never known her to be that interested in men, until she met Andrew that is. And even with him, I felt the attraction was – how shall I put it? – intellectual rather than physical. I think she thought she had found her soulmate."

"And what about him: Mr Fuller? How do you think he felt about it?"

"To be honest, he was already seeing so many women that I don't think he was that worried about it. I think Liz appealed to him as a friend, and maybe that was enough."

"And did he carry on seeing other women after he was married?" Metcalfe asked.

Bradley nodded and giggled.

"Oh yes, there was never any secret about that. You know what you're getting with Andrew. He's utterly charming but utterly faithless. He'll give you a great time, but by your second or third date he's already eyeing up the woman at the next table. That's just the way he is. That's why it was such a perfect arrangement for him you see. It gave him exactly the licence he wanted to do whatever he liked with whomever he liked."

"Hang on, I'm getting confused here," Desai interrupted. "If he was simply bedding women left right and centre then what was the point of the relationship with Angela Bowen? Surely she can't have been very happy knowing that he was just using her."

Bradley shrugged and raised her eyebrows.

"It's very difficult to explain if you don't know Andrew," she said rather helplessly. "He has this amazing charisma. While you're with him he makes you feel that you're the most important person in the whole world. It's a wonderful feeling, and not one that you have the opportunity to experience very often. To be honest, I think Angela was just grateful to be able to spend time with him. So grateful that she was happy for it to be on his own terms. He was very honest about things you know. He never made any secret of the fact that he was seeing other people at the same time. Nobody can ever say that he misled them; at least, not so far as I'm aware."

Desai shook her head and busied herself with her notes. Metcalfe could almost feel the waves of disapproval emanating from his colleague beside him. Knowing her as he did he felt that they were probably directed at least as much at the women in Andrew Fuller's life as at the man himself.

"I'm afraid we have to touch on some rather delicate ground now," he said carefully. "I need to ask you to be completely honest about the nature of your relationship with both Mr and Mrs Fuller. Is there anything at all you can tell us about that? Anything which you didn't tell DS Willis, perhaps because you felt it wasn't necessary or relevant?"

"Oh dear, this is all getting rather personal isn't it? Is this strictly necessary?"

"Miss Bradley, I should make it clear that you're not under any obligation to answer our questions," Metcalfe said at once. "And so far as we are concerned at the moment you are being interviewed as a witness, not a suspect. That's why I didn't caution you before we began. But we are anxious to eliminate as many people as possible from our enquiry and anything you can tell us may be a great help to us in doing that."

He fell silent and gazed at her steadily. The pause threatened to become oppressive, but still he said nothing. Was it his imagination or was she fidgeting slightly in her chair?

He may or may not have been amused to know that beside him Desai was thinking how very similar to Superintendent Collison he was beginning to sound.

"Will anything I tell you be treated in confidence? Really strict confidence I mean?" Bradley asked at last.

"So far as our investigation is concerned, yes absolutely," Metcalfe assured her, "but if it becomes necessary for it to be given in evidence in court then that's another matter of course."

"I see."

She still seemed unsure, but again Metcalfe waited and let the pressure build.

"Well, all right, but I really don't want this to go any further. You see Andrew and I had been having a bit of a fling over the last month or so. I really don't know how it happened, it just did. I was feeling a bit down – there's stuff going on at work, problems with a few colleagues – and I asked Andrew if he'd like to go out for dinner one evening. Suddenly about halfway through the main course I realised that I'd really like to go to bed with him, so I asked and of course he said yes. It all seemed very natural somehow. After all, we already knew each other so well as friends."

"I see. Thank you for being so honest with us and I think you've done exactly the right thing in telling us about it. Is it still going on or is it over?"

"You tell me," Bradley said wryly. "We haven't discussed it. It would hardly seem appropriate in the circumstances would it? But I expect it's over. A few weeks is par for the course with Andrew. He loses interest in women very quickly. Oh, he's happy to go on being a charming friend all right, but I think a lot of it is just the thrill of the chase with him. He once told me that having sex with a woman for the first time was often a very disappointing experience. I remember thinking how sad that was, if he really felt that ..."

"How well did you know Angela Bowen?" Metcalfe asked, deciding to change the subject.

"About as well as I knew Liz actually. We occasionally used to meet up for a drink or something, the three of us together."

"If she had something really important but very sensitive that she needed to discuss with anybody, who would she turn to do you think?"

"Goodness, how very mysterious. I'm not sure that she had any really close friends. I think her mother is still alive because I remember her saying that she was going to visit her last Christmas, but I have no idea how close the relationship is. What are we talking about anyway? Is it something she could discuss with her mother?"

"Possibly," Metcalfe said noncommittally. "I'm just trying to build up a picture, that's all. Had she mentioned anything to you at all? Anything out of the ordinary?"

Bradley thought hard and then shook her head.

"Nothing I can think of, no. It would be easier to answer your question though if I knew what you were getting at."

Metcalfe reflected for a moment.

"Something concerning her health, say. Something serious. Is that the sort of thing that she might talk to the Fullers about?"

"Yes, of course. Why not? Liz was probably her best friend, and she was sleeping with Andrew for Pete's sake. If not them, then who?"

"Well, that's exactly what I'm trying to get a feel for. So you don't think there's anybody she might have told other than the Fullers?"

"No, so far as I'm aware; they were her best friends. But what is it? Was she ill, really ill I mean? Did she have something terminal? Surely you're not suggesting that she killed herself?"

Metcalfe felt that he had waited long enough.

"Actually, she was pregnant," he announced, observing her closely.

"Good God! Surely not?"

"It's true, I'm afraid. It showed up during the post-mortem. There can't be any mistake."

"Well," she said slowly, "that's a turn up the book and no mistake."

"You didn't know then? This could be very important Miss Bradley, so please think very carefully before you go on record. Did you know that Angela Bowen was pregnant?"

"No I did not," she said emphatically.

"And did you ever hear either or both of the Fullers mention the possibility of her being pregnant?"

"Again, no."

"OK, now I'm afraid I have to ask you something really personal, for which I apologise in advance."

"Go on."

"When you had sex with Andrew Fuller was it unprotected?"

"No, of course not. He used a condom."

"Each time?"

"It's only happened twice, actually. But yes, both times."

"And I appreciate that this may be a very difficult question as well, but did Angela Bowen ever give you any indication as to whether she used contraception with Andrew Fuller?"

"No she did not. It's not exactly the sort of thing you discuss over afternoon tea, is it? But I would certainly have assumed that they did. After all, Angela was a very sensible girl."

"And yet she got pregnant," Metcalfe observed dryly. "So either not sensible enough or not careful enough, presumably."

"Yes," Bradley replied sadly. "So it would seem."

"Did she ever mention the possibility of having children? Was it something she hankered after, do you know?"

"No, I don't remember it coming up in conversation at all. I just sort of assumed that she had accepted that it was probably too late for that sort of thing – in practical terms if not in physical – and that she had come to terms with it."

"And knowing her as you did, how do you think she might have reacted to the knowledge that she was pregnant? Would she have wanted to keep it, for example?"

"Oh yes, I'm pretty sure she would. Though I'm not sure why I'm saying that. It's not as if she was particularly religious or anything. Actually, on second thoughts, I really don't know one way or the other."

"But assuming Andrew Fuller was the father, do you think she would have told him about it or kept it to herself?"

"Well, she could hardly keep it to herself forever, could she? If she'd decided to have it, that is. But I think she would have told him anyway. She was a very direct person; too direct sometimes. She could upset people by being too honest with them. She always said what she thought without really stopping to consider the consequences. Perhaps it had something to do with being an academic. She felt that the truth had something pure and intrinsically valuable about it, that you could never get into trouble by being honest. Of course what the rest of us learn very quickly is that often telling a white lie or keeping quiet altogether can save somebody's feelings, but she never really saw things like that. That's probably why she didn't have any close friends."

"Thank you, that's all very helpful. I know this can't be easy for you so thank you again for having been so honest with us. Now, if we could just circle back to the night in question for a moment, there is something I need to ask you formally."

"Gosh, sounds serious but go on."

"Did at any time either Andrew or Liz Fuller ask you to lend them the duplicate key to room 16?"

"No, absolutely not."

"Did anybody, whether the Fullers or somebody else, go into your office either to fetch or return the duplicate?"

"I can't possibly answer that. You were there; you know that I was flitting about from one place to another. It's possible that someone could have slipped into the office without being seen, although there is the CCTV camera in the entrance hall, of course, and there was somebody on the desk until about 11. But even then, people were walking backwards and forwards through that area because of the event. They'd have to go through it to go downstairs to the loos, for example. The only period I can vouch for is from about midnight onwards, because I was in the office from then until about 6:30 in the morning, when I went upstairs to have a shower."

"Unfortunately," Metcalfe said with feeling, "it's precisely the period before midnight that we are interested in. But thank you again, Miss Bradley, you've been most helpful."

"Well, I do hope so. And do please give my regards to Karen."

CHAPTER 19

When Metcalfe returned to the incident room it was to find a small group of officers clustered round a man who was typing briskly on a computer keyboard. They dispersed guiltily as he approached.

"Hello," he said, "you must be John Watt. I'm Bob Metcalfe. How are you getting on?"

"Not bad actually," the other replied, though looking at Willis. "Come and see."

Metcalfe stood beside him to look at the screen.

"So how does this work?" he asked.

"On this side of the screen you see a list of available information sources," Watt explained, pointing at the left-hand side of the screen.

"I never knew we had so many," Metcalfe observed. "There must be 20 or 30 there."

"Oh these aren't all on your police system. One of the things the software does is to search for databases which are publicly accessible, or at least available for official search purposes. I think you might find that a very handy little device to have. You've got things like the land registry here, for example, as well as the electoral register, so one of the things the package would automatically do would be to cross-reference people's postcodes to see if any of them lived at the same address, or somewhere close."

"I see. Yes, that would be very useful. At the moment we have to do all that sort of stuff manually."

"And over here, on the right-hand side, you see a list of what we call samples. These are simply lists of people contained in a pre-existing file. You input those yourself. The system can accommodate all the usual suspects: Excel spreadsheets as well as all the standard database formats, and should automatically recognise postcode, phone number, and date of birth formats. You simply tick one or more of the boxes on the right, do the same on the left, and voila."

He gazed hard at Willis again, like a dog seeking approval for having performed a particularly difficult trick. She smiled automatically and then turned away to sit at her desk.

"And can it interrogate all the information sources in respect of all the samples?" Metcalfe enquired. "All at the same time I mean?"

"Oh yes, in fact, that's what it's really designed to do although we've never really had a chance to test it properly because of database license issues at the business school. It may take time of course, particularly if some of the online information sources run slowly themselves."

"So what do we need to do now?" Metcalfe asked. "Is it ready to roll?"

"Yes, it is. The setup proved much easier than I was expecting actually. All you need to do is load your sample files, and I've shown this officer how to do that."

He gestured towards Evans.

"Excellent. In that case many thanks, and I don't think we need take up any more of your time."

"I'd be happy to stay and help if you like, just in case anything crops up," Watt said with a further longing glance at Willis.

"Thank you but I don't think we can allow that," Metcalfe replied diplomatically. "This is a murder enquiry, you see, and this is our incident room. Technically nobody is allowed in here who is not a member of the team. We had to get special permission for you to be here for even a limited time. Don't worry though, we've got your contact details should we need to get hold of you. Priya, perhaps you'd show Mr Watt out?"

"It's Dr Watt actually," he said rather plaintively over his shoulder as Desai guided him firmly out of the room.

"Now then," Metcalfe exclaimed rubbing his hands together. "Let's get this thing fired up shall we, Timothy?"

"Right you are, guv," the latter responded, sitting down in front of the same keyboard which Watt had just been using. "I've got our stuff ready in a special directory. It's just a question of copying them across ... Here you go, you see, they've popped up already. Here's the list of guests who stayed the night, and here's the list of people who attended the vintage event. I've added Mr Fuller, since he wouldn't have appeared on either, and I've also got a list from Miss Bradley of all club employees."

"Very good. Well done, Timothy. Now let's see if it works shall we?"

Evans duly ticked all three of the boxes on the right, selected 'all' on the left, and clicked 'OK'. A message then appeared on the screen saying 'working on your search – please wait'.

"I have a feeling this may take some time," Metcalfe said, and went to sit in the spare chair by Willis's desk.

"Do we have anything else on our 'to do' list?" he asked.

"Well, we're still working our way down the club guest list, but hopefully this whizzy new system may give us some help with that. Apart from that, it's simply a question of the governor deciding who, if anyone, we may need to re-interview."

"Hm, OK then."

"We're getting something, guv," Evans called.

He leaned closer to peer at the screen and then started laughing.

"What's so funny?" Metcalfe demanded.

"Sorry, guv, but it's you apparently. The big news according to the software is that you, the DS, and Dr Collins all have the same address."

"Oh, for goodness sake," Willis said in exasperation. "Surely there something else, isn't there? I can't believe that's the only connection between people on the lists."

"That's the only level 1 connection," Evans observed. "It looks like there are three different levels, with level 1 being 'very significant', level 2 being 'significant', and level 3 'probably coincidental'."

"Well, what about the other levels then?" Metcalfe pressed him.

"Dr Tasker is a level 2 connection. That seems to be on the basis that she is the only person on both lists."

"And that really is coincidental," Willis pointed out. "A good job we don't leave investigations to machines."

"You're not wrong, Sarge," Evans agreed. "There is one level 3 connection as well, in case you're interested."

"Which is?"

"A woman called Chloe Jennings. They're both barristers so she and Mr Fuller both appear on something called the bar list."

"Oh, I remember her," Metcalfe said at once. "Wasn't she the bunny boiler?"

"Oh really," Willis admonished him. "She was just a bit upset, that's all."

Metcalfe grinned but then realised that Evans was staring at him blankly.

"It's a film, Timothy," he explained. "It's called 'Fatal Attraction'. Michael Douglas has a one night stand with Glenn Close and she turns out to be a complete nutter who ends up boiling the children's pet rabbit."

"Is that the one with the bird who doesn't wear knickers?" Evans asked brightly.

Metcalfe shook his head sadly.

"No," he said firmly. "It isn't."

"When you two have finished talking about women," Willis interjected, "perhaps we could consider whether this is another random coincidence, or something worth checking."

"Well, there's no address link for a start," Evans replied, turning back to the computer. "You can see Fuller here with an address in Lincoln's Inn, and here's Jennings with an address in Guildford."

"Guildford? There are no barristers chambers in Guildford, are there?" Willis asked in puzzlement.

"Not as far as I'm aware, no," Metcalfe concurred. "That must be her home address surely? When did she qualify, Timothy?"

"Early this year, guv."

"Well there you are then. She's probably doing a pupillage somewhere, and pupils aren't members of chambers are they? So she won't have a chambers address to give."

"What's her Inn of Court?" Willis asked.

"Sorry, Sarge, not with you."

"It should give her Inn alongside her date of call. There are four: Lincoln's, Gray's, Middle Temple, and Inner Temple."

"Oh, I see. Yes, here it is. Gray's."

"Well give them a ring and asked for her practising address. And, assuming she's a pupil, find out who her pupil master is."

As Evans started searching for the phone number, Collison walked into the room and gestured to Metcalfe and Willis to meet him upstairs.

"Well, what do we have?" he asked as they sat down in his office.

"The big news is that Rowena Bradley has disclosed she was having an affair with Andrew Fuller," Metcalfe informed him.

"Good God, her too?"

"Yes, it seems so."

Collison thought from moment.

"You said 'was'. Does that mean it was over? And, if so, when did it start?"

"It was recent. And when we asked if it was over she said she wasn't sure. They haven't had a chance to discuss it apparently. But it sounds as though it was just a casual fling, in her mind at least."

"So nothing that could serve as a motive then?" Collison asked, gazing steadily at them both.

"Not for me, guv," Metcalfe replied. "I think she was on the level with us."

"And you, Karen?" Collison persisted. "What do you think?"

"I wasn't there so I can't really agree or disagree with Bob, but I'd prefer to keep an open mind. After all, if she did have a motive then she'd hardly tell us about it, would she?"

"But she did tell us about the affair," Metcalfe protested.

Willis shrugged.

"Perhaps she was just being sensible. After all, we were probably going to find out about it sooner or later. This way she gets brownie points for having volunteered the information. Don't get me wrong, my instinct is the same as yours, but I'm not sure we should take her off the list completely."

"Okay, agreed," Collison nodded. "So it looks like we're still focused on the Fullers, then."

"How did you get on with Adrian Partington?" Metcalfe enquired.

"Nothing that we can use as evidence of course, but a lot of useful background. Apparently it's common knowledge at the bar that the man is a sex maniac, perhaps even to the extent of some sort of mental illness. Adrian commented that our conversation reminded him of the catalogue aria, and that's a pretty apt observation. In his words, Fuller can't keep his trousers up."

"It would be interesting to get Peter's views, now that we have this additional information," Metcalfe suggested. "Rowena Bradley told me something pretty strange which might have a bearing on all of this."

"Which was?"

"She said Fuller once told her that when he bedded a woman for the first time it was almost always a disappointing experience. I'm sure I remember reading about that somewhere, that it's a symptom of some sort of mental condition."

"If he finds it so disappointing," Collison observed dryly, "one has to wonder why he persists in trying it so often."

"But I think that's the point, guv," Willis said seriously. "It's almost as though it's a compulsion with him. After all, as you say, if he doesn't enjoy it then why do it?"

"It certainly a sensible suggestion to revisit Andrew Fuller's state of mind with Peter," Collison agreed, "but I'm not sure it takes us very much further, does it? I get the feeling that we're spinning our wheels a bit here. I've been thinking about this a lot and I can't shake the feeling that a lot hinges on whether Bowen told either or both of the Fullers that she was pregnant."

"And that's exactly what we can't find out, isn't it?" Metcalfe observed gloomily. "The Fullers both say she didn't and the only person who could contradict them would be Bowen herself, and she's dead."

"What did Bradley say?" Collison asked. "Did she know?"

"She says not, and I tend to believe her," Metcalfe replied, glancing uncertainly at Willis, "her surprise seemed genuine enough. But, as Karen says, she could just be putting on a very good act."

"Oh, damn and blast," Collison said mildly. "What we need is a break, something which points the finger specifically at one or both of the Fullers. Or anyone else, for that matter."

As if on cue there came a knock at the door.

"Come in!" Collison called.

The door opened to reveal Evans clutching a notebook and wearing a rather smug expression.

"Yes, Timothy? I hope you've got some good news for us; we could use it."

"I think so, guv, yes. The DS asked me to check up on Chloe Jennings."

"Chloe Jennings?" Collison echoed. "Who's she?"

"She's a rather frightening young lady with piercing green eyes who attended the vintage dinner dance," Metcalfe explained. "Our new software threw up the fact that she was a barrister, and therefore appeared on the same database as Andrew Fuller."

"Just a coincidence surely?" Collison queried.

"That's what we thought, guv," Willis replied, "but we thought it was worth checking up on anyway. What have you got, Timothy?"

"Turns out you and the DI were right, Sarge. The lady is a pupil, at a Chambers in Lincoln's Inn. And guess who her pupil master is? Andrew Fuller."

"Wow!" Metcalfe exclaimed. "How about that for a coincidence? If indeed, it is a coincidence, of course."

"That remains to be seen, of course," Collison said grimly, "but in light of what Adrian Partington had to say about Fuller's pupils she would certainly be a person of interest."

"What did he say exactly?" Willis queried.

"That Fuller always chose his pupils himself, that they were always female and attractive, and that they rarely lasted the course. After a few months they get transferred to one of his colleagues."

"Well, there can only be two explanations for that," Metcalfe observed. "Either they resist his advances and so things get very difficult, or they sleep with him and then things end messily – perhaps when they find out about his other escapades."

"It would seem so, wouldn't it?" Collison agreed. "But in any event let's bring Miss Jennings in for a chat, shall we?"

Metcalfe and Willis nodded and rose to leave.

"By the way, Bob," she said as they closed the door behind them, "they're contact lenses, you know. Nobody has eyes naturally that colour."

CHAPTER 20

"So where the hell is Chloe Jennings?" Collison asked irritably the following evening.

"Your guess is as good as mine, guv," Metcalfe replied. "We've left numerous messages for her but she hasn't got back to us."

"That's unacceptable," Collison replied. "This is a murder enquiry and we've been trying to get hold of her for 24 hours now. Try leaving one more message, Bob. Make it clear that we want to interview her about a murder to which she may be a material witness, and that if she doesn't get back to us straightaway we'll have to try to contact her through her head of chambers."

Metcalfe nodded approvingly.

"That should do the trick all right."

"Let's hope so. Now, what do we have on apart from that?"

"We're still interviewing the various club members who stayed the night. It's all pretty futile. Nobody heard anything or saw anybody wandering the corridors at the relevant time. Most of them say they were in their rooms by about 10 o'clock and didn't come out again until the next morning. So there's nothing really."

"I didn't honestly expect there would be," Collison said

wearily, "but it has to be done even if only so that we can say we've ticked all the various boxes."

"Talking of ticking boxes," Metcalfe replied. "I realised this morning that we never actually took a formal statement from the receptionist who was on duty that morning. She was off work when Karen went to see Rowena Bradley – shock at what had happened, apparently. I'm sure she'll only confirm what we've already been told by Bradley and the doctor, but we need to get something down in hardcopy nonetheless, if only to paper the file."

"I agree. Why don't you detail either Timothy or Priya to drop in at the club tomorrow?"

"Is there anything else we should be doing, guv? I can't help feeling that we're not getting very far. Are we missing something, do you think?"

Collison sighed.

"Oh yes, of course we're missing something, Bob. Or, at least, there's something we don't know which we need to know. Most obviously, did Bowen tell either of the Fullers that she was pregnant? Unless we can break one or both of them down in interview I really don't see how we're ever going to get the answer to that question. And without it, we can't really establish a motive for either of them, let alone both."

Metcalfe pondered this for a moment.

"Here, talking of motive, what about Chloe Jennings? What reason might she have had for murdering Bowen? She might not even have known that Fuller had a long-term mistress."

"He might have told her, I suppose, perhaps as a ploy to get rid of her once he thought the affair had run its course. That's what we need to ask about. But don't forget that according to the room list room 16 was occupied by the wife, not the mistress. We need to find out if Jennings had ever met either woman. If not, and she is our perpetrator, then Bowen may simply have been the victim of mistaken identity."

Now it was Collison's turn to think.

"You know, there may be something here that we have missed after all, Bob. What about that room list? Was Bradley carrying it about with her when she went roaming? What I'm getting at is this: how easy or difficult would it have been for anybody else to take a look at it either during or after dinner?"

"During dinner pretty difficult, I think, at least without attracting attention. After dinner relatively simple. I remember Rowena leaving it on the table. So anyone at the table, or even passing, could have taken a look at it. And you're right, of course. It did show room 16 as being occupied by Professor Fuller."

"I see. Well, in that case it's more important than ever that we should see Jennings as soon as possible. Leave that message straightaway will you? If she hasn't responded by the morning I think we should go round and see her at Chambers, no matter how embarrassing that may be either for her or Fuller."

In the event such embarrassment proved unnecessary. Jennings contacted Metcalfe at about 9 o'clock saying in a very offhand manner "I think you've been trying to reach me."

"We have indeed, Miss Jennings," Metcalfe said formally. "As I made clear, we need to take a statement from you about the events which took place during that vintage event which we both attended. As I'm sure you will have seen from the media, a woman was murdered upstairs in her room."

"Of course I know. It's been all over the news. But what's it got to do with me? May I ask what you want to question me about?"

"We have the list of all the attendees of the event from the organiser," Metcalfe said, choosing his words carefully. "We are intending to speak to everybody on the list sooner or later. But given your connection with Andrew Fuller it seems sensible to speak to you straightaway before anybody else."

"My only connection, as you put it, with Andrew Fuller is that we are in the same Chambers," Jennings responded. "I really don't see why that should single me out for special attention. Anyway, I'm very busy at the moment. I'm in court all day tomorrow."

"I know enough about the legal profession, Miss Jennings, to know that the presence of a pupil barrister in court can be easily dispensed with. You're only there to take notes, aren't you? I suggest you speak to whoever you need to and arrange to be at Hampstead police station at 10 o'clock tomorrow morning."

"That's really not convenient," she persisted.

"To be honest, Miss Jennings, I really don't care whether it's convenient not. This is a murder enquiry and you may be a material witness. We need to interview you, and it has to be face-to-face. Now you can either come along to the nick as I propose or we can call your head of chambers and arrange to see you very publicly at work. But either way we will see you tomorrow. Now, which is it going to be?"

There was a pause the other end of the line.

"Very well, I'll be with you tomorrow."

By the time Chloe Jennings appeared at Hampstead, Timothy Evans was already arriving at the club to take the receptionist's statement, as tasked by Metcalfe.

"You can use my office," Rowena Bradley said at once when he explained what he needed. "I'll cover for Sharon on the desk while you speak to her."

With Sharon seated nervously before him, Evans sat at Bradley's desk, his notebook poised.

"Now then, Miss Jones – it is Jones, isn't it?"

"It is, yes."

"I just need to take a formal statement from you recording what you can remember of the events of that morning."

"Oh, it was so awful, wasn't it? I've still not got over it, you know. I'm still all shook up."

"I'm sorry to hear that," Evans replied, thinking it was the sort of thing that Collison would say. "I really don't want to upset you any further, but I do need to just take you through what happened. Now, what time did you come on duty?"

"My shift starts at seven, but I always get here a bit early, say about 10 minutes or so. I nip down to the kitchen and grab a cup of tea before I start."

"Okay, now I think the first thing that happened was that the maid, Maria, couldn't get into room 16. Is that right?"

"No not really. What happened was that the lady in room 16 – who we all thought was Mrs Fuller, of course – wouldn't answer the phone when I rang with her alarm call. So Miss Bradley sent Maria up to take a look."

"With the key? The duplicate from her office?"

Evans nodded at the keys hanging neatly on their numbered pegs on the wall.

"Yeah, that's right. Maria took the key and went upstairs. I think Miss Bradley would have done it herself, but she was dealing with a guest at the time."

"What happened then?"

"Well Maria came running back downstairs, didn't she? Looked like she'd seen a ghost. Well of course we all asked what was wrong – Miss Bradley did anyroad – and she said she thought she'd snuffed it. Then Miss Bradley asked me to call Dr Tasker in her room and ask her to come back down. So she did. Miss Bradley was busy trying to deal with Maria, so she gave Dr Tasker the key and asked if she minded going up on her own. Then the guest realised that something bad was going on, so she offered to look after Maria and said whatever it was she was asking Miss Bradley about could wait."

"So Miss Bradley ended up going upstairs pretty soon after the doctor?"

"Yeah, that's right. Then she came back downstairs a few minutes later looking very upset. She went into the office and closed the door. I think she said she had a telephone call to make. The doctor came back downstairs again a bit later and asked me for the guest's details to put in a report or something."

"That would be her note to the coroner," Evans observed. "Yes, go on."

"Well, there's not much to tell, is there? According to the computer the lady in room 16 was Professor Fuller, so it was her name and address that I gave the doctor. I wasn't to know there'd been a mix-up, was I?"

"And at what stage did you realise that a mistake could have been made?"

"When Professor Fuller herself came waltzing through the front door as bold as brass. Gave me a right turn it did. Gave Miss Bradley a nasty turn and all. Thought we were seeing a ghost, didn't we?"

"It must have been very distressing for you," Evans sympathised. "Now, was there anything else that happened?"

"Was there ever! Miss Bradley made me go up to the room with the body-snatchers."

"Body-snatchers? Do you mean the men from the morgue?" Evans asked with amusement.

"Yeah, well that's what I called them anyway."

"It's not a bad description actually. I'll remember that."

"Yeah, well so will I. Not my job to do something like that, is it? Bleeding awful it was, pardon my French. Never seen anything like it. Hope I never will again."

"What was there in particular that was so awful?" Evans asked curiously. "Or was it just the whole experience? It can't been very nice for you."

"You can say that again. And it all had to be done so secret, didn't it? Miss Bradley didn't want any of the guests to see, so I had to keep running ahead to the next fire door and give the all clear so they could bring the stretcher along."

"Stretcher?"

"Suppose it wasn't really a stretcher. Don't know what it's

called though. Like a big cradle. They strapped the body into it, though I didn't have to watch that bit thank God."

"Okay, yes I think I know what you're referring to. It was presumably so they could stand the body upright in the lift, was it?"

"Yeah, they did. Bleeding awful that was, and all. We all crammed into the lift together, 'cos they needed me to open the door for them at the bottom, and that's when it happened."

"When what happened?"

"Her bleeding arm only fell out, didn't it? Hung down on me all limp, it did. Miss Bradley gave me a hard time later because I screamed. Said somebody might have heard: one of her precious guests, I expect she meant."

"Was it a loud scream then?"

"Course it was. Nearly wet myself didn't I? You ever had somebody's dead arm hanging down on you, have you?"

"Can't say I have," Evans replied with a smile.

"Bet you've seen some really horrible things though, haven't you?" she asked eagerly. "Stands to reason in your job."

"Well, I haven't been doing it very long."

There was a silence while Evans's note taking caught up with Sharon's narrative. She used this opportunity to appraise him.

"You ever arrested anyone, then?" she asked suddenly.

"I have, actually," he said, closing his notebook.

"What, lots of people?"

"A few, yes."

"Cor," she said, digesting this information while he put his notebook and pen away in his jacket.

"You know," she went on, as if having come to a decision, "you could always ask me out for a drink or something if you like. I've never been out with a copper before."

CHAPTER 21

"Am I here as a witness or a suspect?" Chloe Jennings demanded at once, her green eyes flashing from Metcalfe to Willis.

They both laughed.

"Have I said something amusing?" she asked, flushing.

"I'm sorry," Metcalfe replied, "it's just that it's usually only criminals who ask that question. I suppose we should add 'and lawyers' to that. We don't get to interview many, you see."

"The answer to your question," Willis explained, "is that you are not officially a suspect. If you were, we would have to interview under caution, as you know. However, with your permission, we do propose to tape record the interview."

Jennings nodded reluctantly and Willis went through the usual rigmarole, inserting the tapes and getting the attendees to announce their names.

"Now then," Metcalfe began, "as DS Willis has just explained, we are interviewing you as a possible material witness to the murder of Angela Bowen at the Athena Club. For the tape, I should explain that both DS Willis and I were present at the building in which the killing took place in our personal capacities, as indeed were you. So we have met before, haven't we?"

"Yes, we sat and drank for a while after dinner."

"Exactly. Right, now we've got that out of the way for the record, I would like you to talk us through everything you can remember from about 10 o'clock onwards."

"Well, at 10 o'clock we were still having dinner, weren't we? I'm sure I remember dinner finishing about half past because a few people were making a fuss about not having enough time left to dance."

"Who were you attending the event with?" Willis enquired. "I don't remember you having a partner."

"Oh, I was there with a girlfriend, somebody I was at bar school with. She's very into all that vintage stuff. Her bloke let her down at the last moment – I think he's in private equity or something and had to work late suddenly on a deal – so she asked me, and I thought it sounded fun so I said yes."

"Did we meet her at all?"

"No, I don't think so. By the time we were sitting together it was quite late wasn't it? I think she'd already left. To be honest, I'd had a bit too much to drink I think."

"Can you concentrate on what you can remember about your own movements?" Metcalfe asked her. "You say you left the dining area some time soon after half past ten. What happened then?"

"I had a couple of dances with a few of the men who'd been on our table for dinner, but I'd never met any of them before and frankly I didn't like them very much. Jen – my friend, that is – didn't either. I think that's when she said she was going."

"Why was that?" Willis asked curiously.

"Oh I don't know, they were very full of themselves if

you know what I mean. They were investment bankers or something and they seemed to think they were all very grand. One of them was getting rather fresh; I think he'd had too much to drink too. That's why I started roaming around the room upstairs. I was looking for someone more interesting. I liked the look of that bloke you had on your table: he seemed different somehow. So I asked him to dance."

"Yes, I remember that," Willis said neutrally.

"He looked a bit shocked, poor bloke, I don't think he was used to a woman taking the initiative like that. He was very polite, though, and a lovely dancer. We had a couple of dances together and then he asked me back to his table for a drink. That's when we met, wasn't it?"

"Yes, it was," Willis confirmed. "Can you remember who else was sitting at the table when you arrived and sat down?"

Jennings paused for thought.

"Well, the two of you were there, another woman – nicely dressed, very 'girl next door' if you like that sort of thing – and an older woman. I'm sorry, Peter did introduce me, but I can't remember her name. I think she said she was a doctor."

"Charlotte Tasker?"

"If you say so. I honestly can't remember."

"Dark hair or blonde hair?"

"Dark, definitely and not very well-kept either. She reminded me a bit of that old actress, Joyce Grenfell I think her name was. There was something rather intense about her, as if she was about to interview me for a job or something."

"Yes, that was Charlotte Tasker all right," Metcalfe said with a smile. "Now, this may be important so think carefully:

are you sure there was nobody else at the table? Perhaps another older woman with blonde hair?"

"Oh dear, I was a bit squiffy as I say so I might not be remembering everything perfectly, but no, I really don't think there was."

"OK, so think about this. Do you remember seeing any papers on the table? Documents, I mean, not newspapers."

Jennings thought hard once more.

"Yes, actually, now you come to mention it. There was some sort of typewritten list, attached to a clipboard I think."

"Did you read it at all, or even glance at it?"

"No, I didn't."

"Can you remember whether all the people you just mentioned remained at the table while you were there?"

"Oh no, they didn't, I'm sure. You went and danced with Peter didn't you? And didn't you dance with that other girl?"

"Yes, I think you're right. What about Charlotte? Did she stay with you at the table while we were dancing?"

"Yes she did. All the time. It was almost as though she was desperate for company. I think at one point I said I'd be going and she said 'oh, don't go' straightaway. She said I should wait for Peter to come back to the table so I could thank him for the drink."

"Maybe she thought that would just be common politeness," Willis murmured.

"What?" Jennings asked, clearly having either not heard or not understood.

"Never mind," Metcalfe said quickly. "Now, for how long were you at the table do you think?"

She shrugged.

"I honestly don't know. I'm not sure I was even wearing a watch. I remember wandering off somewhere else fairly soon afterwards, and that was still a while before I went home."

"When did you leave the club?" Willis asked.

"I think it must have been around midnight, or just after, because I remember getting a cab and the driver saying that it was after midnight. I think the fare goes up, or something. Actually, I think he was in two minds about taking me. Perhaps he thought I might be sick in the back of the taxi."

"And I'm sorry to press you on this, but do you remember anything in particular you might have done, or where you might have gone between leaving our table and leaving the club to get a taxi home?"

"No, it's all a bit of a haze really. I think I ended up back on the table having a drink with those awful investment banker types. I remember one of them asked me to go home with him. I told him where to get off."

"Did you go downstairs at all – to the loo perhaps?"

"Oh yes, I'm sure I did. A few times. Like I said, I'd had a lot to drink."

"And when you got across to the other side of the club, you're sure that you went downstairs not upstairs?"

"Yes of course. That's where the loos are, isn't it?"

"All right," Metcalfe said, "let's talk about something else, shall we? What can you tell us about Andrew Fuller?"

She shrugged again.

"What's there to tell? 'His fame precedes him', as they say. Surely you lot know him? You must come across him in court all the time. He's brilliant, by the way. As a lawyer, if that's what you mean."

"We know he's a very well respected member of the senior bar," Metcalfe said cautiously, "but that's not really what I meant. What I'd like you to describe is the nature of your relationship with him, as it is now and also as it was on the night in question, just in case anything has changed in the meantime."

Jennings flushed once more.

"I thought I'd made it clear on the phone that our relationship is a purely professional one. He's my pupil master."

"Still?"

"What you mean?"

"I think it's a very simple question, Miss Jennings. We know that Andrew Fuller was your pupil master. Perhaps he still is officially. But is that the case in practice? Which particular barrister are you shadowing? Is it still him, or has he handed you off to somebody else?"

"It's not really a question of 'handing me off'," Jennings said, bristling. "You make me sound like the baton in a relay race or something."

"I'm sorry, I didn't mean any disrespect, but please answer the question."

"It's true that I'm spending a lot of my time with other members of chambers, but that's not unusual. If somebody else's in court that day and he's not then it's natural for me to go with the other person. The whole point of pupillage is to get as much experience in court as possible."

Willis and Metcalfe exchanged a glance.

"This really could be very important, Miss Jennings, and I do urge you to think very carefully because what you are saying now is going on tape, and therefore on record. What I'm asking you, as I think you very well know, is whether at any time you have had a personal relationship with Andrew Fuller as well as a professional one. A sexual relationship, in fact."

"No, I haven't."

"That was a very quick response."

"That's because I'm very sure. I'm aware that Andrew Fuller has a certain reputation at the bar, but I'm not part of it."

"You say that Andrew Fuller has a certain reputation," Willis observed, "and by 'a certain reputation' I assume you mean with women. Now, you're clearly an attractive woman, are you really saying that he's never made advances to you?"

"No, I'm not saying that at all. As a matter of fact he tried it on almost at once. What I am saying is that we have never had any sort of sexual relationship."

"Define 'tried it on', will you?" Willis asked curiously.

"Well, we used to go for a drink in the evening after work, particularly if we'd been in court. Always champagne, naturally; that's his style. It wasn't long before he had his hand on my knee. Oh, I don't mind that particularly, it's almost a normal part of going for a drink with a man isn't it? But he asked me out to dinner with him and he made it pretty clear what he had in mind after that. So I said no. He asked again another evening and I said no again. After that, he seemed to lose interest."

"So, just to be clear," Willis pressed her, "you have been out for a drink with Fuller on a few occasions in the evening, but you've never had dinner with him or had any other sort of interaction other than of a purely professional nature?"

"Exactly, yes."

"I'm still curious," Willis went on after a pause. "From what we think we know about Andrew Fuller – about that sort of man, perhaps I should say – I would have thought that once you had rejected his advances he would lose interest in you personally."

"I'm not sure I know what you mean."

"Well, put it this way. Was it from about this time that he started suggesting that you spent time with other members of chambers?"

"Well, I suppose it was, yes."

"And do you think there was a connection between the two events?"

"It's not really for me to say, is it?"

"Can I ask this, then?" Metcalfe proffered, struck by a sudden idea. "Has Andrew Fuller taken up with another pupil since? Perhaps one who is officially attached to a different member of chambers?"

"He's started going to court with someone else, yes," Jennings admitted reluctantly.

"A young lady by any chance?"

She nodded.

"For the tape, please."

"Yes, he has."

"And is she attractive?" Willis enquired.

Jennings tossed her head.

"I suppose so, in a rather mumsy way, if you like that sort of thing."

CHAPTER 22

"And did you believe her?" Collins asked.

Willis shook her head at once, so he glanced enquiringly at Metcalfe.

"Hard to be sure," Metcalfe said slowly," but I think not. Don't forget all that stuff she was coming out with at the dance. Of course there could be an innocent explanation, but if Fuller wasn't at the bottom of that then who was?"

"Perhaps we should have asked that," Willis suggested.

"I thought of it actually, but I decided it would be better to keep it for later. She had had a lot to drink, remember, and so it may be she doesn't remember exactly what she said to whom. If we end up having to re-interview her – and I think we will – then it could be useful to have something up our sleeve."

"What about you, Peter?" Willis asked, intrigued. "After all, it seemed to be you that she was drawn to."

He considered the question carefully.

"The fact that she was so desperate to strike up a conversation with people she had never met before – let alone to ask one to dance – suggests that she was feeling lonely, and that's certainly the impression I received. Not just at the dance I mean, but generally. I think she was angry as well, although that was already pretty obvious from what she was saying. It's curious, when we were dancing together she wasn't relaxing at all. There was a hardness about her – an intensity, I suppose you might say – a sort of focus, as if she was concentrating her anger into the business of the dance itself. Curious, because she knew what she was doing; she'd obviously had dance lessons at some stage."

"Would she be capable of murder, do you think?" Metcalfe enquired curiously. "Or maybe that's an unfair question, Peter?"

"It is an unfair question," he acknowledged with a smile, "but let me try to answer it anyway. Of course I only met her very briefly and as you know my theory is that any one of us is capable of murder if pushed to a sufficient pitch of anger, desperation, or both. However, I found the degree of her anger, albeit expressed as determination, quite striking. It was almost as if she felt a grudge against the whole world just because of what one person had done to her. So yes, if the situation were to present itself I think she would be capable of just about anything. That's a purely unofficial view, of course. I'd need to get to know her much better to be able to present a professional opinion."

"It's useful nonetheless," Metcalfe replied. "And you agree presumably, Karen?"

She nodded.

"I do. Oh, I couldn't present the sort of detailed assessment that Peter has just given, not least because I wasn't really listening that hard to what she was saying. To be honest, I was just hoping she would get up and go away. I find drunk people moaning about their unhappy love affairs very wearing, don't you? But back when we were interviewing her I had the very strong impression that she was lying about her relationship with Andrew Fuller. I think we need to suggest to the guvnor that we find a way of investigating that a bit more."

"Of course the mere fact that she may be lying about a relationship with Fuller isn't necessarily a sign of guilt," Collins observed mildly, gazing into the remnants of his Chardonnay. "She's a professional career woman and should she want to conceal the fact that she had had an affair with her pupil master – her boss in effect – then I could quite understand that. Put yourself in her shoes. It's really a no-win situation, isn't it? If you succeed then there will always be snide people suggesting that you did so because of granting someone your favours, rather than because of your own ability."

"But she's a barrister," Willis pointed out. "She must understand the possible consequences of lying during a police interview."

"I know, I know, Harriet," Collins responded, flapping his free hand helplessly. "Were she to have lied to you today – and she may well have done for all I know – then that would indeed be a very stupid thing to have done. But it would still not be any conclusive evidence of guilt so far as the murder of Angela Bowen is concerned. I didn't see her today, but on the evidence of what I saw the other night I think she's a very unhappy and very confused person right now."

"She's a suspect though, isn't she?" Willis persisted. "You'd have to concede that surely, Peter?"

"I concede that you have to treat her as a suspect, yes. And if nothing else I suppose that takes a little of the heat off Andrew Fuller himself for the time being. What about Rowena Bradley, by the way? Do we think she's in the clear?"

"Nobody is in the clear," Metcalfe said decisively, "at least, not yet. That's the problem with this case. We've not been able to narrow anything down. All we know for certain is the time of death – or approximately anyway – and we have four suspects all of whom we can place at the club at the relevant time with possible access to room 16."

"There's something I'm not sure we've considered about that, by the way," Collins observed. "It just occurred to me earlier. If Andrew Fuller is indeed our perpetrator then Angela Bowen could have been killed anytime up to about 11 o'clock. But on his own evidence he was in the room with her until about that time. So if he is not our murderer then whoever did it had to have been in the room after 11 o'clock and – according to the forensic evidence – before about half past. In other words, if we are looking for somebody other than Fuller then we can narrow the time window down to a specific 30 minutes or so."

Willis and Metcalfe looked at each other.

"You're right you know," Metcalfe acknowledged. "We should have thought of that. Instead of asking the other suspects about their whereabouts earlier, we only really need to know what they were doing from the time Fuller left the club via the back door."

"Unless of course," Willis pointed out, "that two of them were in it together, in which case it's quite possible that she could have been killed at the very beginning of the time window."

"You mean that Fuller might have sat in the room alongside a dead woman, just to mislead everybody about the possible time of death?" Metcalfe asked incredulously.

"Why not? If you've got the nerve to murder a woman in cold blood, then surely the adrenaline would kick in and it might be just the sort of thing he would have thought of. He's an intelligent man, don't forget, and a lawyer to boot."

"The more I think about it," Collins mused, "the more I think Simon is right. The key here surely is whether Bowen told anybody else, and particularly either of the Fullers, about her pregnancy. And ironically it seems that's about the one thing that we can't know. Not unless somebody cracks in interview and tells us, and why should they? There'd be incriminating themselves for sure, whether they did it or not."

"There's the duplicate key as well," Metcalfe reminded him. "Surely that's the other really important point. Because the guest key was found inside the room then we know that our murderer must have had access to the duplicate. They couldn't have locked the door behind themselves without it. And try as we might we can't place anybody with the key, other than Rowena Bradley that is."

"So if you're right, then that brings us right back to Rowena doesn't it?" Collins asked, gazing at the empty wine bottle with bleak disfavour.

"Not necessarily. It just means that we can't place anybody else with access to the room and also with the means to lock the door behind them. But yes, I get your drift, Peter."

"Could there be another key I wonder?" Collins conjectured. "Perhaps it might have been possible for somebody to borrow the key and have it cut, or the good old bar of soap or lump of plasticine might have been employed to advantage..."

"Well, that would blow the case wide open certainly. If we could find a third key..."

"Oh, but how likely is that really?" Willis asked briskly. "Apart from anything else, aren't we treating this as something of an impulse killing? To have had a duplicate of the duplicate made in advance would point to premeditation and forward planning."

"Which would presumably mean that Bowen had already told somebody about her pregnancy, and that our murderer had seized upon her night at the club as a convenient opportunity for doing away with her," Collins went on. "Yes, I see the difficulty, old thing. It's hardly the basis we've been proceeding on so far, is it now?"

They sat and considered this in companionable silence, Willis sniffing contemplatively the last few drops of her wine as she swilled them around in the glass.

"But to have had a duplicate made," Metcalfe said at length, "would still require access to the one in Rowena's office, wouldn't it? And we've already seen how difficult it is to get in and out of there without anybody noticing."

"Well, not necessarily," Collins demurred. "We've seen that when everybody thinks very hard about a certain period of time then they will tend to remember whatever they saw, particularly under the impetus of some particularly shocking event. But if we are now saying that this might have been a premeditated crime then being able to prearrange the removal and return of the key on a planned basis would be a very different thing to having to nip in and out of the office on the spur of the moment with lots of people milling around because of an event going on."

"Why yes, that's right," Willis agreed. "For all we know there may be certain points in the daily schedule when it's fairly easy to get in and out of the office. Or during the night, for that matter. We know that Rowena didn't usually occupy the office overnight."

"But somebody else did," Metcalfe pointed out. "There's always a night manager and they always use that office. It's just that on this particular night Rowena had to cover the nightshift herself."

"Our killer could have had an accomplice to facilitate copying the key," Collins suggested. "Someone who could go in and out of the office without being challenged. The night manager for one. Cleaners for two. Secretarial and reception staff for three ... why, their line stretches to the crack of doom."

"And with a third key anybody could go in and out of room 16 any time they wanted," Metcalfe commented. "Their only challenge would be to get their key safely out of the building, and since it was unlikely the murder would be discovered until about 8 o'clock then all our killer had to do was to make sure they were out of the club before then just in case the police were called straightaway and the building sealed off. Just as Elizabeth Fuller did, in fact."

"True," Collins nodded. "But there's the manner of death to be considered as well. One possible reason for choosing smothering would be that the means of death – the pillow – would lie close at hand. But another might be the hope that the death might be written off as natural causes, as was in fact the case, and thus no hue and cry would be raised at all."

"But it would still make sense to get out of the building as quickly as possible, wouldn't it?" Metcalfe insisted. "Just to be on the safe side."

"Yes, I think it would," Collins conceded, "which would certainly point the finger of suspicion at Elizabeth Fuller, as you say, but don't forget that her husband left the building even earlier and so would have had every opportunity to dispose safely of a third key."

"I think this is taking us down a completely different line, isn't it?" Willis demanded after finishing her wine. "Until now we've been assuming that this was an opportunist killing, perhaps sparked by sudden news of Angela Bowen's pregnancy. If we are to start conjecturing about somebody taking the trouble to create a further duplicate key in advance then we are into a planned, premeditated murder. What do we think about that?"

"It would suggest there's something we haven't found out about yet," Metcalfe suggested. "It would suggest that the killing might have been about something other than the pregnancy. After all, she might only have just found out about it herself, so the idea of her being to tell somebody about it even a week or two earlier is unlikely."

"I wonder if she did know about it?" Willis asked suddenly. "We are assuming that she did, but perhaps she didn't. It was still at quite an early stage..."

"That's an interesting thought in itself," Collins said diplomatically, "but if we stick to this new angle just for a moment, then I have to agree with Bob. It strongly suggests that there is something behind the killing, some motive, of which we are as yet unaware. Surely a leading QC wouldn't evolve an elaborate plan to bump off his mistress when he could simply have ended the affair any time he wanted, just as he had ended countless others?"

"Correct," Metcalfe agreed. "So we need to dig much more deeply into Bowen's background. Logically the answer would have to lie there somewhere."

Willis sighed.

"Good luck with that," she commented gloomily. "We've pretty much drawn a blank there. Apart from her relationship with Fuller she doesn't really seem to have had much of a private life at all."

"Two observations," Collins commented, holding one finger up in the air.

"First, we should remember that because of the switched rooms Bowen may not have been the intended victim. That would of course assume that neither of the Fullers was involved in her death, and right now that's looking unlikely, but it's worth remembering all the same."

The others nodded.

"Second, just because it would have been so much easier to copy a further key in advance, it doesn't necessarily follow that that is what happened. An instinctive, opportunistic killing still feels more likely to me, in which case the whole question of access to room 16 – or rather, if one is being pedantic, egress from it – remains of vital importance. So by all means this new idea should be investigated, but if I were in Simon's place I would still be focusing my efforts on trying to find out exactly who could have access to room 16 between 10:30 and 11:30."

"And as to that at the moment," Metcalfe said sadly, "we seem to be no further forward. We are completely in the dark in fact."

"Well, I know this will sound very unhelpful," Collins replied, "but I don't see that you can do anything other than keep bashing on and just hope that a chink of light will present itself."

CHAPTER 23

"So on balance we don't believe Chloe Jennings when she says she wasn't having an affair with Andrew Fuller?" Collison enquired.

"That's about the size of it, guv, yes," Metcalfe replied.

"And what are you proposing to do about it?"

"Well, the obvious thing would be to get Fuller back in for a further interview and put the question to him."

Collison reflected on this, drumming his fingers softly on the desk.

"Yes," he said slowly. "That would be the obvious thing to do but I'm not sure it's the right thing. At least, not yet."

"Why's that then, guv?"

"Well, look at it this way. Fuller is still our main suspect, isn't he? He's the only one we can place at the crime scene at or about the right time. And yet when you look at it, we've actually got nothing on him. Nothing other than circumstantial evidence that is. If it went to court he would simply swear blind that Angela Bowen was alive and well when he left her room, and the chances are that a jury would believe him. Why wouldn't they? No, I wonder if there's a way we can get something stronger. Catch him out in a lie, for example."

"You mean find out first whether they were having an

affair and then put the question to him, hoping that he denies it?"

"Yes, Bob, exactly that."

Metcalfe sat back in his chair and whistled contemplatively.

"Well, it's a great idea," he admitted, "but how do we go about it?"

"I'm tempted to ask Rowena Bradley, but it's a difficult one isn't it? After all, she is still officially a suspect herself and it's entirely possible that she was an accomplice to Andrew Fuller."

"Do you really believe that, guv? Is that what your gut tells you?"

"Oh, I don't know," Collison said helplessly. "There's something strange about this case, almost as if we're missing something somewhere. I really don't know what to think."

"It is a difficult one," Metcalfe concurred. "I wonder if there's some way we might be able to get what we need from her without making it obvious what we're asking, or why?"

"That's an idea," Collison replied approvingly. "I know. What about saying that we need to corroborate her story and ask her for the name of the restaurant where Fuller took her for dinner?"

"And that helps us how?"

"Oh, you never know. It's just possible that Fuller's a creature of habit and tends to take his women to the same restaurant. At the very least, he might have a small number of favourite restaurants. If we could find out which they are then we could put some photo packs together and ask if they've seen him with each of the women."

"Okay, guv. Leave it to me. I'll get onto that straightaway. Perhaps I'll get Karen to ask. They seem to have quite a good relationship and it may sound better coming from a woman."

"Fine, whatever you think. Now, where are we with everything else?"

"We've finished speaking to the various guests who stayed at the club that night. In some cases it's been no more than a few words on the phone, but we have managed to track everybody down. That's the good news. The bad news is that nobody remembers anything out of the ordinary, such as raised voices, or anybody walking the corridor after about 11 o'clock. Of course that's not conclusive. I'm assuming that if you took your shoes off you could walk along the corridor without disturbing anyone, but it might be worth asking Karen to check that when she goes to speak to Rowena Bradley."

"Yes, let's do that. Oh dear, that's a pity. I wasn't really expecting anyone to have heard anything, but it's disappointing nonetheless. Where does that leave us, I wonder?"

"Well, if you include Chloe Jennings then we have four possible suspects, but right now we can't place any of them except Fuller himself in room 16. More difficult still, we can't place anyone except Rowena Bradley herself in her office either taking the key or putting it back. For me, the most likely perpetrator is Fuller, possibly with assistance over the key from Bradley. But like you say, we can't actually prove anything, only show that it would have been possible..."

"Well, I'm not going to start making formal accusations against a senior member of the bar without some real evidence," Collison said decisively, "and I'm pretty sure the ACC would take a similar line."

"Understood, sir. Well, let's do as you suggest and see what we can come up with on the Chloe Jennings angle."

"Right you are, Bob. Keep me posted of course. By the way-"

He hesitated and then, as Metcalfe looked at him enquiringly, shrugged and went on.

"I'm sorry, you can tell me it's none of my business if you like, but I was just wondering how things were going with Lisa Atkins."

"I don't mind you asking at all, guv. Very well indeed actually. In fact, so well that I'm sort of worried."

"What on earth do you mean?"

"Well we've covered a lot of ground very quickly so to speak and it's already starting to feel quite serious."

"Well that's good. Or isn't it?"

"Yes of course it's good, but I don't have to tell you that it takes a very special sort of person to be the partner of a copper. You've been lucky of course. So has Karen, but then Peter is a very special sort of person and they don't exactly have a normal sort of relationship. With me it's always been different in the past. I've found it difficult to hang onto people. You know what the job is like. When you're on an active investigation it takes over your life."

"Yes I do know what you mean."

Collison looked at him thoughtfully before continuing.

"But perhaps she is different, Bob? Perhaps she's that special sort of person that we are all looking for?"

Metcalfe smiled.

"That's what I'm hoping, yes," he said as he opened the door.

After Metcalfe left the room Collison stood up, gazed out of the window, and sighed. He knew enough by now to realise that murder enquiries fell into two categories. There were those with one obvious suspect that were resolved quickly, usually either a domestic argument that went too far or a different sort of crime that went horribly wrong. Then there were the others, those which could last for months or even years and which dragged in police resources pursuing increasingly stale lines of enquiry with little to show for it. In these more complex investigations there were periods such as this, where the possible perpetrators had been identified but nothing specific could as yet be pinned on anyone. Often the vital clue would be unearthed almost by accident. Worst of all were those when sooner or later a senior officer had to call a halt to proceedings, recognising at least privately that nobody would ever be held to account.

The jangling of the telephone interrupted his thoughts. A respectful voice asked him to hold for the ACC.

"Simon, Fuller is playing hardball," the latter began without preamble. "I've just had a call from Max Willough-by-Forbes. I assume you know who he is?"

"He's quite a prominent solicitor, I believe."

The ACC chuckled.

"He's probably the most prominent solicitor there is. He

acts for the Royal family, you know. He was made a CVO in the last Honours list for personal services to the Queen – for handling yet another Royal divorce actually. And now he's acting for Andrew Fuller."

"Is he now? Interesting that Fuller should feel the need of a solicitor."

"That's as maybe. But it makes things even more tricky. Willoughby-Forbes has the ear of every editor in London. Do you think anyone's going to turn down the chance to talk to the Queen's solicitor? Well anyway, he's putting us under pressure."

"What did he say, sir?"

"I think his precise words were that it would be extremely helpful if we could issue a statement for the press confirming that Fuller was not a suspect in our investigation."

"But that's ridiculous, sir. Fuller knows damn well that he's a suspect. On his own admission he was alone in a hotel room with Angela Bowen at about the time she died."

"I know that. You know that. Fuller knows that. Willoughby-Forbes knows that. Like I say, he's putting us under pressure. He's putting the message across that as far as he's concerned we only have a limited amount of time to find something on Fuller. The implied threat is that if we don't put out a statement ourselves then he will, saying something like so far as he is aware his client will not be charged in connection with the death of Angela Bowen."

"I see," Collison said flatly.

The ACC chuckled again.

"Don't take it to heart, Simon. This is what expensive

lawyers do, it's why people hire them. You could have been one yourself, remember."

"It's not a decision I've ever regretted, sir."

"I know that, and private practice's loss has definitely been the Met's gain. But listen, that wretched man has a lot of clout and we can't just ignore what he says. It's too dangerous. Now where are we on Fuller exactly? Anything new?"

"We're not sure but we think he may have been having an affair with his pupil, who just happens to have been present at the club at the right sort of time. Actually, she was attending a vintage event there and met Collins, Metcalfe, and Willis, albeit briefly. She was in the proximity of Rowena Bradley's room list – though she hasn't admitted to having read it – which showed the room number of every guest who was staying at the club that night. And she was flitting around quite a bit, so it's entirely possible that she might have been able to slip into the office and remove the duplicate key."

"But you can't prove any of that?"

"No, sir, we can't. Not yet anyway. But I've just been discussing with Bob Metcalfe the possibility that we may be able to kill two birds with one stone."

"How's that?"

"We going to try to find independent evidence of the affair. Jennings has already denied it, so perhaps that means they've discussed a party line together."

"In which case Fuller would also deny it and you'd be able to catch him out in a lie?"

"You've got it exactly, sir."

"Hm, not sure that gets us where we want to go, does it?

It just shows that he's told a lie, not that he murdered Angela Bowen."

"Unless he and Jennings were in it together, that is. They may have agreed that she would get the key and bring it to the room because she was less likely to be recognised than him. I think he was quite a regular visitor to the club."

"But there's no evidence of that?"

"No, sir. I'm just thinking aloud."

"Careful, Simon, we're walking on thin ice here. If we are going to make any move against Fuller at all then we need to be very sure of our facts."

"I do understand that, sir. At the moment the most likely hypothesis seems to be that Fuller killed Bowen, but that's all it is: a hypothesis. We can't show a motive because neither he nor his wife will admit to having been told about Bowen's pregnancy. And we can't show how he was able to lock the door behind him because we haven't been able to prove anybody took the key and then returned it. Without at least one, and preferably both, those pieces of evidence it's very difficult to see how we can make a case stick."

"That would be for the DPP to decide, but I agree with you. I don't think they would bring a case based purely on circumstantial evidence, especially not against such a high profile defendant. So where do we go from here? I don't want to put you under undue pressure, but I get the feeling we may be running out of time. If we don't come up with something in the next day or two then it may prove very difficult to keep Willoughby-Forbes at bay."

"I do understand the situation, sir, but I think that whatever happens we need to interview Fuller again."

There was a silence at the other end of the line.

"Have you thought," came the response at last, "about how that might place you in a difficult position? If you interview him again, particularly with his solicitor present, aren't you going to have to make a decision as to whether to treat him formally as a suspect and interview him under caution?"

"I hadn't got to the stage of thinking about that, sir, but you're right of course. And yes, I think it would have to be under caution. To be honest, I was thinking about it the first time and it was probably a borderline decision."

"Willoughby-Forbes wouldn't like that at all. You know, that gives me an idea. I think I will call him back, say that I have just spoken with the SIO, and that we're planning to re-interview his client under caution. I can then suggest that if he is prepared to give us a little more time we may be able to find out what we need to know elsewhere and spare his client that embarrassment."

Now it was Collison's turn to laugh.

"That sounds like a plan, sir."

"It is that. All right, Simon, best of luck and let me know as soon as you find out anything of interest."

Collison replaced the receiver. Then on impulse he picked it up again and dialled Willis's extension.

"Karen? It's Simon Collison. I think you're going over to the club to see Rowena Bradley, aren't you? Do you mind if I come with you? I've never actually been there, you see, and I wouldn't mind just wondering about a bit in case I'm suddenly struck by a brainwave. Unlikely, but you never know."

CHAPTER 24

As Collison and Willis approached the club having walked along Curzon Street from Green Park station, the former said "half a mo, Karen, I just want to make a quick phone call."

While they dawdled along the pavement he placed a call to Adrian Partington at his chambers.

"Adrian? It's Simon. Listen, I hate to do this to you but we're making some discreet enquiries about Andrew Fuller and you might be able to help ... Yes I know, I do appreciate your position ... That's understood, Adrian, but I only want to ask you something very innocent and everyday. Do you happen to know what his favourite restaurants are? In particular, is there one special one that he takes his women to?"

There was a pause while he listened, nodding as he did so.

"Okay, Adrian. I'll wait to hear from you – and many thanks indeed. Don't worry, tell your friend it will be completely confidential."

"What did he say?" Willis enquired.

"He said he knew lots of women whom he thought had had affairs with Fuller," Collison replied with a laugh, "but only one for certain. Apparently she makes no secret of it. He's going to ask her and then get back to me. At least that will give us a bit of a check on whatever Rowena Bradley is going to tell us."

Rowena Bradley met them in the lobby and Willis made the introductions. Conscious that various members were eyeing them excitedly while pretending not to, she ushered them quickly into her office and closed the door behind them.

"This is all rather delicate, and to tell you the truth I'm not entirely sure how best to proceed," Collison confessed at once. "You see there is something we need to find out about Andrew Fuller and I'm hoping that you may be able to help us."

"Oh dear," Bradley said, looking awkward at once. "I was rather hoping that we had finished with all this. Are you still treating Andrew as a suspect then?"

"He's someone who was present at the crime scene at or about the time Angela Bowen died," Collison said carefully. "As such, we are anxious to eliminate him from our enquiries. As an experienced barrister, I'm sure he would understand that. It's how criminal investigations work. If he is indeed innocent then I'm sure he would appreciate anything you can do to help us in that regard. However, I must make it clear that you are under no obligation at all to answer our questions. It's entirely a matter for you."

Though flustered, Bradley seemed somewhat mollified by the explanation.

"Well, I'm anxious to help Andrew of course. Why don't you tell me what it is you want to know and then I can decide whether to tell you or not."

"Fair enough. It's really very simple. You mentioned in your statement that Mr Fuller took you out to dinner."

"Yes, he did."

"Would you mind telling us where you ate? At which restaurant?"

"Not at all. We ate at Scott's, around the corner in Mount Street."

"Does he often eat there do you know? Is he a regular customer of theirs?"

"Yes, I think so. Certainly I can remember Angela telling me that she had been there with him."

"That's really very helpful," Collison said warmly. "Thank you very much. Are there any others by the way? Any other restaurant he particularly likes?"

"He's very much a creature of habit, I think. He certainly eats at Scott's fairly often, judging from the reaction of the waiters there. I think when he's in Hampstead he eats at Villa Bianca."

"Doesn't everyone?" murmured Willis appreciatively.

"Was that everything?" Bradley asked in surprise. "Was that all you wanted to know?"

"Well, you might be able to help us with one other thing," Collison replied. "So far as you know was Mr Fuller having an affair with anybody else recently? At much the same time as he was with you, I mean?"

Rowena Bradley burst into peals of laughter, which took a few minutes to subside.

"Oh dear, I'm sorry. You obviously don't know Andrew at all. Yes, I'm sure he would have been because he always is.

But no, he would never have mentioned it to me because he is far too well-bred. Would I have minded? No, absolutely not. You know exactly what you're getting with Andrew. While you're with him he's attentive and charming and gives you the impression that you are the most important person in the world – which is exactly what we all want, isn't it? But at the same time he's impulsive – just like a child really – and utterly faithless. If you went out with him expecting to be the only woman in his life then he'd make you very unhappy very quickly."

"Did Angela Bowen think she was the only woman in his life?" Willis enquired.

"Oh no, not for a moment. Angela was a very intelligent woman and she had Andrew all worked out. He offered exactly what she was looking for: an occasional handsome and charming companion but with no commitment whatsoever on either side. I don't think she had any ambition, or illusion, about being his wife or anything like that. Anyway, Liz was her friend and she knew that they would never get divorced; that was all implicit in the arrangement."

"But do you think her attitude might have changed when she realised she was pregnant?" Collison asked quickly.

Bradley shrugged helplessly.

"God knows. But did she know she was pregnant, do you think? She certainly never mentioned anything to me at all nor, so far as I know, to Liz or Andrew."

"Now there," Collison commented ruefully, "is one thing we really would like to know, but unfortunately the only person who could tell us for certain is dead."

There was a brief silence while they all looked at each other. Then Collison slapped his thighs and stood up.

"While I'm here," he said, "would it be a huge imposition to ask for a quick walk around the club? I've never been here you know, and it might help to see where things actually happened that night."

"Not at all, and I'd be delighted to show you around. Karen's had the tour already, of course. I think room 16 might actually be vacant at the moment if you'd like to take a look inside."

"I would indeed, thank you."

As he stood aside to allow the women to go through the door first, he took the opportunity to study the board hung with duplicate keys, noting that each one, in addition to being on a numbered peg, was attached to a simple stiff cardboard label with the room number upon it.

"Miss Bradley," he enquired as he caught her up, "are the actual room keys in the same format as your duplicates? In other words, do they just have those quite narrow labels attached to them?"

"Oh yes, we don't go in for all that metal knob business. Though perhaps we should. They're designed to stop people taking their keys with them when they leave, you know, and it's really most inconvenient to us when people do that. If there's no key at reception then the cleaners can't know for certain that a room is unoccupied. So first they have to go and find out, and then they have to come and get the duplicate from my office. Our regular guests know to leave their key at the desk, but even they forget sometimes."

Bradley paused at the self-same desk and asked for the key to room 16, which she clasped in her hand as they moved on.

"So do I understand then," Willis asked her, "that the cleaners are slipping in and out of your office with keys all the time during the day?"

"Not all day, no. Cleaning is supposed to be finished by 2 o'clock, but most of it is usually done by midday."

"But during that time," Willis persisted, "would it be true to say that access to and control over the duplicate keys is not really under your direct control?"

"Why yes, I suppose it would," Bradley replied looking puzzled. "But why is that important? I thought we were talking about the period leading up to midnight."

"Yes, well ... you never know I suppose," Willis said vaguely.

She saw Collison looking at her in bemusement and mouthed 'tell you later'.

"Well here we are at the foot of the stairs," Bradley told Collison rather unnecessarily. "The main staircase, that is. The one on the other side leads up to the library but does not go any further."

"And as I understand it there is no access from that staircase to any of the guest rooms?"

"Yes, that's right. The only way you can access the accommodation is by heading up this staircase here."

"And downstairs from here, again as I understand it, are the loos. Is that right?"

"Yes, quite correct. That would have been the original back stairs: the servants' staircase, I expect."

"So if somebody had been attending the dinner dance," Collison said, looking around to get his bearings, "they would have walked through this lobby, past your office and then the reception desk, and would have arrived exactly where we are standing now?"

"Yes."

"And in order to go to the loo, they would continue along that narrower part of the hall to the rear staircase and go down one floor?"

"Yes, exactly."

"So, just to be clear, is this staircase the only means of access to the accommodation above?"

"No, don't forget the lift. That's just at the back there, immediately beyond the rear staircase. That's how poor Angela was brought out. There is a service door one floor down at the back: ground-level is lower at the back of the building than at the front."

Collison nodded. This was of course usual with period buildings in London, with the earth excavated from foundations being piled up at the front of the building and eventually going towards the bedding for a roadway. He looked around the hall, and then went to inspect first the lift and then the back stairs. Then he nodded again.

"Thank you. Shall we go upstairs now?"

Rowena Bradley led the way to room 16. Then she unlocked the door and stood aside.

"Please do come in," Collison urged her as she hung back.

With every appearance of reluctance, she edged just inside the door.

"I'm sorry," Collison said. "I know this room must hold very unpleasant memories for you, but while you're here could you just explain exactly what you saw that morning?"

"I was only here just for a moment," she replied very tightly, as if keeping her emotions in check with difficulty. "Charlotte told me it was okay to wait outside."

"Yes, I've seen the statements on file. But while you were here – and I appreciate it was only very briefly – what did you see?"

"Angela – of course I didn't know it was Angela then – was sort of sprawled on the floor beside the bed. The whole upper part of the body was covered by the duvet. Charlotte was kneeling down beside her. She turned as I came into the room. I think she saw straightaway that I was upset – it's ridiculous I know, but I'd never seen a dead body before – and told me that she could take care of things by herself. I waited in the corridor and almost at once she came out and confirmed that she was dead."

Collison appeared to be thinking deeply about something.

"Right, thank you. Now, I'm sorry to be darting around from one thing to another, but do you happen to remember seeing the room key while you were in here for those few seconds?"

"Yes, now you come to mention it I did. It was on the floor behind Charlotte. She must've had to step over it in order to get to the body."

"Could you just indicate for me exactly where on the floor you mean?"

She ventured a few steps into the room and, kneeling down, briefly touched a spot on the carpet.

"Sorry, I'm darting around again," he said, "but do I remember reading that the corridor lights are dimmed in the evening?"

"Yes, we dim them some time after 9 o'clock. Sometimes people want to go to bed early, either because they've just come in from the airport after a long journey, or because they're making a very early start in the morning. We used to get complaints that they were being kept awake by the strip of light showing underneath their doors."

Now it was Collison's turn to kneel down while he inspected the lower part of the door to room 16. Facetiously, Willis was tempted to ask if he would like a magnifying glass.

"Karen," he said suddenly, "you be our victim will you? Just sit on the bed as if I've been paying you a visit in your room and now I'm leaving. Miss Bradley, could I trouble you for the key? And would you mind stepping outside with me so we can leave Karen here alone?"

He closed the door from the outside and locked it. Bradley watched curiously as he squatted down, slid the key under the door and gave it a firm push. As it disappeared from view he stood up again and tapped on the door.

"Karen," he called out, "can you please make a note of where the key is now and then unlock the door and let us in?"

From within came a little cry of excitement and then the sound of Willis fumbling with the key in the lock. As the door swung open she pointed to a lipstick which was lying on the carpet about equidistant between the bed and the door.

"Miss Bradley," Collison began, "is that roughly where –"

There was clearly no need to continue however. Rowena Bradley had slumped backwards against the wall, her eyes wide and a hand over her mouth. Wordlessly, she nodded.

CHAPTER 25

"Very interesting," Peter Collins observed after listening to Willis's account later that evening.

Lisa Atkins, who had taken to staying at the house more and more, was away with her mother and thus for once the three of them were able to discuss the case quite freely, something which they had not always been able to do, not only because Peter Collins himself had only from time to time been officially involved with investigations but because Lisa's presence, though welcome, imposed similar limitations.

"And to think," he continued, sniffing his wineglass appreciatively, "that here I was coming up with ways in which Chloe Jennings might be our perpetrator."

"Really?" Metcalfe enquired. "You mean that she might have been able to get away with both taking the key from the office and then replacing it, both incidents happening before midnight – indeed, presumably by about half past eleven, given the known time of death – and both times without being noticed?"

"Yes, it's a bit improbable, isn't it? That's exactly what I was thinking, and then it struck me that there was a way in which she might have been able to lower her chances of detection quite considerably; by about fifty percent in fact."

"I'm intrigued, Peter dear," Willis said as she tucked

her legs up on the sofa and settled comfortably against the cushion. "I'm sure we should be able to work this one out for ourselves, but I'm just too tired at the moment so why don't you tell us?"

"Well it's just an idle thought of course, I have no evidence at all to support it, but how about this for an idea? Jennings happens to notice, while sitting at our table and glancing idly at Bradley's guest list, that Andrew Fuller's wife is spending the night in room 16. She also hears Bradley announce that she will be in her office from after the event kicks out into the street until about 6.30, at which point she intends to head off in search of a shower."

"Both quite possible, of course," Metcalfe commented.

"Indeed, but now comes what might be the clever bit. She slips away and gets the duplicate key from Bradley's office, managing to do so unobserved. She then heads upstairs, fortuitously after Andrew Fuller has left, and does the business, thinking of course that she is smothering Liz Fuller whereas it is in fact Angela Bowen. She then comes back to the event, still carrying the key – presumably in her handbag – waits until a quiet moment near the end and then slips into the secret room without anybody seeing her do so."

"Oh," Willis said at once. "Not the secret room, Peter? You're not serious?"

"Well, it's an intriguing possibility, isn't it?"

"But very risky, surely? What if somebody had come in and found her?"

"Not that risky perhaps. I'm sure she could have some cover story ready in case somebody came in. For example, she could say that she had dropped an earring, had been in the room briefly before dinner, and was looking for it because she thought it might have dropped off while she was in there. And certainly not as risky as trying to make it into Bradley's office for a second time without getting caught."

"So your idea is that she might have spent the night in an armchair in the secret room, going downstairs quietly at some time after 6.30 to replace the key?" Metcalfe asked.

"That's about it, yes. Making her exit through the service door at the back just as Fuller had done the night before."

"Wow!" Willis said admiringly. "That's not a bad idea, at that."

"But how on earth would we prove it?" Metcalfe queried. "If she said she'd been in the secret room before dinner – and who's to contradict her if she hadn't? – then finding her DNA or fingerprints in there would mean nothing."

"And surely if Rowena Bradley had noticed the key to room 16 was missing, she would have said so?" Willis pointed out. "Particularly as she must realise that she is in the frame herself. After all, it would let her off the hook, wouldn't it?"

"She might not have noticed," Collins countered. "Why should she? She had no reason at that stage to think that the night would be any different to any other, and unless she had reason to go to the keyboard for another key, why should she necessarily have noticed that one was missing?"

"It's a very interesting theory," Metcalfe admitted, "and it certainly keeps Jennings alive as a suspect."

"It's all a bit tenuous though," Willis objected. "I mean, it needs a lot of things all to fall into place very neatly. It needs

Jennings to have seen the room list, recognise the significance of the occupant of room 16, decide in that moment to do away with Liz Fuller, know that the duplicate keys were kept in Bradley's office, realise the significance of her being absent from 6.30, and to have got into the office unobserved, and to have had the determination to get into room 16 and not bottle out of what she wanted to do, and realise the potential of the secret room ... Like I said, it's all a bit far-fetched, isn't it?"

"It does seem so doesn't it?" Collins conceded. "And yet if you think about it doesn't fate often seem to work out like that, a seemingly random coming together of connected events? As for bottling out, by the way, I'm not sure that's an issue. Once the murderer was in the room and the victim was disturbed, it would be pretty tricky to try to explain what you were doing there, wouldn't it? You could hardly claim to have been sleepwalking."

There was a short pause during which they all took the opportunity to raise their glasses and sip.

"Oh, I don't know," Collins said distractedly, "maybe it's just my love of crime fiction trying to persuade me that the murderer can't possibly be the most obvious suspect. Now, how about dinner?"

...

"Very interesting," the ACC echoed the next morning, having listened intently to Collison's report. "What do you think, Jim?"

Collison, recognising the possible significance of what he

had discovered, had invited DCS Murray to accompany him to the meeting.

"It strengthens our case, clearly," Murray said carefully, "but it doesn't alter the fact that all our evidence is pretty much circumstantial. In particular, we still can't prove any specific motive. The threesome had been running for some time, and all the witnesses, including the surviving parties to the relationship, seem unanimous in the view that everybody was perfectly happy with the state of affairs. So why would Fuller suddenly decide to murder Bowen? How do you explain that to a jury, Simon?"

"It's a problem, I admit. But we shouldn't be afraid of setting a precedent. After all, the Krays were tried for the murder of Frank Mitchell even though the prosecution couldn't produce a body."

"They were acquitted," the ACC pointed out sourly.

"Yes they were, of course, but if you can have a murder trial without even being able to prove the death of the victim, then surely you can ask a jury to infer a motive when a possibility is obvious?"

There was a silence while the ACC reflected.

"Is there any way at all that we can prove that Angela Bowen had told somebody – not necessarily either of the Fullers, but just anybody – that she was pregnant?"

"No, sir, not that I can think of."

"Can we even show that she knew she was pregnant? Have we spoken to her doctor, for example?"

"Yes we have, and she hadn't been into the surgery for some time. So if she did know she was pregnant, it wasn't from the doctor She must've worked it out for herself – done one of those tests from the chemist or something."

"Hm."

The ACC fiddled with his reading glasses. Gazing into the distance, he began speaking as if to himself.

"The reason we're having this discussion, of course, is that the suspect is a prominent QC. There are obvious concerns that if he is tried but acquitted it would be a black mark against the criminal justice system, as well as having the potential deeply to damage Fuller's career prospects. For both those reasons, we need to think very carefully about what we're doing here."

"But isn't that the point, sir?" Collison asked. "If our suspect was not a prominent QC then we wouldn't be having this discussion. Shouldn't we actually be treating this case just like any other one? Why should we effectively give Fuller special treatment? Justice is blind, and all that."

"Nice try, Simon, but it won't work," the ACC replied with a smile. "The practical situation is that this case has the potential deeply to embarrass the Met if we get it wrong. The Commissioner put his head into my office only this morning to ask me how we were getting on. He wouldn't do that unless somebody from the Home Office was leaning on him. And, knowing that Fuller is up for consideration as a High Court judge, that presumably means that someone from the Lord Chancellor's Department is leaning on the Home Office. That's an awful lot of important people with a direct interest in this case."

"But it might be an interesting exercise nonetheless,"

Murray suggested, "if we were to review where we are with the evidence, regardless of who our suspect might be."

"Fair enough," the ACC acknowledged. "Just what do we have, Simon, as you see it?"

"Well," Collison replied, "I think the clincher for me is that on his own admission he was with the victim in her room for at least half of the hour or so within which we think her death must have occurred. So he had opportunity and, given what we know about the duplicate key situation, I'm inclined to favour any candidate whom the deceased would have admitted readily to her room. He falls into that category."

"As do his wife and this Bradley woman," the ACC pointed out. "And from what I've read in the file neither one of them really has an alibi. The wife claims to have been alone in her own room and could presumably have knocked on our victim's door after Fuller left the building. Bradley was flitting about all over the place and nobody can be quite sure of exactly where she went, or when."

"All that is true, sir, and I'm not ruling out the possibility that he may have done it jointly with one or even both of those women, but he does seem the most obvious suspect. He had opportunity. The means was ready to hand: a pillow. As for the motive, that's the bit we would need the jury to infer. What strikes me about that is that we have not been able to establish any other possible motive for anybody wanting to murder Angela Bowen."

"If they were indeed trying to murder Angela Bowen," said the ACC. "I'm sorry, Simon, I don't necessarily disagree with you, I'm just trying to anticipate all the various points I would make if I were the defence counsel."

"I appreciate that, sir, and I have considered the mistaken identity point. It seems to me that it only has relevance if the murderer is somebody other than our three main suspects. They all either knew that Bowen was in room 16, or would have recognised her instantly. The mix-up with the rooms only comes into play if our murderer was someone who had never met Bowen before."

"But you do have just such a suspect, don't you? This young barrister woman."

"We do, sir, and I'm not ruling her out, but there is the question of the key to be considered. In my view the problem around obtaining the key in the first place and then putting it back subsequently is a huge issue. It's only fair to point out that some of the team have very recently come up with a hypothesis under which Chloe Jennings ran the risk of detection only once, spending the night concealed upstairs in order to be able to put the key back unobserved in the morning, but ..."

"A bit far-fetched, surely?" the ACC interjected.

"Yes, sir, I tend to agree. Another reason why I see Fuller as the main suspect. After all, if we were able to show that Angela Bowen had confronted him about her pregnancy, then I think would all agree that we had a very strong case."

"But we can't, can we?"

"No, sir, we can't."

"So it comes to this, does it?" the ACC concluded, suddenly sounding very like a barrister himself. "We can put

Fuller at the crime scene at the right time, with the murder weapon readily to hand. However we can't prove any specific motive, nor can we rule out the possibility that other people might have had access to the crime scene after he left."

"Yes, sir, that's about the size of it."

"Well," the ACC said, "if there's one thing my career in the Met has taught me, it's never to take a decision unless you have to. I propose that we pass our file on this to the DPP with a recommendation that they take counsel's opinion – very discreetly, of course – on the chances of conviction."

"And what about the ongoing investigation, sir?" Murray queried. "I may be a bit old-fashioned but it worries me that we still have other active suspects out there whom we've not been able to eliminate from the enquiry."

"This is a very unusual enquiry, Jim," the ACC pointed out, "but yes, I agree. Clearly the investigation must continue, at least for some time. There's always the possibility that some new piece of evidence will come to light. Perhaps you should wind it down a bit, Simon, but I leave that to your discretion. After all, you're running the show under the new guidelines, aren't you?"

"That's true," Collison said ruefully. "I'm beginning to regret having written that paper already."

"You know, at the end of the day," said the ACC quietly, "it may just be that this is one of those cases where you have a pretty good idea – copper's nose and all that – who the guilty party is, but equally know full well that you'll never be able to prove it. We all hate those cases, but we know they happen. And in this one, what with the confusion as to the cause of death and everything, the odds really were stacked against us from the start. We lost a whole 24 hours – the most important 24 hours at that – during which the crime scene was hopelessly contaminated. With a murder enquiry, timing is everything."

"That's true, of course," Collison agreed. "Not that it makes me feel any better about it."

CHAPTER 26

The next morning Collison and Metcalfe sat drinking coffee together in a companionable sort of way in a cafe just across a small side street from the King William IV pub, known universally as "the Willy". Though they could always speak privately in Collison's office in the largely deserted police station whenever they wanted, they both found it pleasant to get out and about in Hampstead and feel themselves surrounded by people who had other everyday concerns than the successful conclusion of homicide enquiries.

"So that's how it's going to be, Bob," Collison was saying.

He broke off as a very young child at a neighbouring table began giving a passable imitation of an air raid siren. He winced involuntarily, and found himself wondering if his own child would ever behave in such a way. Metcalfe, who had guessed himself what he may be speculating, grinned broadly.

"As I was saying," Collison continued, raising his voice over the mother's ineffectual attempt to mollify the child's indignant rage, "the ACC is suggesting that the DPP takes counsel's opinion as to whether we have enough to proceed against our man."

He carefully avoided mentioning Fuller's name given that they were in a public place.

"Who will they use, do you think? Alistair Partington perhaps, since you've already consulted him informally?"

"No," Collison replied, shaking his head decisively. "On something big like this they'll want a QC. I've suggested Patrick Barratt. He may be a pompous so-and-so but he's a damn good lawyer. Probably as good as Fuller, if not better. The DPP needs us to prepare a full briefing note which they can turn into some formal instructions. I was thinking of asking Karen to do that, since it's easier for her to free herself up from day to day stuff than it is for you."

"Fine by me, guv."

"Good, let's do that then."

Collison drained his cup and they stood up, crossed over the road outside the community centre, and began walking down Rosslyn Hill.

"By the way," Collison said casually, "I've been meaning to ask you how it's going with Lisa Atkins."

"Very well I think. She's away you know. Spending a few days with her mother."

"And how is she? No lingering ill effects from her injury I hope?"

"A few days ago I would have said no, none. But her mother rang yesterday to say she'd been having headaches and dizzy spells, some of them quite severe. So she's going back to see the consultant at the Royal Free when she's in town tomorrow. I'm a bit worried, actually. The doctors did make it very clear that there could be all sorts of unforeseen complications following a fractured skull."

"I'm sorry to hear that, Bob, but try not to worry about

it. I'm sure if they think it's anything even potentially serious they'll get her back into hospital and put her under observation."

Metcalfe said nothing but Collison could feel his concern; it was almost tangible.

"If you'd like a few days off, Bob," he proffered, "I'm sure that wouldn't be a problem."

"No thanks, guv, not yet anyway, but thanks for the offer."

They crossed over Downshire Hill, which featured endlessly in those lists of London's most beautiful streets regularly drawn up by bored journalists desperate for copy to submit against a looming deadline, and climbed the steps to the police station. Almost at once it was time for the morning briefing, so Collison went straight into the incident room and spent the next few minutes chatting idly with Priya Desai. He became aware that Timothy Evans seemed to be trying to attract his attention, albeit somewhat half-heartedly, but before he could speak to him Metcalfe was calling the meeting to order.

"As expected, we will not be allowed to take any further steps against Andrew Fuller until counsel's opinion has been obtained," Collison reported when it was his turn to speak.

He glanced around the room meaningfully.

"I'm sure I don't need to make this clear formally, but I'm going to do so anyway. Please remember that nobody in this room has authority to discuss this case, or indeed any case, with anybody who is not officially a member of the investigation. For our purposes that includes Peter Collins, but nobody else. It is absolutely vital that no news should leak out regarding the status of Andrew Fuller within our enquiry. There is already speculation in the press, but there's nothing we can do about that. Please, people, be very careful indeed about what you say, particularly when you are speaking in public and may be overheard."

There was silence as the room digested his words. One or two officers, ones he had never worked with before, looked almost contemptuous that he should be making something so obvious explicit, but most just nodded seriously.

"Karen," he said, turning to her, "I'd like you to take charge of preparing a very full briefing note for the DPP so they can in turn instruct leading counsel. Obviously you need to be thorough, but could you do that as quickly as possible please? With every day that passes the possibility of some leak – accidental, of course – increases."

"Of course, guv. I'll get onto it right away."

"Okay. Bob, what else do we have on our plates?"

"We need to check that restaurant in Mayfair, guv. Scott's, wasn't it?"

"Scott's, yes."

"Priya, why don't you do that? You don't have very much on at the moment, do you?"

"Not that much, guv. So yes, leave it to me. I'll pull some photos together and go over there later."

"Probably best to avoid lunchtime," Collison suggested. "They're likely to be too busy to give you their proper attention."

Metcalfe checked on progress in tracking down the few remaining residents of the club on the night in question, and assigned a few routine tasks. As he drew the meeting to a close he couldn't help feeling that there was a flatness about the atmosphere, a passive consensus that they were marking time rather than making any real progress. Investigations were strange like that. It was almost as though they acquired a life of their own, or at least the ability to influence the emotions of those taking part. In the case of a long enquiry with a frequently changing team, such as the hunt for a serial killer, the senior officers could be faced with mounting a constant struggle against depression and a sense of futility.

Willis was already methodically calling up witness statements from the computer folder in chronological order, a pen and notebook ready for use. Desai was similarly busy searching the database for similar photographs to those of the women in question to use for identification purposes. They were the only signs of obvious industry in the room, however. For the others the prevailing emotion seemed to be one of listlessness. Metcalfe didn't like it, but there wasn't much he could do about it either. Frowning, he went to his desk.

A couple of hours later Willis looked up from her computer screen in the direction of Timothy Evans. She waited for him to finish his telephone conversation and then crossed the room to speak to him.

"Timothy, when you took that statement from Sharon Jones at the club, are you quite sure that you got it word for word?"

"Pretty sure, Sarge. Why, what's up?"

Willis reflected. On the one hand she knew Evans to be a conscientious police officer. On the other hand he had commented in no uncertain terms on his return to the station on how unexpectedly enjoyable his interview had proved to be. She was only too well aware how distracting the presence of an attractive woman could be to most men. She sighed.

"It may be nothing," she said, "but there again it may not. I think we may need to re-interview her."

Evans shifted uneasily in his seat.

"Ah," he commented uneasily.

"What is it?"

"Well, there was something I meant to mention to Mr Collison."

"Which was?"

"I really did mean to speak to him, Sarge. I even tried just now."

"Just tell me what it is, Timothy," Willis adjured him with the air of a mother addressing a slightly backward child.

"Well, the fact is that Sharon and me are sort of going out."

"Sharon and I," Willis corrected him automatically, "and what you mean – 'sort of'? Either you are or you aren't."

"We are," Evans confessed unhappily. "She sort of asked me out that day I took her statement and ... Well, one thing lead to another, Sarge. You know how it is."

Willis sighed again, this time with more than a little irritation.

"Well clearly you can't re-interview her. I'll have to do it myself."

She thought quickly.

"I'm going to have to talk to Mr Collison about this myself. Not to snitch on you, but to ask him how I should prioritise things. So if I were you, Timothy, I'd run upstairs pretty sharpish and tell him straightaway. All right?"

"Yes, Sarge," he acknowledged, and darted out of the room.

She waited until he came back a few minutes later and then went upstairs herself and knocked on the door.

"Come in, Karen," Collison called.

"So you were expecting me then?" she asked as she went in.

"Timothy did just hint that you were likely to be pretty close behind him, yes," he said with a smile. "Sit down, won't you? What have you found?"

"It may be nothing, but look."

She put a print-out of the statement in front of him and pointed at the relevant passage.

"It's curious on the face of it, I agree," he said after a pause while he read it through twice, "but I would imagine it was either a slip of the tongue or Timothy wrote it down wrongly."

"I think so too," she concurred, "but it gives me an obvious problem, which is why I've come to see you."

"What problem?"

"Well, as you know, I'm now under time pressure to produce this briefing note for the DPP. Ordinarily I would ask Timothy to go back and re-interview Sharon Jones but, as I'm sure he's just told you, they now seem to be in some sort of relationship together so clearly that would not be appropriate. But if I do it myself instead, then that's time I have to spend away from my desk and away from the briefing note. So what should I prioritise?"

Collison thought hard.

"Yes, I see the issue. Even if we were to send somebody else to re-interview her you would still need to wait to find out the answer, rather than going ahead and preparing the briefing note straightaway."

"Exactly."

"All right. Given the urgency of the situation, go ahead and prepare the briefing note on the assumption that it was just a slip. But as soon as you can, go and speak to Sharon Jones yourself and make sure. After all, if it does turn out to be something, we can always ask the DPP to delay sending out the instructions to counsel."

"Right you are, guv. I hope to be finished with this by this evening, by the way. I'll stay as late as I need to in order to get it done."

"Thank you, Karen, I really appreciate that. By the way, I'd prefer it if you didn't mention this to anybody else in the team for the time being. Bob, yes of course, but nobody else. It will probably turn out to be nothing anyway, but either way I think it would be better to keep it on a 'need to know' basis until we're certain one way or the other."

She stood up to leave, but then hesitated.

"Was there something else?" he enquired.

"Actually, guv, I just had an idea. There might be something else we could do today so as not to lose time later."

"Which is?"

She told him, a suggestion which prompted him to whistle and then gaze reflectively at the desk for a few seconds.

"That could be very embarrassing, you know, if it turns out it was just a mistake," he observed.

"I'm aware of that, guv, but we could stress the need for absolute confidentiality to all involved."

He thought hard again.

"All right," he said, coming to a decision. "But for goodness sake be as discreet as you possibly can."

CHAPTER 27

Metcalfe's phone rang, his mobile not the handset on his desk. Glancing at it quickly he saw the incoming caller identified as Lisa's mother. Without knowing why, he was gripped by a sudden premonition that something may be wrong. He stood up as he answered it, and headed out of the room.

"Hillary?"

"Bob, is that you?"

"Yes, it's me. What's wrong? Has something happened?"

"Oh, Bob. Please try not be too upset. Lisa's had some sort of a fit or a seizure or something. It happened during the night."

"Dear God! How is she?"

"She seems okay physically, although she has a nasty headache and she's bitten her tongue, but she's very upset and very confused. I'm taking her back to the Royal Free this afternoon. I've just been on the phone to the specialist there."

"Is there anything I can do to help? Can I give you a lift?"

"No thanks, I have a taxi booked. I thought it would be easiest that way. Look, I'm sorry to have disturbed you but I knew you'd want to know. I'll let you know as soon we're finished at the hospital, I promise. OK? I'd better go now, I need to get Lisa ready."

Bob found himself saying "yes, of course" into a dead phone.

"Bob, dear, what's wrong?" Willis asked as she came down the stairs from Collison's office. "You look dreadful."

"That was Hillary, Lisa's mother. Lisa's had some sort of a fit – during the night apparently."

"My God, that's awful. I'm so sorry, Bob. What's happening? How is she?"

"Hillary is taking her back to the Royal Free to see the specialist. I expect they'll want to run some tests or other."

"Why don't you go and see the guvnor and asked for the rest of the day off? That way you could be with her at hospital."

"I don't know," he said doubtfully. "Perhaps I'd just be in the way. What do you think?"

"I think you should go," she said at once. "Of course you won't be in the way. I'm sure it would make a big difference for Lisa to be able to see you, and her mother would probably be glad of the company too."

Metcalfe felt numb. It was a struggle somehow even to be having this conversation, taking in what Willis was saying and finding the words with which to reply. He was haunted by the image from a few months ago of Lisa being struck viciously on the head and falling to the ground as if poleaxed.

"You're in shock," Willis commented, gazing at him shrewdly. "For goodness sake go and see the guvnor, tell him what's wrong, and then ring Peter. You need to be with someone, and it can't be me because I have this note to do.

Please, Bob, don't hang around here. You're in no state for work right now."

Metcalfe nodded dully and headed upstairs, his mobile phone still clutched unnoticed in his hand. As she heard him knock on Collison's door, she pulled out her own, thumbed Collins on speed dial and, when he answered, informed him tersely of what had happened.

"Don't worry, leave it to me," he replied at once. "I'll come straight down to the nick and meet Bob as he comes out."

Willis found her hand trembling slightly as she returned her phone to her bag. She liked Lisa very much, and this was upsetting news, particularly as it was precisely the sort of development they had all feared. The specialists had been at pains to point out the possibility of all sorts of unexpected complications following a fractured skull. Yet even if she had not been as fond of Lisa as she was, Metcalfe's anguish was so palpable that it would have been impossible not to share it.

She paused for a moment in the corridor and gazed out of the window at the traffic heading down the Hill towards the Royal Free. She gripped the window ledge with her free hand and struggled to pull herself together. She heard the door of the incident room open and close and felt, rather than saw, someone gaze at her curiously, but it didn't seem to matter somehow. By the time she turned, they had gone. She dabbed quickly at the tears which were forming in her eyes and then walked briskly into the room.

"What is it, Sarge?" Desai asked at once as Willis approached her desk.

"It's nothing, don't worry. Just someone I know has had

some bad news, that's all. Listen, there's something I need you to do. I've just spoken to Mr Collison and he's OK with it, but this has to be just between the three of us for the moment – and the DI as well – OK?"

"Of course, Sarge, if that's the way the guvnor wants it. What you want me to do?"

After Desai had gathered up her photos and left, Willis struggled to concentrate on her briefing note. There were times when she found herself staring blankly into space, when going to the canteen became an excuse simply for getting up from her desk, the journey up and down the stairs coming as a welcome respite from the thoughts going round in her head.

Collins had met Metcalfe as promised and took him home to await the appointment at the Royal Free, having established from Hillary Atkins that it was for 2 o'clock. He flooded Metcalfe first with idle chat and strong espresso, and later with urgent entreaties to have some lunch. Unsurprisingly however, Metcalfe had no appetite. Refusing Collins's offer to come with him to the hospital, he walked down the hill until he came to Pond Street and turned left towards what is surely one of the ugliest buildings in London.

Fortunately he had been with Lisa to the specialist before, or he would never have found his way through the labyrinthine branching corridors. Hillary was waiting in a little anteroom, holding a book but not reading it. She stood up with a sad smile and kissed him.

"Am I late?" he asked.

"No, not at all. It's just they've taken her off for some

sort of scan – an EEG I think they said. What's that, do you think?"

He shrugged helplessly and they sat down. They made conversation rather listlessly and then after about twenty minutes Lisa came in from the corridor. She was making a determined effort to look cheerful but as soon as she saw him the act fell away and she clung to him, weeping silently. He sunk his face onto the top of her head and inhaled the smell of her hair, feeling helpless and afraid of what might be to come.

"Miss Atkins," a woman said as she came into the room, "the doctor will see you now."

Seeing her distress, she produced a box of tissues and proffered them to Lisa who nodded gratefully, took two or three and wiped her eyes.

"Can I borrow your hanky, Bob?" she asked quietly.

"Yes of course."

She blew her nose noisily and then let her arm fall limply to her side, the handkerchief still screwed up tightly in her hand.

"You can take this lady and gentleman in with you, if you like," the woman suggested.

"Yes," Lisa answered softly but firmly. "I'd like that please."

So it was that the three of them went into the room together. Mr Stern, whom they had all met before, rose and greeted them. Once they were all sitting in front of his desk he sat down himself.

"Now then, Lisa, why don't you tell me what you can remember of what happened last night?"

"There's not a lot to tell. I remember going to bed but then the next thing I can remember is lying all curled up having bitten my tongue. Mummy was there beside me. She said I'd been crying out and shaking."

"Is that right, Mrs Atkins?"

"Yes, it is."

She glanced quickly at Lisa and then went on.

"Actually, she was moaning rather than crying out and the shakes were very convulsive. She was trembling violently."

"And how long did this go on?"

"Once I was in the room perhaps three or four minutes, although it felt a lot longer. I don't know how long it took me to hear what was going on in the first place, but not long I think. The house was quiet and I'm a light sleeper."

"I see, thank you. Now, Lisa, did you feel anything out of the ordinary before you went to bed? Were you particularly tired, for example? Did you have a headache, or anything like that?"

"No, I felt fine. I really don't understand what's happened to me, Doctor. What is it, do you think?"

"Well," the doctor said carefully, "the scan you've just had measures brain activity. It's not a physical scan, rather it records the electrical impulses which your brain produces. Yours are quite disturbed, even though it's a few hours now since you had this little episode, whatever it was. From what you've told me, both of you, and from the results of the scan, the signs point to some sort of epileptic fit."

"Is that normal in the case of a fractured skull?" Metcalfe asked, trying to sound calm.

"Nothing is normal in a case like this, I'm afraid. The after effects of a serious injury such as Lisa sustained are completely unpredictable. But certainly it's not unusual for people to develop epilepsy – or epilepsy type symptoms, which comes to much the same thing – after a physical head trauma."

"And is this a one-off incident do you think, Doctor?" Hillary enquired. "Or is it likely to happen again?"

The consultant shook his head.

"It really is impossible to say. I treat a lot of epilepsy patients, most of whom have had it since infancy, and with some of them it just stops for no apparent reason. The problem is that you can't take any chances. You have to assume that it will happen again, rather than that it won't. I'm sure you understand."

"But what does that mean for how I live my life?" Lisa asked quietly. "Will I have to be forever worried that it may happen again?"

Stern hesitated, clearly trying to decide how best to phrase what it was he had to say.

"For the time being, I'm afraid yes, it would be only sensible to assume that it may happen again. But I'm going to give you some tablets to take every day which should significantly reduce the chance of that. It's called Epanutin and it's what's known as an anticonvulsant. I get very good results from it with my epilepsy patients. For many of them, it keeps it completely under control. I'm also going to give you some sleeping pills, not to take every night, but just when you might have trouble sleeping. It's very important that you should not allow yourself to get tired. That's when it's most likely to happen."

"Oh," Lisa said helplessly and started to cry again.

"I'm so sorry," she said, bringing Metcalfe's handkerchief into play, "I didn't mean to be so useless."

Metcalfe reached across and took her hand.

"If it's any consolation, Lisa," the doctor commented, leaning forwards towards her, "what you've had is actually a very mild episode. Most of my epilepsy patients have something called petit mal, which means the symptoms only ever occur while they are asleep. Distressing, yes of course, but not actually dangerous. In these cases, for example, I am usually happy to sign a doctor's certificate to allow them to have a driving licence. But for those unfortunate cases who have fits during the day, and repeatedly, life can be very difficult indeed. All you have had so far is one isolated incident of petit mal. What we need to do now is to get you taking your pills every day and then monitor the situation for a few months."

Lisa nodded through her tears and said "thank you".

The doctor hesitated again.

"Forgive me if this is an intrusive question, Lisa, but do you sleep alone?"

She and Metcalfe looked at each other and then at her mother, who smiled.

"When I'm with Mummy, yes, but recently I've been sleeping with Bob, here in Hampstead."

"I'm very glad to hear that," the doctor observed. "It's always a reassurance to know that there will be someone on the scene should you need them. Now then, Mr Metcalfe, there are three things you need to bear in mind. First, you must make absolutely sure that Lisa takes her pills every day. Second, you must look out for signs of her becoming overtired or having any trouble sleeping. Third, and I do hope this might never become necessary, keep something beside the bed that you can slip into Lisa's mouth if you wake up and become aware that she is having a fit. The only way in which she might do serious harm to herself is if she bites off her tongue. During an epileptic episode the jaw clamps together extremely tightly. You need to be very quick about getting something between her teeth before it does so. Do you understand all of that?"

"Yes, I think so," Metcalfe replied slightly shakily.

"Please try not to worry," the doctor assured him. "I'm telling you all of this because you need to know, but that doesn't mean you're ever going to need to actually put it into practice."

Metcalfe nodded silently.

"Now," the doctor said, drawing a prescription pad towards him, "let's see about getting you your pills, shall we?"

CHAPTER 28

Across London in the elegant environs of Mount Street, Priya Desai sat in the rarefied atmosphere of Scott's oyster bar. The effect of the interior had been so dazzling when first she had entered the room, that she had stopped and simply stared around in awe. In the centre of the room stood an immense rectangular bar, though unlike any bar she had ever seen before. It was finished in leather and stainless steel, and red barstools were arranged around it, each exactly squared away as if slotted into pegs on the floor. Around the edge of the room were tables placed in discreet little alcoves, and everywhere there was glass. One side of the room was a continuous window, shaded by an immense dark awning outside. The other walls had to make do with gigantic mirrors in which the electric lights sparkled as though winking at her, and adding immeasurably to the perception of size in what was already a very generously proportioned room.

For a moment she found the experience completely over-whelming. She simply could not believe that she had any business walking into an establishment like this. Everything about it reeked of wealth, privilege, and exclusivity. Had its interior designer been made aware of her feelings he would doubtless have smirked quietly to himself, since this was indeed the very effect for which he had been striving. Little though she knew it, however, there was little about her that looked out of place. Her trim figure in a smart trouser suit was drawing admiring glances from the waiters drinking coffee at a corner table – for this was the dead period of the late afternoon when even the most persistent lunch guests had returned to their offices – and as the manager, Giovanni, approached he was struck by the strength of her features, which was somehow accentuated rather than diminished by her lack of make-up. Like all managers of exclusive restaurants, Giovanni was used to sizing people up in an instant so as to be able to decide whether (or not, as the case may be) to make a table available to them. He appraised her quickly, and liked what he saw. He sensed a strength, almost a fierceness, from her expression and the way she was holding herself. Yet beneath this lurked a hint of insecurity, perhaps accentuated by the strangeness of her surroundings. It was an appealing combination.

Now she sat at one of those peripheral tables with Giovanni. She had refused his offer of a glass of wine, but was sipping gratefully at a sparkling water, the name of which she had failed to recognise, but which had been served with a flourish by one of the waiters – summoned effortlessly by Giovanni with no more than a glance – from a bottle with a label which in other circumstances could have been mistaken for an entry in an international art competition.

"So you see," she was concluding, "that's really all there is to it. We don't want to put you to any trouble, but it would be very useful to us to know whether Mr Fuller had any connections we don't know about. I understand he is a regular customer here?"

"He is indeed," came the reply. "Not as regular as some of our customers, of course. Some of them come here for lunch every day, or at least every day when they are in town. He usually comes in the evening, perhaps once or twice a week."

"And always with a lady?"

"Oh yes," Giovanni said emphatically, "always with a lady. Never alone."

"And is this always the same lady?" Priya enquired innocently.

"Oh no. Sometimes one particular lady, but most of the time we see them just the once."

Priya reached into her bag and produced four brown envelopes.

"I'd like to show you some photos," she said hesitantly. "It won't get you into trouble or anything. It's just for our own purposes at the moment."

Giovanni smiled indulgently.

"We've survived being bombed by the IRA," he informed her, "so I think we can handle a small matter like this – but very discreetly I hope?"

"Yes, of course. In fact I was going to ask you to treat this whole enquiry confidentially. I'm sure you understand."

She paused and looked around.

"Were you really bombed? When?"

"It was back in the early 1970s. Can you imagine what it did to all this glass?"

"But why? Who would want to do such a thing?"

He shrugged.

"It was quite common back then you know. There was a club just a few blocks away which had a machine gun fired through the window one night. The IRA thought that if they could close down places like Scott's and deprive the establishment of their sole meuniere then the British government would give up and sue for peace. Needless to say, that didn't happen."

"How awful. I mean, I know this stuff all happened before I was born, but I never knew things were so bad here in London."

"We lived with terrorism for decades," Giovanni said matter-of-factly. "People forget that now. All these awful things which happen around the world, they were commonplace here in London for many years. There was so much hatred coming out of Ireland – on both sides."

There was a silence while Priya digested this.

"Now," he went on gently, "how can I help?"

"I'd like to show you a selection of photos. In each case I've chosen photos of women who are as close a match to each other as I can manage. And I'm going to do this four times, with four different selections. In each case there is one of the photos that I'm hoping you might be to identify as being a woman whom you've seen here with Andrew Fuller."

"Okay, let's go."

Priya opened the first envelope and started to spread the photos.

"No need," Giovanni said straightaway. "This one here is

the lady he comes with quite a lot. I think her name is Angela. I'm sure I've heard him call her that."

"Okay, thank you."

Priya made a careful note on the back of Angela Bowen's photo and then gathered the first selection back into their envelope. Then she picked up the second one and spread its contents carefully onto the table, feeling strangely like a conjuror attempting a card trick as she did so.

Giovanni took more time than before, but then identified Rowena Bradley without difficulty.

As she spread the third selection on the table Priya felt a mounting excitement, which she struggled not to betray. She gazed fixedly at the table top while Giovanni considered the selection. For a moment he picked up the image of a WPC in plainclothes whom Priya had been forced to press into service to stand in front of the camera, but having gazed at it he put it down again, and turned back to Chloe Jennings.

"This one – but only the once, I think."

Priya found that she had been holding her breath. Now she let it out.

"Thank you," she said, carefully marking the photo before putting it away with the others.

She picked up the fourth envelope and then hesitated.

"This is a bit of a longshot," she confessed. "To be honest, it's based on a hunch that one of my colleagues has. And I must stress that this one is really, really confidential."

Giovanni nodded and she slowly arranged the pictures in front of him. He gazed carefully at each one, and then concentrated more carefully on two in particular. Again, Priya held her breath. One of them was the one she wanted him to pick. To her relief, he picked it up and waved it vaguely in her direction, a few inches above the table top.

"I'm pretty sure that I've seen him with this woman as well," he said. "But again, only the once."

Priya felt a sudden rush of elation, but then caution kicked in.

"You say you're pretty sure," she said carefully. "What does that mean exactly? Could you swear to it?"

Now it was Giovanni's turn to hesitate.

"In court you mean? No, I'm not sure that I could. Like I said, I'm pretty sure but I couldn't say for certain."

He gazed at her sadly.

"I'm so sorry. I sense that this is important. It is, isn't it?"

"Yes, it is," she said with a thin smile, "but you mustn't say anything you're not absolutely certain about. After all, like you say, you might be asked to swear to it in court."

"That first lady," Giovani ventured. "Am I correct in thinking that she was the poor soul who died one night just around the corner from here?"

"Well, since you've identified her anyway, I suppose there's no harm in telling you. Yes, she was. In fact, we believe she may have been in here that very evening – the evening before she was found dead."

Giovanni tutted.

"What a terrible thing. And such a nice lady too."

"Really? Did you know her then?"

He shrugged.

"Not personally, no. But obviously you get chatting to

regular customers, and she was in here quite a bit. I liked her, and I can't say that about all my customers and their guests."

"What sort of person would you say she was?" Priya asked curiously.

"She was a quiet person. She spoke softly but very seriously. I would imagine that she was very intelligent."

"Did you know that she was a Professor?"

He whistled softly.

"No, I didn't know that, but it doesn't surprise me. Like I said, she seemed very intelligent. Him too. I don't mean to suggest that he wasn't, but he's a very different character. Very outgoing, very charming, and making la bella figura, as we say in Italy."

"What does that mean?"

"Literally it means to make a good figure. It describes a man who is always very well dressed, very well presented. I know that you don't usually think of men like that in London. It's usually women who make the effort to be very elegant."

"Hm I see, thank you."

She darted a glance at him. He felt that she was suddenly conscious of her lack of make-up and was trying to ascertain if he was making fun of her. This upset him, as he had spoken quite innocently but was conscious that his words might be misunderstood.

"They seemed very happy," he went on a little awkwardly, "but then I suppose that's not really very helpful for you is it? You deal in hard facts, evidence."

"Anything you can tell us is helpful," she replied diplomatically. "It's certainly useful to know that there was no sign of them having a row, for example."

"Far from it. They seemed to have that quiet, settled happiness of an established couple. It's strange, until I read about her in the newspapers I'd always assumed that they were married, even though he brought other women here. It had that sort of feeling about it. They seemed very comfortable together. Do you know what I mean?"

"I think so, yes."

She gathered up the last set of photos and slipped everything back in her bag. She wriggled free from her banquette and Giovanni escorted her to the door.

"I'm so sorry I couldn't be more helpful," he said as they shook hands.

"Not at all, you've been very helpful. It's just that we obviously have a bit more work to do, that's all."

"I'm sure you're very busy at the moment," Giovanni ventured, "but when you have the time perhaps you and your boyfriend would like to come and have dinner here one evening? As my guest, I mean."

Priya was completely taken aback.

"Thank you," she said awkwardly, "that's incredibly kind of you, but actually I don't have a boyfriend."

Giovanni stared at her in obvious disbelief.

"Not at the moment, I mean," she went on hastily.

He shook his head sadly. Somehow she felt the urge to say more.

"I don't know," she said with an attempt at a laugh, "maybe

it's the job – the police I mean. I just never seem to meet the right sort of man."

As he opened the door for her, Giovanni engaged in a brief but intense inner debate. As he gazed one last time at her coal dark eyes, he came to a decision.

"If you would do me the honour of leaving me your card," he suggested quietly, "I will see what might be arranged."

CHAPTER 29

Collison saw Evans in his office the next morning, with Metcalfe and Willis looking on.

"I must say you've put us in a rather difficult position, Timothy," Collison observed. "Surely it must have occurred to you that it was improper to start a relationship with someone who is a material witness in an ongoing investigation with which you are involved?"

"I'm sorry, guv," Evans said wretchedly. "I just didn't think about it. Everything happened so fast."

"Well, we're about to go into the morning meeting and I'm going to have to tell people that there are things which cannot be shared openly within the team. I'm not going to mention your name, Timothy, but I don't mind telling you that I don't like having to do this."

"I really am very sorry, guv."

"There's something else. I must ask you to have no further contact with Sharon Jones until the investigation has been formally concluded."

"May I tell her why?"

"No, you may not. I repeat: I want you have no further contact with her at all. No phone calls, no messages, nothing. I'm sorry, I know how that will look to her but there's nothing I can do about that."

"Yes, guv."

"Okay, you can go now."

Collison waited for Evans to leave the room and then gave a deep sigh.

"Why, oh why do these things have to happen? I always thought Timothy was such a sensible fellow."

"I think he is basically, guv," Metcalfe volunteered. "It sounds as if the girl made the running and took him by surprise before he had a chance to think about things properly. I hope you're not going to make this official ...?"

"I can't answer that at the moment. It rather depends on how things turn out, doesn't it?"

Metcalfe nodded.

"Now then," Collison went on, "from now on the three of us have got to be very careful what information we share with the rest of the team, at least until we get an opportunity to re-interview Fuller and Jones."

"I think we can include Priya," Willis suggested. "After all, she knows the most important bit already."

"Agreed, but let's swear her to secrecy. It will certainly be useful have an extra body on hand. Karen, I saw your list of suggested further enquiries and it all looked very sensible. Can you and Priya handle that between you, do you think?"

"It depends what you're talking about, guv. Do you mean interviews, or just background research?"

"Just background research at the moment," Collison said determinedly. "We could be in very dangerous waters here and I don't want to go off half cocked. I think the obvious step is to ask Fuller's brief for a further interview, but we need to know as much as possible about all this other stuff in the meantime."

"Perhaps Priya and I could simply drop out of sight for a couple of days," Willis proffered. "There'd be no need for anybody to know where we are. There are plenty of empty rooms up here; we could take one of them over. If you don't mind that is, guv?"

"I don't mind at all. In fact I think it's a very good idea. Now, is there anything else before we go and see the troops?"

"No, I don't think so," Metcalfe said.

As they stood up, Collison looked at him with concern.

"Are you sure you're okay, Bob? I was so sorry to hear the wretched news about Lisa."

Metcalfe managed a smile.

"Actually, it may not be so bad. Obviously we'd all prefer that nothing had happened, but if something did have to happen then at least so far it doesn't seem too serious. Apparently lots of people have mild epileptic fits while asleep. As long as it doesn't progress beyond that, I think we can handle it OK."

"All right then, but do let me know if there's anything I can do."

Willis spoke quietly to Desai before the morning meeting, and they slipped out of the room together as Metcalfe gave the usual update and assigned responsibilities. If anyone wondered where they had gone or what they were doing, they kept their thoughts to themselves. Nor was there any immediate reaction when Collison explained that for the time being certain information was going to have to be treated on a 'need to know' basis, for this was quite a common occurrence which any seasoned officer would have experienced before. Evans however looked deeply unhappy and stared at his desk.

When Collison returned to his office it was to find a message to call the ACC.

"Fresh developments," the latter said briefly when he answered Collison's call. "Fuller's brief is getting restless again. He's pressing for a statement."

"Actually, sir, I was going to call you anyway. Willis has spotted something that may be significant, and it seems to have been confirmed – partly anyway – by a conversation one of the team had yesterday afternoon."

"Go on."

The ACC listened silently apart from the occasional grunt as Collison updated him. Then there was a pause while he thought things over.

"Don't you think you should put this to Fuller?" he asked at length. "After all, if it really is true, we need to know why he withheld the information. Did we ever ask him about it, for example?"

"No, of course not, sir, because we didn't know about it ourselves. I agree that it would seem to make sense to ask him formally now in interview, but what happens if he denies it? Remember, our witness couldn't be sure."

There was another grunt at the other end of the line.

"Normally I would share your desire for caution, Simon, but right now we have other concerns. The Commissioner is keeping the Home Office off our backs for as long as he can, but we really don't have the luxury of time. You're the SIO, so at the end of the day it's your call, but I would strongly suggest that you get Fuller back in and agree with his brief whether it's going to be under caution or not."

"And what do you reckon about that, sir?"

"Obviously I would prefer it not be under caution," the ACC said simply, "but again it's your call – you're the SIO."

"It's a difficult one, isn't it? He's still our main suspect, although we now seem to have the possibility that he could have done it jointly with various other people."

"But he hasn't actually lied to us about anything, has he?" the ACC pointed out. "Not so far as we know, anyway. I would suggest that unless and until you do think he's been untruthful, then you could probably hold off cautioning him. I'm sure his brief would prefer that too."

"Very well, sir, thank you for the advice."

Collison rang off and called down for Metcalfe.

"The ACC 'strongly suggests' that we should re-interview Fuller straightaway, Bob. Apparently his brief is growing fractious."

"And the ACC's strong suggestion is our command, eh guv?" Metcalfe asked with a grin.

"Something like that, yes. Set it up, will you? I think you and I should do it together. Make the arrangements with his brief. Make it clear that we would prefer to continue to treat him as a witness, but that if what they want is for him to be interviewed as a suspect under caution, then so be it. And for God's sake try to keep it quiet. Don't make the call from the incident room."

"Right you are, guv."

As Metcalfe left the room, Willis put her head round the door.

"Sorry to trouble you, guv. Just checking if you'll be around later. I think we're going to need a court order, and I'll need your signature on the papers."

"Yes, I should be, though I may be in an interview room with Bob. We're going to re-interview Fuller."

"Straightaway? I thought we were going to wait."

"The ACC thinks it would be a good idea," Collison replied.

Willis grimaced and departed.

In the event it seemed that Andrew Fuller was fully engaged in court all day, and indeed all week. His lawyer suggested that an appointment might be arranged that evening, a suggestion to which Collison was forced to agree.

Having phoned his wife to break the bad news, he received a call from Peter Collins, suggesting that they might meet for coffee. They arranged a rendezvous at The Coffee Cup, the team's habitual home from home.

"You know, Simon, I've been thinking about Chloe Jennings," Collins began after the usual greetings had been exchanged. "If she really was lying about having a relationship with Andrew Fuller, then that doesn't look very good, does it?"

Collison shrugged.

"No, it doesn't, but it doesn't necessarily make her a murderer. After all, she's got all sorts of very good professional reasons for not wanting people to know that she's slept with her pupil master. A bit tacky to say the least, wouldn't you agree?"

"Agreed, yes. But would you tell a lie to a murder investigation? She is a lawyer, don't forget. So she knows the possible consequences of what she's done."

"Oh, Peter," Collison chuckled, "I'm supposed to be the pompous one, remember? Yes, she lied. Actually we've always suspected that. Karen did, in particular. The thing that will interest me is whether Fuller lies about it too. If both of them try to cover it up, then that does look very strange indeed given, as you say, that it would be within the context of a murder enquiry."

"I sensed an inner rage in her, you know. Or the capacity for it, at least. She strikes me as someone who has always been given what she wants. That sort of person can very easily fly out of control."

"But doesn't that argue for someone who acts on impulse, on the spur of the moment?" Collison asked. "As I understand it, your theory for her involvement hinges on her having spent the entire night in a secret room upstairs. Doesn't that argue for premeditation? Or might it still have been an impulse action prompted by anger?"

"Yes, that would seem to make sense," Collins admitted. "Though if she and Fuller had prearranged matters – if they were in it together, as it were – then anger wouldn't really enter into it. She'd presumably be doing it in the expectation that after a decent interval she would take Bowen's place at his side."

"Do you really think her feelings for him would be strong enough to get her to act completely out of character – to kill?"

"As to the first question, yes, at least assuming that it was indeed Fuller she was moaning about to me. It was clearly someone who had affected her very deeply. As to the second question, doesn't it really depend exactly what her character is? Anyone who is capable of strong hatred or strong jealousy is capable of murder, surely?"

"Yes, I suppose so," Collison said as he took a quick sip of his coffee which was still really too hot to drink, "but I must say I'm unconvinced, Peter. It all seems a bit far-fetched, doesn't it? Of course, if they both deny the affair then that's different. In that case I might be prepared to listen to all sorts of theories about secret passages, or even mysterious Chinamen, and missing Oriental daggers. But right now, we just need to carry on gathering facts."

"Fair enough," Collins nodded.

"Do you remember those conversations we all used to have about the second murder?" he asked suddenly, his finger idly tracing a trail on the table in some spilt sugar.

"Yes of course. What of it?"

"Oh, nothing really. I was just thinking how jolly convenient it would be if there should be a second murder in this case. Awful really, to wish somebody dead, but it might make things much clearer, mightn't it? Particularly if it was one of our suspects who got bumped off."

Collison laughed.

"That was Miss Marple, wasn't it? In the poisoning case at the hotel. And yes, I know her prediction came true, and helped us to solve the case too, but I think that might be rather too neat an outcome to hope for a real-life murder case, Peter – particularly for a second time. This one is unusual, admittedly, in that we have various credible suspects. Also, sadly, in that we have no forensic evidence to speak of as the crime scene was spoiled before we could get to it. But at the end of the day it all comes down to good old-fashioned police work. We just carry on pursuing the truth until we have enough of it to charge somebody and make it stick.

"What about this new line of enquiry, though? That's a bit of a turn up for the book isn't it?"

"Potentially, yes," Collison said calmly, "but let's not get carried away. All we have at the moment is one apparent discrepancy – and a fairly trivial one at that – and a half identification which we can't rely on in court, and which may not mean anything anyway."

"Oh, how very vexing," Collins replied, clearly disappointed. "Why, I was getting ready to start forming all sorts of new theories ..."

Collison laughed again.

"Don't worry, Peter. If there is anything there, Karen will get to the bottom of it. Of that I have not the slightest doubt whatsoever."

CHAPTER 30

"So where are Priya and the DS?" Evans asked curiously that evening.

"They are pursuing lines of enquiry which are nothing to do with you, Timothy," Metcalfe answered coolly. "Given that you chose to get involved with a person of interest to the investigation, Mr Collison understandably decided that there were certain things which could not be mentioned within the Incident Room."

Evans flushed.

"I know what's going on you know," he said gruffly. "Yeah, OK I made a mistake, but I'm not stupid. I can put two and two together the same as anyone else."

"What are you talking about?"

"This new line of enquiry. It's about Sharon, isn't it? That's why I can't know anything about it. I reckon you think that she was having an affair with Fuller, that she spent the night with him at his place in Hampstead, and that he gave her the key to bring back with her in the morning and slip it into the office while that manageress woman was upstairs having a shower."

"I'm only going to say this once, Timothy," Metcalfe replied crisply. "Whatever the DS and Priya are up to is nothing to do with you. End of story. Understood? Because if not I'll happily invite Mr Collison to have a word with you himself."

Evans muttered something inaudible which Metcalfe chose to interpret as a grunt of consent.

"OK, now get on with whatever it is you're supposed to be doing."

As if appearing promptly on cue, Collison opened the door.

"Bob," he said, "we're on. Fuller and his brief are downstairs."

Metcalfe picked up his notebook and pen and followed Collison downstairs. He was curious to meet the celebrated Max Willoughby-Forbes of whom he, like everyone else, had heard a great deal. If he had been asked to describe him in his mind he would have been proved remarkably accurate. The solicitor had the tailored suit and expensive haircut of a 1950s film star but there was an unmistakable strength behind the glamour. He gave a firm handshake, and there was a steel behind his eyes, the calm assurance of a man who was used to getting his own way.

"My client is here in a spirit of full and frank cooperation," he stated for the tape as soon as the ritual announcements were over, "and with every intention of assisting with your enquiries."

"Thank you, Mr Willoughby-Forbes, we appreciate that. Before we begin I should mention that a possible new development has arisen. As we are still pursuing some lines of enquiry which this may suggest, I'm afraid I can't be more explicit about what it may be. However we would very much like to question Mr Fuller about it. Oh dear, I'm explaining this rather clumsily aren't I? I suppose what I really mean is that we may not be able to explain why we are asking a question, only to assure you that so far as we can see it has relevance to the investigation."

Fuller and his solicitor glanced at each other and exchanged a subtle nod.

"We are happy to proceed on that basis," Willoughby-Forbes said, speaking deliberately towards the microphone.

"Very well, thank you," Collison acknowledged. "Mr Fuller most of what we want to speak to you about this evening concerns your relations with various ladies. I apologise in advance if you should find any of this difficult or embarrassing but, as I've already said, I can give you my personal assurance that it's relevant to various aspects of the case."

"Go ahead," Fuller said flatly.

"Can we start please with a young lady named Chloe Jennings?"

"I know Chloe Jennings of course. She is – or was until recently – my pupil."

"And did you have an affair with Chloe Jennings?"

Fuller shifted uneasily.

"Is this really necessary, Superintendent? I'm sure you'll appreciate that this is all very sensitive territory. She is a member of chambers after all."

"I'm very sorry, Mr Fuller, but there is a specific reason for my question. Of course if you do not wish to answer it, that is your prerogative."

Willoughby-Forbes darted an urgent glance at his client.

"No, I said I'll cooperate fully, and I will. Yes, I did have an affair with Chloe, but a very brief one."

"Why was it brief?"

"Because I decided to bring it to an end almost immediately."

"And why was that?"

"To be honest, Chloe turned out to be rather unstable. Despite me having made my situation perfectly clear she seemed obsessed with the idea of me leaving my wife and setting up house with her. So I ended it."

"And presumably that was the reason she ceased to be your pupil?"

"Yes it was. In fact technically I think she may still be my pupil but by mutual consent she stopped coming to court with me and started going with other members of chambers instead. She's still in Chambers. I think she has a couple of months still to go."

"And presumably she won't be considered for a tenancy?" Collison enquired wryly.

"That will be a decision for Chambers, of course, but I would imagine not. Quite a few members have commented that they find her manner rather abrasive."

"Just a background point we need to check, Mr Fuller, but did you ever take her for dinner to Scott's restaurant in Mayfair?"

"Yes I did. I go there a lot; it's one of my favourite places."

"Thank you. As a matter of interest, did you know she was at the club that night?"

"No, I most certainly did not. What was she doing there? She wasn't – she wasn't following me was she?"

"Why?" Collison asked curiously. "Was she in the habit of following you?"

Fuller laughed uneasily.

"Well, it all seems a bit melodramatic to talk about stalking, doesn't it? But yes, I had noticed her following me a few times. In fact I was debating whether to confront her about it or not. Rightly or wrongly, I decided not to."

Metcalfe tapped his pen discreetly on the table. Collison glanced at him and nodded.

"You say that you noticed her following you a few times?" Metcalfe asked.

"Yes, that's right."

"Were you on any of those occasions with Angela Bowen?"

"I'm not sure."

"Please think very carefully, Mr Fuller," Collison said, suddenly catching Metcalfe's drift. "The question of whether she may have seen you together with Angela Bowen could be very important."

"Actually," Fuller said slowly, "I rather think she had. I'm pretty sure that one time I met Angela for a drink at the Savoy I thought I saw Chloe hanging around at the entrance to the American bar. There's a little sort of anteroom there, where people wait for tables."

"Yes, I know it," Collison said at once. "And was anything said? While you were both waiting for a table I mean?"

"I didn't have to wait for a table," Fuller said simply. "I know the head waiter and I always give him a decent tip.

But as we walked into the bar I thought I saw her out of the corner of my eye. There are some mirrors there at the end of the corridor and I'm pretty sure I noticed her reflection as she waited just round the corner."

"Thank you," Collison said, "that's really very useful. In answer to your question by the way, she was there at a vintage dinner dance which was attended by coincidence by two of my officers, including DI Metcalfe here."

"Now moving on," he continued, "there's another lady we'd like to ask you about. Could you confirm the nature of your relationship with Rowena Bradley?"

"Rowena and I have been friends for years. She's also – I suppose I should say she was also – good friends both with Angela and my wife. I think they may have all been at university together."

"But did the nature of that relationship changed recently?"

"Yes it did. We embarked on a brief fling. It's over now."

"Was it over at the time of Angela Bowen's death?"

"As far as I was concerned, certainly."

"But what about Rowena Bradley? Was it over as far as she was concerned? Had you communicated your feelings to her?"

"Well no, not exactly, not in so many words."

"So Rowena may well have imagined that you were still interested in her? That her relationship with you had a future?"

"I really don't know. When you say 'a future' she knew full well that I had no intention of leaving my wife. After all, she knew all about my relationship with Angela."

"But might she have thought that at least the position as your long-term mistress might be up for grabs? I'm sorry if that sounds flippant, it's not intended to be. But you get my point? She might have thought that you were prepared to transfer your affections from Angela Bowen to herself?"

Fuller shrugged.

"I really don't know."

"But you hadn't specifically told that you had no further interest in seeing her – as a girlfriend I mean?" Collison pressed him.

"No, I hadn't."

"OK, thank you. Now there is one further person I need to ask you about. Do you recognise this lady?"

Collison pushed a photograph across the table. Fuller and his lawyer both leant forward to look at it.

"For the benefit of the tape," Collison recited, "I'm showing Mr Fuller photograph reference PW/4/4."

"Yes, I do," Fuller acknowledged, looking up with a confused expression, "but what does this have to do with anything?"

"Let's take one thing at the time shall we, Mr Fuller? Could you please confirm for the tape the identity of this lady?"

"Her name is Charlotte Tasker. She's a lady I know slightly. We met on a case where she was an expert witness. It never went to court though; the parties settled."

"Can we be clear please, Mr Fuller? Did you have a sexual relationship with Charlotte Tasker?"

"Yes, but again only a very brief one."

"And why didn't you mention this before? Didn't think it might be important?"

"No, of course I didn't or I would have done. What's Charlotte got to do with all this?"

"Surely you know that Charlotte Tasker was the doctor who reported Angela Bowen's death to the coroner's office?"

Fuller and his brief gazed at each other in consternation.

"No, I hadn't the slightest idea that it was Charlotte. What on earth was she doing there?"

"Attending the same function as Chloe Jennings, DI Metcalfe here, and incidentally Rowena Bradley."

"Dear God, no. I had no idea."

"You didn't go to the inquest?"

"No. I was told it was going to be adjourned and I was booked to be in the Court of Appeal all week. So do you mean that Charlotte Tasker spent the night at the club as well?"

"Yes, she did."

There was a pause.

"Bit of a coincidence, isn't it?" Collison commented gently. "A small club like that, and yet on that one evening no fewer than four women were there with whom you had – or were having – a sexual relationship. That must be some sort of record, don't you think?"

"You can't possibly expect my client answer that question," Willoughby-Brooks cut in at once, "and if I may say so I think it's an improper one. My client is being completely open with you. I don't think it's appropriate to comment on aspects of his personal life."

He gave Collison the benefit of a well-practised stern glare, the effect of which was rather lost on the tape recorder.

"If so, I apologise of course. But you do see the difficulty which all of this places us in. We have a multiplicity of your client's partners with access to the crime scene at the critical time, not to mention your client himself."

"We sympathise with your difficulties of course, Superintendent," Willoughby-Brooks replied, he stern glare melting into an equally well-practised understanding smile, "and we're doing everything we can to cooperate. But at the end of the day we can only do so much. We can only tell you what we know. The conduct of the investigation is a matter for you. As for me, my job is simply to protect the interests of my clients who, as I'm sure you're aware, include the Royal family."

He paused for the full weight of this grave announcement to sink in. Both detectives knew what was coming next.

"Mr Fuller is of course also something of a public figure in his own right. He's one of the most eminent QC's of his generation. He is a Bencher of his Inn. He has already sat on various occasions as a deputy judge of the High Court. It really is quite intolerable that he should continue to have this situation hanging over him. We are already holding various newspaper editors at bay only by the active threat of injunctions for defamation. The time has come for the police to make a decision, I fear. Are you planning to charge my client? Because, if not, I really would urge the release of a statement to that effect. I am quite happy to press this point with the Commissioner himself tomorrow morning, but I'd like to give you an opportunity to respond first."

Collison stared down the twin barrels of the Royal family and the Metropolitan Police Commissioner but stood firm.

"You must appreciate, Mr Willoughby-Brooks, that I'm in a difficult position here just as much as your client is. This is an ongoing investigation and as yet we have not been to rule out any of our principal suspects. It remains my fervent hope that it will prove possible to do that in respect of your client as soon as possible, but right now we simply don't know enough to be able to take a view."

"I'm sorry," Willoughby-Brooks said firmly. "That's not acceptable."

"Then I really don't know what to say to you," Collison said simply. "I've stated our position. If it would satisfy you, at least in part, I'd be happy to recommend to my superiors the release of a statement confirming that Mr Fuller is cooperating fully with our enquiry and that we are grateful to him for his input. But I'm not prepared to go any further than that."

Willoughby-Brooks seemed about to reply, but then hesitated. He looked at Fuller, who gave an almost imperceptible shake of his head.

"I will take instructions on that overnight, Superintendent. Now, is there anything else?"

"No, I don't think so. It only remains to thank you and your client once again for coming here in the evening and assisting with our enquiries. Interview terminated at 21:56."

CHAPTER 31

"I hope you realise that you're putting me to great inconvenience," Chloe Jennings told Metcalfe and Evans in the same interview room the next morning. "I was supposed to be in court today."

"I'm sorry about that, Miss Jennings," Metcalfe replied. "Now, I know that you're a barrister but let me just confirm for the tape that this interview is proceeding under caution, a caution which I administered to you when I switched the tape recorder on. Do you understand that?"

"Yes, of course I understand."

"I'm sorry, but I do have to go through this just so there's no mistake. Because you're being interviewed under caution you have the right to have a legal representative present. Do you wish to exercise that right?"

"No, I don't."

"Very well. We've asked you to come back to be re-interviewed because we're not very happy with some of the things you told us last time."

"I can't help that. I told you the truth. If that's not good enough for you, I'm sorry."

"Well actually we're not so sure about that, that you told us the truth that is."

"What are you talking about?"

"Well, let's focus on Andrew Fuller, shall we? Do you remember that when you spoke to us last time you said that you had never had a sexual relationship with him? I can show you the transcript if you wish."

"No, that won't be necessary. I remember what I said."

"And would that still be your response if you asked the question again today?"

"Yes, of course it would. My relationship with Andrew Fuller was purely professional; I was his pupil."

"And do you remember that you also said that, while you had been out for drinks with him, you'd never been out for dinner together?"

"Yes I do."

"Then, Miss Jennings, I have to put it you that I think you are lying on both counts. First, I should tell you that the manager of a restaurant in Mayfair – Scott's to be precise – has identified your photograph as being that of a lady who dined in his restaurant together with Andrew Fuller."

"How can that possibly be a valid identification? You probably just showed him a photograph and asked if he remembered it. Why, he must have hundreds of women pass through the restaurant in the course of even a single week."

"Yes, but Andrew Fuller is a regular customer of his and he pays particular attention to his choice of companion. It is his job, after all. And I can assure you that he was shown a selection of photographs, which were as similar to you as we could manage. I do have the package on file if you would like to see them for yourself."

Chloe Jennings gave a snort of derision. Metcalfe waited, his eyebrows raised.

"Do you wish to make a comment for the tape, Miss Jennings?"

"Only to say that I do not admit to having dinner with Andrew Fuller. As I said, our relationship was purely professional."

"Very well, Miss Jennings. In that case I am bound to tell you that together with a colleague I interviewed Andrew Fuller in this very room yesterday evening. Do you know what he said when we asked about you?"

"I really haven't the slightest idea."

"He confirmed that you and he had indeed had a personal relationship, not a purely professional one as you allege."

"The bastard!" Chloe Jennings spat out.

"Is that a yes or a no, Miss Jennings? Did you or did you not have a sexual relationship with Andrew Fuller?"

"Has it ever occurred to you," she asked sarcastically, "that a middle-aged man like that might want to boast about bedding a young woman? It's pure male ego."

"Are you saying that he's lying?"

"I'm asking how you can be sure that he's telling the truth."

Metcalfe gazed at her levelly.

"I know you're a barrister, Miss Jennings, but please don't let's engage in sophistry. Let me put a question to you. Don't you think it's likely that Mr Fuller, as a very senior criminal lawyer, might recognise that it makes good sense, not to mention being a matter of professional duty, to cooperate with the police in the course of a murder enquiry?"

"I can't comment on what he may or may not think."

"Look," Metcalfe said, trying a different tack, "we do realise that this must be very difficult for you. It's obviously very sensitive from a professional point of view for other people in the legal profession to think that you've had an affair with your pupil master. But if you have, then I can't believe that you're the first. In fact, from what I hear, it goes on all the time. If you tell us the truth, we'll try very hard to keep what you tell us confidential. Obviously if it becomes relevant to the proceedings then we may not be able to do that. But if you do tell us the truth then it's possible we may be able to eliminate you from our enquiries."

There was a long silence. Chloe Jennings stared at them mutinously, but it was clear that she was close to tears.

"Yes, all right," she blurted out at last, "I did sleep with the bastard."

"Why do you say 'bastard'?" Metcalfe enquired. "Did he behave badly to you? Did he lead you up the garden path for example?"

"He led me to believe that he cared for me, yes. Then he dumped me unceremoniously as soon as I wanted things to get a bit more serious."

"Were you aware of his reputation with women?"

"Yes I was. That's the really stupid part about it. I was warned by one of my lecturers at bar school when they heard who my pupil master was going to be. I was very excited of course. Who wouldn't be, to be Andrew Fuller's pupil? But this woman said that he wasn't to be trusted, and that one of his specialties was seducing young women barristers – not just barristers, but solicitors as well."

"But you went ahead in spite of that warning?"

"Oh, I know it makes me sound like an idiot, but he made me think that I was different, that he really cared for me. He can do that, you know. He has this amazing ability to make you feel cared for, looked after, special…"

Metcalfe and Evans glanced at each other.

"Well now that we have that out of the way, Miss Jennings, can we come back to the night in question? You remember, the night that you and I met at the club."

"What about it? I've already told you everything I know, everything I can remember."

"Let's just try again, shall we? For example, can you remember what time you left?"

"No, not exactly, but I know it was late. I'd had a lot to drink. You might remember."

"Yes, I do indeed. But let me put this to you: are you sure that you did actually leave the club, that you didn't stay the night there?"

"No, of course I didn't. I didn't have a room. I went home. I can remember waking up at home the next morning."

"Very well, let's try something else. While you were at the club did you at any time go to any of the floors where the residential accommodation was? I'm talking about the period after dinner."

"No, of course not. I was with you and your friends wasn't I?"

"For some of that time, yes. But I'm talking about the

whole period. You said your friend went home early. Is there anyone else who can vouch for where you were in the club at any particular time?"

"I was talking to different blokes at different times, but I'd never met any of them before, so I wouldn't know how to go about contacting them. One of them was your friend Peter Collins."

"Yes, I'm aware that you spent some time with Peter Collins, but it can't have been more than 20 minutes or so, was it? What I'm trying to establish is where you were for the whole time, not just the short period you spent on our table."

"Well, to be honest, I can't account for every last-minute. I can remember meeting various people, but things were getting a bit fuzzy by then."

Metcalfe consulted his notes.

"When last we spoke you said you remembered seeing a clipboard lying on the table, with a typewritten list on it."

"I think I said I remember the clipboard," Jennings said cautiously. "I can't remember what was on it."

"Then let me assist you. It was a list of names and room numbers. Do you remember looking at it, at all?"

"No."

"No you didn't look at it, or no you don't remember?"

"I don't remember."

"So you don't remember seeing the name of either Elizabeth Fuller or Angela Bowen?"

"No, like I said I can't remember."

Metcalfe and Jennings stared at each other. He sensed that

there was fear now behind that green-eyed mask of self-confidence. He deliberately let the silence build.

"Is there anything you'd like to tell us, Chloe?" he asked finally.

"If you mean am I going to cough to murder, the answer's no," she said defiantly. "Look, I'm sorry I wasn't entirely straight with you before, but clearly I had my reasons. I'm very sorry about what happened to that poor woman, but it was nothing to do with me. I had dinner, I had too much to drink, I had a few dances, and I went home. That's it. Now, either charge me or release me. I'm not prepared to answer any more questions."

"In that case," Metcalfe replied, "I will terminate the interview at 11:18".

Evans reached out and stopped the tape. Jennings sat in silence while he took one of them out of the machine, logged it, initialled it, and gave it to her. She put it in her bag and stood up.

"Am I free to go?" she asked with a touch of her old bravura.

Metcalfe nodded.

"DC Evans will show you out," he said.

As her high heels clacked away towards the reception area with Evans in tow, Metcalfe walked thoughtfully upstairs and knocked on Collison's door.

"Any luck?" the latter enquired.

Metcalfe shook his head.

"She's come clean finally about the affair – she could hardly do anything else – but that's it. She's sticking to her story that she never went up to the rooms and that she can't remember the guest list. She is also adamant that she left the building. Says she can remember waking up at home the next morning."

"So what do you reckon?"

"God knows. I sensed that she was frightened, but I'm not sure what to make of that."

"Hardly surprising, is it? She's a barrister and she knows that she's lied to a murder enquiry. That's not good. Even if we can't make a formal complaint we could always have a quiet word with her head of chambers. And then there's the affair. That's not exactly good for her career either, is it?"

"You're right of course. But we clearly can't rule her out. Not unless and until we can come up with an alibi for her anyway."

"Oh," Metcalfe added, "she won't admit that she saw the bedroom list either, but I saw her looking at it myself. Looking at it pretty carefully, in fact."

Collison nodded, and appeared deep in thought.

"You think she's capable of it – murder I mean?" he asked.

"Yes, actually I do. There's an intensity there behind those bright green eyes of hers. I think she's probably capable of great extremes of feeling, whether that's jealousy, anger, or love for that matter. I'd be interested to know what Peter thought of her when he met her. He's a professional, after all."

"Well, perhaps we should ask him. Now, have you heard anything from Karen and Priya?"

"They're both away from the nick, guv. Karen told me this

morning that they were planning to serve that court order, so hopefully they may have some news later today."

"Good."

Collison crossed the room and gazed absently out of the window.

"We need something to fall into place, don't we?" he commented. "It might be something quite small that suddenly makes a connection and enables us to see things clearly. Right now I feel that we still have four or five different possible explanations. Was it Fuller? And, if so, did he act alone or with one of these women? And do we need to think differently about Charlotte Tasker now that we know she was one of Fuller's conquests? And did Sharon Jones just make a couple of slips of the tongue or is Karen right about it being something significant? And why is Chloe Jennings so reluctant to tell us the truth?"

"Well, like I said, we may get what we need from Karen and Priya. There again, they may turn up nothing at all in which case we'll be no further forward."

"Yes," Collison said slowly, "and in which case we'll come under fresh pressure to make a decision about Fuller."

He fell silent as he watched a bus stop at Pilgrim's Lane and discharge a lady with a pushchair which was surely large enough to double as a golf cart. Then he came to a decision and turned round.

"I don't see any alternative, Bob. If Karen and Priya haven't come up with anything by tomorrow morning then I think we have to send the briefing note to the DPP. After that, it's up to them."

CHAPTER 32

"Thank you so much for inviting me around," Collison said that evening in the house in Frognal.

"Well, you said you wanted a word," Collins replied, "and I thought this would be much more civilised than a pub, as well as a lot more private."

"Speaking of private," Collison said, looking around, "where is Lisa this evening?"

"She's visiting her mother," Metcalfe explained. "She'll be back in a while, but we should have enough time to talk before then."

"Okay then, let's crack on. Peter, I thought it might be very useful if you could tell us whatever you've been able to surmise about our leading characters from a psychological point of view."

"I'll do what I can, of course, but remember that there are some of them I've never met, and others whom I've met only briefly."

"Of course that's understood. All right then, by all means generalise if you need to. Let's start with Fuller himself. What on earth are we to make of his frantic womanising? Is it some sort of addiction?"

"A lot of people think that it can be, yes, particularly some of the writers in American journals. I have an open mind on the issue. I suppose it depends in large part on exactly what you mean by 'an addiction'. For me for something to be a true addiction it must be not only something that somebody cannot do without, or feels they cannot do without, but is an actual emotional crutch of some kind. Alcoholism is a good example. Alcoholics don't drink specifically to get drunk but because it gives them confidence, or eases their fears. In short, addiction tends to answer an emotional need."

"And could that be an answer here?"

"I'd need to know a lot more about Fuller to be certain, but it's a strong possibility that it speaks of the need for self-validation, a constant proving of himself as it were. It's also possible that he was starved of affection by one or both parents while he was growing up, and feels a compulsive need to be liked or valued."

"But how common is it? I mean, we're hardly talking about normal behaviour are we?"

Collins winced visibly.

"You should know by now, Simon, that psychologists get terribly twitchy when people start labelling behaviour as 'normal'. At the end of the day, isn't normal behaviour simply what most people do? It doesn't necessarily make it right or morally attractive."

"All right, my mistake. Forget 'normal'. Is it common?"

"No, it's not. Certainly not to this degree, anyway. With him it seems to be almost a compulsion which goes way beyond any usual male desire for sex. That's largely physical of course, and all the more powerful because of that. But if my theory is correct what we're looking at here is psychological in origin."

"But how do you rate him as a possible murder suspect?" Willis cut in.

Colin shook his head.

"It's really impossible to say. I did have one thought though."

"Which is?"

"Well I'm no forensic expert, but the fact that our deceased was smothered with a weapon which was close to hand – the pillow – suggests an opportunistic killing, surely? And also one which was presumably conceived more or less on the spur of the moment. If your suspicion, Simon, is correct, namely that she had just told one or both of the Fullers that she was pregnant, then Fuller might have seen this as a potential obstacle to him being able to continue to pursue his obsession and killed her almost without even thinking about it. It's tenuous I'll admit, because being married to one woman hadn't stopped him, so why should being married to another prove any different?"

"But it's possible?" Metcalfe asked.

"Of course it's possible, but no more than that. And, as I understand it, we can't currently show that either of them knew about the pregnancy anyway."

Collison nodded sadly.

"What about the wife?"

"I simply don't know enough about her to give any valid opinion. But I would venture a conjecture if you like."

"Go on."

"Well she and the deceased were good friends of long-standing, weren't they? I would imagine that they understood each other very well. They both knew exactly what the relationship was, and what it wasn't. But if she did know that Bowen was pregnant, she would have realised that this could change the dynamic dramatically. If Fuller 'did the decent thing' and divorced her to marry Bowen, might she lose him altogether, even the companionship which she clearly valued very highly? When anyone is threatened with the loss of something which they crave more than anything else in the world, nobody can be really sure how they might react. Perhaps she panicked and decided to get rid of her. Or perhaps she went to her room to reason with her but then lost her temper because Bowen wasn't prepared to be cooperative. Who knows?"

"And of course we come back to the fact that we can't prove that either she or her husband knew about the pregnancy," Metcalfe said.

"Too true, Bob," Collison said.

"Rowena Bradley?" he enquired, turning back to Collins.

"Unless I'm reading her all wrong I really don't see her as the type, do you? Of course it's always possible that she is really just exceedingly cunning and that she's just putting on some fluffy bunny rabbit act to hide a hard, calculating personality. But without spending a lot more time with her I really couldn't say. She strikes me as a fairly pragmatic sort, who understood that having sex with Fuller was just that and no more, but as I say I don't really know her well enough to say that with any certainty."

"Talking of bunnies," Metcalfe asked with a grin, "what about Chloe Jennings?"

"Ah, now you're talking, Bob. She really is a very interesting character indeed. I would say that she is self-obsessed, generally dismissive of others, and has a very quick temper which is probably made worse when she's been drinking."

"Which of course she had been that evening," Collison pointed out. "Are you saying that she's unstable, Peter? And, if so, do you think she's capable of committing murder?"

"Again, I'd have a slight problem with your choice of words. 'Unstable' can mean different things to different people. If you mean could she do something really awful – murder for example – if she was sufficiently angry then I'd say yes. But I have a slight problem with her as a suspect for the murder of Angela Bowen."

"And what's that?"

"Well if she was bitter and angry with Fuller – and she clearly was – wouldn't it make more sense for her to seek to murder him, rather than his wife? I'm assuming that it was his wife she was intending to murder, by the way. We know that she looked closely at the room list and Angela Bowen's name would have meant nothing to her, whereas she could probably have put two and two together sufficiently to work out that Liz Fuller was Andrew's wife. She wasn't to know that they had accidentally swapped rooms."

"But mightn't she have just lashed out blindly, thinking that by killing the wife she was somehow hurting the husband? She might even have been sufficiently lucid to work out that he might be the obvious suspect in any murder enquiry."

"It's possible, yes. It seems to me though that at the moment you can't show that she ever actually went anywhere near Bowen's room at all. Once she moved away from our table none of us saw her again. She might just have gone back to that table full of Hooray Henrys she'd been with before. She might have just gone downstairs and left the club. We don't know, do we?"

"No, we don't. We've circulated her photograph to black cab drivers in the hope that somebody might remember picking her up – she's a very attractive woman after all – but nobody's come forward. There's also the problem of the key. She might have got away with going into the office once unnoticed, but it's almost impossible to believe that she could have done it twice."

"Unless you buy the possibility that she stayed the night in the concealed room and put the key back in the morning while Rowena Bradley was upstairs having her shower."

"Oh dear," Collison groaned theatrically. "I do so hope that we're not going to end up with a solution featuring a concealed room. We'd never be taken seriously in the Met again."

"Well, I'm sorry about that, Simon," Collins responded, "but whether we like it or not it is a viable possibility."

They all looked at each other thoughtfully while Metcalfe refreshed their glasses.

"And what about the new entry in the Athena Club Stakes?" Collison asked the room in general. "How do we view Dr Charlotte Tasker? Karen, you've been doing a lot of work on this, so why don't you go first?"

"Well, we have lots of interesting snippets of information, but the question is do they fit together or not?"

"For example?"

"For example both of her patients who died recently had within the few weeks prior to their deaths made new wills leaving her significant amounts of money. In one case they even left her their house."

"Is there any suggestion that she influenced these wills at all, or might even have forged them?"

"No, there isn't. I've spoken to both the lawyers concerned. In each case it was their client who approached them with instructions to make the new will and in each case they were satisfied that they had proper testamentary capacity."

"That they knew what they were doing, in other words?" Metcalfe asked.

"Yes, exactly, and in each case the will was signed in the lawyer's office and witnessed by some of the staff there, so there's no question about due execution. No, the wills were valid right enough."

"And was Dr Tasker informed in either case that she was now a beneficiary?"

"Not so far as the lawyers were aware. I did ask them about that and they said that it wasn't normal practice to notify beneficiaries unless they were specifically asked to do so by their client."

"And how did these patients die?"

"According to the death certificates, of heart failure. One of them also had cancer at quite an advanced stage, but that wasn't given as the cause of death."

"And was there a post-mortem in either case?"

"No, because in both cases they had seen a doctor in the few hours before their death and she was able to sign the death certificate."

"The doctor in each case being Charlotte Tasker of course?"

"Yes, exactly."

"If I was playing devil's advocate," Collins said after a pause, "I could think of quite a few objections to this line of thought. First, didn't she herself say that it was customary in that sort of private practice for patients to remember their doctor in their will?"

"Oh come on, Peter," Willis replied briskly, "being mentioned in a will is one thing, but being left someone's house is quite another. Anyway, we don't know for sure that it was customary. We only have her word for that, and it's a pretty self-serving thing to say, isn't it?"

"Very well," Collins conceded, holding up his hands in mock surrender, "but second, can we actually prove that she caused the death of these patients? And, even if we can, does that naturally make her a likely suspect for the murder of Angela Bowen?"

"If she smothered them, then no. There would be no evidence left by now. However, there is one ray of hope. The records of her drug supplier show that she was in possession at one stage of large amounts of diamorphine. If she used that, then it's just possible that it might show up if we went for an exhumation."

"Hm, I think we'd need to take some advice on that,"

Collison observed. "People don't take too kindly to you digging up their relatives."

"Are the suppliers sure about the diamorphine?" Metcalfe enquired.

"Oh yes, in fact they were rather nervous about it. After the Shipman case new guidelines went out to stop doctors ordering excessive quantities. This was before those came into force of course, but they were very sensitive about it nonetheless."

"Well, we have her coming in for re-interview tomorrow," Collison said, "so we won't have to wait long for an opportunity to put this to her, but suppose she simply denies any wrongdoing in their deaths? After all, this is just supposition on our part, isn't it? And unless you're right about the diamorphine there doesn't seem the slightest possibility of being able to prove any of it."

"And just because she was having, or had had an affair with Fuller," Collins observed, "it doesn't necessarily follow that she would have wanted to murder his wife. If that was so, the poor woman would have had people queueing up to bump her off."

"And – and I hate to be boring – what about opportunity?" Metcalfe interjected. "Wasn't she with us the whole time? Didn't we all moan about it the next morning? And if she was with us on one side of the building, then she can't have been murdering Angela Bowen on the other side of the building at the same time, can she?"

"Maybe, maybe not," Willis answered cryptically.

She broke off as they heard the sound of the key in the

front door. It opened and closed and then Lisa Atkins walked into the room. She looked pale and rather pinched.

"Oh please don't get up," she said quickly as the men did exactly that, "I don't want to disturb anybody or interrupt you."

"Not at all," Collison said at once. "In fact we'd just finished, and I must be going, so you're not disturbing anybody at all."

"How are you feeling?" Metcalfe asked anxiously.

"Rather tired, I'm afraid, and I have a brute of a headache. Would you mind if I went upstairs and had an early night?"

"Of course not. Can I get you anything? A cup of tea?"

"No thank you, Bob, dear, I really do think that a good sleep is what I really need. Good night, everybody. Goodbye, Simon."

As she went upstairs there was a taut silence in the living room. Nobody really wanted to look at anybody else, although Willis and Collins exchanged a furtive glance.

"Well," Collison said self-consciously. "I was telling the truth. I really do have to go now. Thank you for the wine, Peter. Don't worry, I can show myself out."

CHAPTER 33

"This interview with Dr Charlotte Tasker is commencing at 10:34," Metcalfe intoned for the tape. "Present are Detective Inspector Metcalfe and Detective Sergeant Willis. Dr Tasker, would you please confirm your name and address for the tape?"

She did so.

"Just before we begin, I have a duty to inform you that you are attending the police station voluntarily to assist with this enquiry and that you are of course free to leave at any time. First of all, thank you very much for coming to see us this morning. I hope we haven't inconvenienced you too much?"

"No, not really. I had to come into town today anyway to see a patient."

"Will you be staying at the club?" Willis asked.

"No, I'm going back on the train this evening."

"I hope the dreadful experience you had last time hasn't put you off staying there?"

"No, not at all. Remember, I'm a doctor. So, while what happened was very unexpected, I did at least have experience of that sort of situation."

"Yes, and recently too I believe?"

"I have, as a matter of fact. I've lost a couple of patients in the last few months. Not entirely unexpected – they were both elderly and one of them had cancer – but sad nonetheless. My father had been their doctor before me, and I thought of them more as family friends than patients."

"And I understand they both made generous provision for you in their wills?"

"Yes, certainly," the doctor said looking surprised, "there's no secret about that. It used to be traditional in private practice for your patient to remember you in their will. It happened to my father all the time."

"But this was very generous, wasn't it?" Willis pressed. "In one case I understand they even left you their house."

"Actually, they left me the whole estate which of course included the house. I was very surprised naturally. But they had no close friends and no immediate family left, so I suppose they just decided to leave everything to me. Patients do form a very close bond with their doctor, you know. Particularly if they sense the end is coming."

"Yes, I've no doubt. But let's ask you about something else. I understand that you're in the habit of ordering quite large amounts of diamorphine. What do you use it for?"

"For my patients of course. If you have terminal cancer then diamorphine is about the only thing that can be used. It's a very effective painkiller and while it's addictive that's hardly a consideration when the patient is going to be dead in a few months anyway."

"But wouldn't it be usual for a patient to obtain their own diamorphine under prescription?"

"Yes, I suppose so. But sometimes the patient is elderly – and obviously very unwell – and it's easier for me to give it to them than for them to have all the trouble of going to the chemist. To be honest, I can leave them larger amounts as well, so they don't have to worry about it so often."

"Do you ever administer diamorphine to a patient yourself?"

"Yes, I frequently administer it by injection while I'm visiting."

"But isn't that very unusual? Wouldn't a terminal patient usually be connected to a drip, and be able to regulate the flow of the drug themselves?"

"Sometimes they do and sometimes they don't. Some of them prefer me to give them an injection."

"But unless you were there every day, and several times a day at that, how would that work? They would still have to self-administer all the rest of the time wouldn't they?"

"I'm not sure what you're getting at," Dr Tasker said with a quizzical look. "I thought you asked me here to help you with that awful business at the Athena club."

"Quite right, so we did. We've been re-interviewing all our witnesses. We find it's a useful process. Sometimes they might remember some little detail which they overlooked first time around. I wonder if you could walk us through the events of that morning once more?"

"Well, as I said before, my first intimation that something was wrong was when the telephone rang in my room and I was asked to go downstairs to take a look at a lady guest about whom the maid was concerned."

"And can you remember when that was exactly?"

"Sometime after seven certainly. I was getting ready to go downstairs for breakfast."

"I see. Are you quite sure about that?"

"Yes, of course. Why shouldn't I be?"

"Well, you see we have another witness who says that you were downstairs earlier. Sometime between 6:30 and 7 o'clock in fact."

"Oh, you must mean the receptionist. Yes, she did see me downstairs earlier. I went in search of breakfast but there was no-one in the restaurant – no-one to serve breakfast I mean – so I was heading back to my room when she saw me."

"So you thought that breakfast began at 6:30?"

"Yes, foolish of me perhaps. But I thought that with guests sometimes having to make an early start – to go to the airport for example – well, you know…"

Willis and Metcalfe exchanged a glance.

"I have to tell you, Dr Tasker, that we find that a little strange," Metcalfe said quietly. "You see we have various witnesses – including ourselves – who distinctly heard Rowena Bradley tell you the night before that breakfast began at seven."

"Did she? Well then, I must've forgotten."

There was a silence.

"Dr Tasker," Metcalfe went on, "I am now going to caution you. You do not have to say anything, but it may harm your defence if you do not mention when questioned something which you later rely on in court. Anything you do say may be given in evidence."

The doctor looked shocked.

"What's happening? Are you arresting me?"

"No, not at present anyway. You are still free to leave at any time if you wish to do so. You also have the right to receive legal advice and to have a solicitor present for the rest of the interview. Do you wish to exercise either of those rights?"

"No, I don't think so. Why should I? I've got nothing to hide."

"Fine. You have the right to change your mind at any time by the way. Now, just to be quite clear, we are as you know investigating the death of Professor Angela Bowen at the Athena club and we are asking you to account for the fact that you were downstairs before 7 o'clock that morning, something which is inconsistent with your original statement. Do you still say that you thought breakfast would be served from 6:30 onwards and that this was the reason why you were downstairs at that time?"

"Yes, I do."

"And you have no recollection of Rowena Bradley having told you very distinctly the night before that breakfast did not begin until 7 o'clock?"

"No, I don't."

"Then why did you tell us, both originally and again today, that when you received the telephone call in your room – which by common consent was sometime after 7 o'clock – that you were getting ready to go down for breakfast having set your alarm for 7 o'clock? Yet if you had already been downstairs once, then you must have got ready some considerable time before that, mustn't you?"

"Well, it was just a figure of speech I suppose. I think I was sitting down reading a book when the telephone went. Why, what you think I was doing?"

"I think you were waiting for the telephone call because you knew it was going to come. Because it was you yourself who had killed Angela Bowen."

"But that's nonsense! Why, I was with you and your party all the time until I went to bed, and by then it must have been getting on for midnight. So I can't have killed her. You know the time of death as well as I do. It must have been some time before midnight."

"Yes, that's what we've all been assuming isn't it? But if you think about it, the only basis for that assumption was the body temperature which you recorded when you inspected the body the next morning. But in fact she didn't die before midnight, did she? You murdered her sometime between 6:30 and 7 o'clock the next morning."

Dr Tasker looked at him blankly.

"You see, not only did you know that breakfast did not begin until 7 o'clock, but also that Rowena Bradley would be absent from her office for about half an hour before that. She told you that too – told us all in fact – before you went to bed. So what actually happened was that you came downstairs shortly after 6:30 and took the key from her office. You went upstairs, smothered Angela Bowen with her pillow, probably before she even had a chance to wake up properly, and went downstairs again to return the key. It was just bad luck that the receptionist came early that morning. You must have thought that you would have been able to get back to your own room without being seen by anyone. On the spur of the moment you made up the story about breakfast. It nearly worked even so. If DS Willis here hadn't noticed that the receptionist said that you'd come 'back' downstairs then nobody would have suspected you at all."

"But that's ridiculous. What possible reason could I have had for wanting Angela Bowen dead?"

"Well, as it happens, she was the long-term mistress of a man with whom you'd recently had an affair. But you didn't know that, did you? You saw the name of Elizabeth Fuller against that particular room number, and that's whom you thought you were killing. Presumably you thought that with her out of the way you might be able to claim Andrew Fuller's full attention. You weren't to know that, tragically for Professor Bowen, there had been a mix-up and they had accidentally swapped rooms. After all, you had never seen either woman."

"It really was very clever," Willis said since Tasker showed no inclination to reply. "Of course you'd been around sudden death before; every doctor has. So you knew the procedure. You knew that the time of death would be based on the body temperature recorded by the doctor who examined the body. All you had to do was make sure that doctor was you. And that was pretty much a racing certainty, wasn't it? What could be more natural than for the club to ask a doctor who was already on the premises to help out?"

"And your 'mistake' in certifying death by natural causes was a stroke of genius too," Metcalfe said, taking up the story. "It meant there would be no proper forensic examination and that, the way things work with mortuaries and so forth, the body would not be examined for some considerable time, and would have spent a lot of that time under refrigeration anyway, which would muck up the body temperature good and proper."

They both gazed at her hard, but no answer came.

"Oh, and there's one more thing," Willis said levelly. "While the body was being moved downstairs – in the lift actually – an arm fell out of the body bag and hung limply against someone. Someone who remembered it very well, because they weren't used to being around dead bodies. But that's curious, isn't it? If death had occurred when you say it did that would have been impossible, since rigor mortis wouldn't have begun to wear off yet. Whereas if the time of death was sometime after 6:30 then rigor wouldn't have had a chance to set in. So the body temperature you say you recorded can't possibly have been correct can it?" There was another long pause.

"Dr Tasker," Metcalfe said finally, "I must remind you that you are under caution. You may not realise the full implications of that. It means that not only may your answers to our questions be given in court, but also that the court will be entitled to draw conclusions from any failure to answer. We're giving you every opportunity to tell us your side of the story."

There was another silence. Charlotte Tasker had fixed her gaze at a point on the wall off to the left, her lips pursed tightly together.

"I'd never really been in love before," came finally in a sad, flat little voice. "Oh, I know that must sound ridiculous to you. You probably both jump in and out of bed with people all the time, like most people seem to do these days. But it was different for me. I'd been out with a few men, and each time I tried to persuade myself that I might actually like them, but I always knew that I didn't really. And then I met Andrew. He wasn't just the most wonderful man I'd ever met, but the most wonderful man I could ever imagine. That first time I saw him, even though it was quite a short time we were together and there were other people around as well, I knew that he was the man for me, the man I was meant to meet. I never thought he would be interested in me, but he was."

She turned her head and looked at them. A single tear started running down her left cheek.

"I should have known that it wasn't meant to be, for me to be happy I mean. There are some people for whom things just seem to work out in life. I know lots of them, and just for a little while I thought that I might be one of them too. But I should have known better, shouldn't I? My life's never been like that, and why should it change? I'm just plain, boring old Charlotte Tasker rattling around in an empty old house miles from anywhere with no friends and no family. No sort of life at all really."

"And when you did meet the man of your dreams," Willis said gently, "he turned out to be married."

"Yes, I suppose that was inevitable really, wasn't it? Didn't somebody once say that any really attractive man must be either gay or married? The dreadful thing was that I found myself conceiving this really dreadful hatred for a woman I'd never even met, and the only harm she'd never done me was to marry someone years and years earlier. He said he'd never leave her, you see. He said that she'd helped him through lots of bad times in the past and that he owed it to her to stay with her. I never actually thought about killing her, putting her out of the way, until the opportunity suddenly presented itself. I was glancing idly down Rowena's list and there was her name. It was such a surprise I almost cried out. And almost at once it occurred to me that this must be fate, and then when Rowena mentioned going upstairs at 6:30 I saw in a flash how it might be done. How I could do it and not be suspected. Isn't that awful?"

"And how was that, Charlotte?" Willis asked softly, and then held her breath.

"Oh, it was just as you both said, of course, exactly as you said."

Willis exhaled and looked at Metcalfe.

"Dr Charlotte Tasker," he said formally, "I am now arresting you for the murder of Angela Bowen. In a moment I will terminate this interview and take you to the custody officer who will explain all your rights to you. But before I do, is there anything else you'd like to say?"

She shook her head.

"What's the point?"

CHAPTER 34

"So the Tasker woman has confessed?" the ACC asked.

"Yes, sir, a full confession. It's all down to Willis really. She spotted the key clue and it was she and Bob Metcalfe who got the confession. Without it I'm not sure we would really have been able to prove that Tasker had done it. Oh, we had a strong circumstantial case all right but if she'd just sworn blind that she'd got in a muddle about breakfast and so forth, well, I'm not so sure; you know what juries are like..."

"I do indeed, and just as well that this is not going to be left to one. I suppose there's no possible loophole? She didn't have legal representation after all, did she?"

"No, but she was clearly offered it and declined. I've listened to the tape and I'm quite satisfied. Bob even reminded her that she had the right to change her mind at any time."

"Well, that's all right then. I must say that I'm glad it's over. The Commissioner will be very happy too. He's been getting all sorts of pressure from upstairs. Bad business all round though."

"Yes, her confession lets Fuller off the hook right enough."

"Legally perhaps," the ACC replied cryptically.

"How do you mean, sir?"

"I mean that even though there won't be a trial, the full truth will still come out. Even on a guilty plea counsel will have to address the court on sentencing, and all the sordid details will be all over the newspapers. They'll love it of course."

"What will that mean for Fuller? For his career I mean?"

The ACC shrugged.

"As a QC? Who knows. I'm sure solicitors will keep instructing him. And clients will probably love it. He'll be more of a celebrity than ever now. People will want to have been represented by him just be able to tell their grandchildren about it. As a High Court judge? Well, I think he can forget about that. It would be impossible politically. I suspect he must know that."

"Hopefully he'll be too relieved not to be a murder suspect any more to worry too much about anything else."

"Perhaps, yes."

The ACC took off his glasses and fiddled with them.

"Your team did a good job, Simon. Please pass on my thanks and good wishes."

"I will indeed, sir. As I said, I'd like to commend Willis in particular."

The ACC nodded.

"Put it in writing and I'll add it to her file with my recommendation for early promotion. She has that already, anyway, but it can't do any harm. How's Metcalfe getting on? How's that girl of his?"

"They had a bit of a scare actually. It seems that she's developed epilepsy, although they're not sure to what extent. I saw her the other evening and she didn't look too well. Went to bed early complaining of a headache."

The ACC shook his head sadly.

"That was a bad business too. At least we got the murderous bitch who did it. That's some consolation anyway. She comes up for trial next month actually; I've just been reading the file. Apparently she's going to plead to GBH. If I had my way it would be attempted murder, but there you are; everything is run by the lawyers these days."

"Hopefully it won't make too much difference to the sentence, sir. GBH is pretty serious after all."

"Changing the subject," the ACC said suddenly, "I've been giving a little more thought to your organisational paper. I wonder if it might need a little fine tuning?"

"How do you mean, sir? I'm open to suggestions of course."

"I wonder if there's an argument for making each homicide area an autonomous task force, each headed by a DCS. You might like to think about it, Simon. Murder enquiries are getting so damn complicated these days that perhaps it might make sense for major investigations to be headed up by a Superintendent, just as you have done with this one. But if that's going to be the way ahead then it's difficult to see that individual also being able to oversee other enquiries at the same time."

"But you'd still need to put something on top. A more senior officer to whom each force would report: a Commander presumably?"

"Something like that, yes. As I say, you might like to think about it some more."

"Well at least that would offer Jim Murray a step up,

anyway. To be honest I've been feeling a little guilty that my proposals have left him a bit isolated."

"I'm not sure that Jim really wants to be a Commander anymore," the ACC said. "He's an old-style copper, albeit a very good one, and I think he's beginning to realise just how much time he would have to spend sitting on committees and filling out reports. I can't say I blame him, either."

"He's hinted as much to me, certainly," Collison admitted. He thought quickly.

"Do you know, sir, there's at least one obvious merit to your suggestion, in my eyes anyway. It would create a DCS post which would still be operational, still doing proper investigative work, even if at a very senior level."

"Yes, I suppose it would," the ACC said with a smile. "Like I said, think about it, Simon."

...

"You know it was really a very clever idea," Peter Collins observed as the four occupants of the living room in Frognal sampled a glass of Pinot Grigio. "Faking the time of death like that, I mean."

"Well, I suppose the one person you're never going to suspect is the doctor who attends the scene," Lisa Atkins replied. "I'm just jolly glad the whole thing is over, not least because it means you lot can talk to me about it now. I've felt pretty much in the way at times these last few weeks."

"Yes, I'm sorry about that," Willis said with an embarrassed smile. "It's just that we're not allowed to discuss the case with anybody who is not a member of the team, and sometimes – as in this case – even with some people who are."

"Oh, I don't mind," Lisa responded at once. "I understand how it is. It's just nice to be able to be part of the discussion again, that's all."

"I wonder just how much of it she did actually plan in advance," Metcalfe mused, "and how much just happened to work out for. The hotel room being cleaned, for a start. If that hadn't happened we would presumably have been able to pick up her DNA."

"But it would have been there anyway, wouldn't it?" Collins commented. "That's why it was such a wonderful plan. If there had been a forensic examination of the room, and if it had turned up her DNA, what of it? After all, she had been the attending doctor so of course her DNA would have been in the room."

"So you think that she planned it all, even though she had so little time?" Lisa asked.

"She says that it suddenly just came to her – all of it at once," Willis said. "A sort of inspiration as it were. Personally, I believe her. For example, in retrospect it's obvious that she was using us all to create the perfect alibi for the period before midnight. So she must already have had the idea of faking the time of death."

"I think she also knew that if everyone thought it was natural causes then there wouldn't be any sort of proper investigation," Metcalfe cut in. "It wasn't just a question of the room being cleaned as a matter of routine, and the club wanting to get rid of the body as quickly as possible. It created a dead period – no pun intended – of at least a day or so for the trail to go cold. We all know that the first twenty-four hours are crucial in any murder investigation; well, she took them away from us."

"And she very nearly got away with it," Collins reminded them. "If it hadn't been for Harriet here spotting that inconsistency then who knows what might have happened? It wasn't as if we were short of other suspects. Why, I even had that Jennings woman staying the night in a secret room, crazed with murderous jealousy."

"And I had a sneaking suspicion that it was the wife all along," Metcalfe said. "I felt sure that Bowen must've told the Fullers – or either one of them – about her pregnancy. I was getting pretty depressed about it too because I couldn't see any way we'd ever be able to prove it."

"Well, I'm glad of one thing anyway," Collins said as he drained the last of his wine appreciatively. "At least the most likely suspect turned out not to be the murderer. My faith in detective fiction can remain intact."

"Yes, and what an impressive collection of red herrings, Peter," Willis observed, noting with regret that her glass too was empty. "The husband, the wife, the manager, the angry young woman who lied through her teeth ..."

"What about those other people, by the way?" Collins asked. "Those patients who died suspiciously soon after leaving all their spondolicks to Dr Tasker? Did she kill them too?"

Willis shrugged.

"I don't think we'll ever know for sure. She says not, but all that diamorphine takes a lot of explaining. Personally I'd like to pursue it, but the guvnor thinks it's a waste of resources. Sometimes I think he's starting to sound like the ACC."

"I hate to say it, but he's probably right," Collins said sympathetically. "After all, you've got her bang to rights for the Bowen murder, so she's probably going to spend most of the rest of her life in prison anyway."

"Now," he went on, addressing the room in general, "what do we think about another bottle? And, if so, shall we try more of the same or give something else a go?"

Lisa put her hand up, clearly intending to answer the question. However, her response was puzzling and no sort of answer at all.

"Might this be a good time, Bob?" she said brightly.

Metcalfe flushed.

"Oh, yes, I suppose so," he mumbled.

Collins looked bemused, as did Willis, but suddenly she threw both hands up in front of her mouth and gave a little scream.

"Oh, Bob," she squealed.

"Yes," he replied, surer now, as he crossed the room and took Lisa's hand. "We're going to get married."

GUY FRASER-SAMPSON is an established writer, having published not only fiction but also books on a diverse range of subjects including finance, investment, economics and cricket. His darkly disturbing economic history *The Mess We're In* was nominated for the Orwell Prize.

His *Mapp & Lucia* novels have all been optioned by BBC TV, and have won high praise from other authors including Alexander McCall Smith, Gyles Brandreth and Tom Holt. The second was featured in an exclusive interview with Mariella Forstrup on Radio 4, and Guy's entertaining talks on the series have been heard at a number of literary events including the *Sunday Times* Festival in Oxford and the *Daily Telegraph* Festival in Dartington.

THE FIRST THRILLING TITLE IN THE HAMPSTEAD MURDERS SERIES

£7.99, ISBN 978-1-910692-93-6

The genteel façade of London's Hampstead is shattered by a series of terrifying murders, and the ensuing police hunt is threatened by internal politics, and a burgeoning love triangle within the investigative team. Pressurised by senior officers desperate for a result a new initiative is clearly needed, but what?

Intellectual analysis and police procedure vie with the gut instinct of 'copper's nose', and help appears to offer itself from a very unlikely source a famous fictional detective. A psychological profile of the murderer allows the police to narrow down their search, but will Scotland Yard lose patience with the team before they can crack the case?

Praised by fellow authors and readers alike, this is a truly original crime story, speaking to a contemporary audience yet harking back to the Golden Age of detective fiction. Intelligent, quirky and mannered, it has been described as 'a love letter to the detective novel'. Above it all hovers Hampstead, a magical village evoking the elegance of an earlier time, and the spirit of mystery-solving detectives.

THE SECOND GRIPPING TITLE IN THE HAMPSTEAD MURDERS SERIES

£7.99, ISBN 978-1-911331-80-3

The second in the Hampstead Murders series opens with a sudden death at an iconic local venue, which some of the team believe may be connected with an unsolved murder featuring Cold War betrayals worthy of George Smiley.

It soon emerges that none other than Agatha Christie herself may be the key witness who is able to provide the missing link.

As with its bestselling predecessor, *Death in Profile*, the book develops the lives and loves of the team at 'Hampstead Nick'. While the next phase of a complicated love triangle plays itself out, the protagonists, struggling to crack not one but two apparently insoluble murders, face issues of national security in working alongside Special Branch.

On one level a classic whodunit, this quirky and intelligent read harks back not only to the world of Agatha Christie, but also to the Cold War thrillers of John Le Carré, making it a worthy successor to *Death in Profile* which was dubbed 'a love letter to the detective novel'.

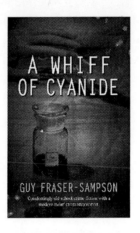

THE THIRD GRIPPING TITLE IN THE HAMPSTEAD MURDERS SERIES

£7.99, ISBN 978-1-911129-76-9

The third volume of the bestselling Hampstead Murders sees the team become involved with a suspicious death at a crime writers' convention. Is this the result of a bitterly contested election for the Chair of the Crime Writers' Association or are even darker forces at work?

Peter Collins, who is attending the convention as the author of a new book on poisoning in Golden Age fiction, worries that the key clue to unlock this puzzle may be buried within his own memories. A character called Miss Marple offers her advice, but how should the police receive this?

Meanwhile an act of sudden, shocking violence and a dramatic revelation threaten tragic consequences...